REQUIEM

A Montague and Strong Detective Novel

ORLANDO A. SANCHEZ

BITTEN PEACHES
PUBLISHING

ABOUT THE STORY

No matter how fast you are, you can't outrun your past.

When Ramirez receives a call from Shadow Company, he uncovers secrets from Simon's covert operative days and an instruction: contact Simon.

An agent Simon thought dead, has resurfaced, looking for vengeance and his help.

Now, together with Monty, Simon must stop this agent from exacting revenge before it's too late and countless lives are lost. Will Simon succeed in keeping his past hidden? Will the past come to haunt his present and destroy his future?

"I have long had the taste of death on my tongue."
-Wolfgang Amadeus Mozart

ONE

I stepped into the lobby of Haven and did a double-take.

I immediately noticed the heightened security strategically placed around the lobby, though they were working hard at trying to blend into the decor of the reception area. This only made them stand out more. I easily counted six security personnel spread out around the space.

Whoever trained this group needed to brush up on the "hiding in plain sight" lesson of the curriculum. I stepped to the closest guard, who eyeballed me warily.

I could tell from his energy signature that he wasn't run-of-the-mill security. This was a group of high-level mages. Roxanne wasn't relying on just wards and runes anymore—she had raised the stakes and she was betting it all on the house.

"When did Roxanne hire your team?" I asked, looking around at the group of mages still trying desperately, and failing spectacularly, to blend in. "She expecting another attack?"

Tall, muscular, and wary gave me the once-over, determined I wasn't a threat, then looked down at my ever-friendly, super approachable hellhound, and paused.

Peaches was giving him his best hellhound grin, and I struggled to keep a straight face. All this did was scare the security mage, who took a step back, letting his hand drift to his side, and to his weapon.

"What kind of dog is that?" he asked, pointing at Peaches, who was doing a horrible impression of Fangs and Cuddles. "I've never seen that breed before. What's wrong with his eyes?"

"He's not a dog, actually," I answered, lowering my voice and leaning in conspiratorially. "He's more of a hellhound. That's why his eyes glow."

"Hellhound, right, sure," the security mage said. "Pull the other one."

I shrugged. I wasn't in the convincing mood, and he was just doing his job. He didn't have to believe me and I didn't have to make him. No harm, no foul.

"Why the extra security? Is the hospital on lockdown?"

"You ask a lot of questions, Mr.—?"

"Strong, Simon Strong. I know Roxanne."

"Who?" he asked. "Do you have some ID, Mr. Strong?"

"No need to get all Fort Knox on me, big guy," I said, reaching for my wallet and stopping when I saw him tense. Things were not developing well. "I was just asking about all the extra security."

"I'm not at liberty to discuss details, sir," he said. "I don't know a Roxanne. No one here does. Please remove the ID slowly from your pocket. Thank you."

"Seriously," I said, handing him my license, "everyone knows Roxanne. I mean *everyone*."

I proceeded to grace him with my best Sting rendition of the classic. Clearly, he was dumbstruck by my virtuosity, because all he could do was stand there in shock.

I had that effect on people.

Then I realized there was a good chance he wasn't on a first-name basis with the Director. It made sense. She may have just hired them. She would have made sure to keep it professional, after all. I paused my version of *Roxanne,* which was so amazing even Sting would weep tears of applause, and clarified my association with Roxanne—the Director, not the one who didn't have to put on the red light.

"Director DeMarco? She's a good friend of mine," I said, looking around. "Is she around?"

I noticed the glance he gave his team. Subtle he was not. The glance was basically a message of, "harmless lunatic on the floor, escort out with minimum attention," to the rest of the team. I saw them move. They were pretty good, and approached at oblique angles. No one had a weapon drawn.

Smart move, kept things de-escalated...except that trying to box me in was the exact opposite of de-escalation. Trying to box in my hellhound—my very overprotective hellhound—was the opposite of a smart move. It bordered on suicidal, unless—of course—you had a large bowl of pastrami in your hands.

However, I did appreciate the effort. It looked like they had paid attention during the "coordinated attack" lesson. It wasn't their fault that they hadn't trained for the possibility of encountering an offspring of Cerberus.

It was hard to plan for every contingency—especially hellhounds.

Two of the team, the ones furthest away from my location, resembled boxers as they slowly bounced on their toes. The other three were forming a cordon to make sure I had limited options of exit. Primarily, my options were limited to the exit they chose.

They approached carefully. I'd like to say it was because I was such an imposing figure, but I'd be lying. It was more likely due to the now *alert* hellhound by my side who sensed the team closing in on our position.

Peaches gave off a low rumble, which stopped everyone in their tracks.

In retrospect, mentioning Roxanne by name may have been a mistake. This team was especially twitchy. It could've had something to do with Haven being attacked by Evers not too long ago. Or having parts of the building blown to bits—none of which, I promise, was my fault. I may have been *on* the scene, but I was definitely not the cause *of* the scene.

I moved my hands slowly into the air in a surrender pose as Peaches entered rend-and-maim mode.

"Listen, we really don't want any trouble," I said. "Trust me on this. What's your name?"

"Everyone calls me Tank," he said, putting his hand on his holster. I was glad I had kept my jacket closed. If he saw Grim Whisper, things would go sideways fast. "You can call me *Mr*. Tank."

"Okay, Tank," I said, extending my hand as he examined my license. "I'm just here to see a close friend. No trouble and no shenanigans. Just here to see a recovering friend."

"What are you?" Tank said, narrowing his eyes at me.

"You're reading all over the place, but I know for a fact that you're no mage."

"No," I said, "I'm a little more complicated than that."

There was nowhere that conversation could go, except south. I opted on the side of discretion and limited my response to the bare minimum.

"I bet," Tank answered slowly, blading his body away from me. "How about we take this conversation into the office? I'm sure we could find this Roxanne friend of yours. Get you all sorted out and on your way."

"You're not paying attention, Tank," I said, repeating his name deliberately to increase his focus. "Your team thinks they are dealing with a threat. I am not, in any way, shape, or form, a threat to you."

"See? That's good," Tank answered, as his team slowly closed in. "The last thing anyone needs today is a threat. I know you don't need one, and I certainly don't need one. Here you go."

He handed me my license, which I returned to my wallet, inadvertently causing my jacket to open. This in turn revealed my oversized holster which held Grim Whisper. This caused Tank to open his eyes, first in wonder, followed immediately by a look of suspicion, and lastly by a decision for overt violence...directed at me.

"I have a perfectly good explanation for—"

"Gun!" Tank yelled as he drew his weapon and aimed at my face. "Get on the floor...now!"

I want to say that what happened next wasn't my fault, but I'd be lying. Some of it was my fault.

Most of the blame lay with Peaches.

TWO

Peaches didn't even wait for the command.

He blinked out and reappeared several feet higher, moving at speed and aimed at the now truly-shocked Tank. He crashed into Tank's chest, unbalancing him. The next moment, Peaches' massive jaws were clamped down so hard on the arm holding the gun, that I heard Tank gasp in pain.

With a few head shakes, Tank was easily disarmed.

Actually, it was incredibly impressive. I had no idea a hellhound could build up that much speed over such a short distance. Peaches slowly began applying pressure. I could tell this because the grunts of pain escaping Tank began increasing in volume.

The jaw strength of a hellhound has not, to my knowledge, ever been measured. I would guess it had something to do with the fact that if a hellhound had you trapped in its jaws, the last thing you'd be thinking about—aside from the excruciating pain and imminent loss of whatever body part said hellhound was latched onto—was, *How much jaw pressure is being exerted on my soft tissue and delicate bones?*

At this moment—from the look of surprise mixed with terror on Tank's face—I would have to say things were not heading in a positive direction for any of us.

<Can I bite him?>

"No!" I said out loud, hoping to assuage Tank. "That's a good boy. But Tank needs his arm. No chewing."

<He tried to hurt you. I should hurt him. A small bite?>

Tank looked at me in confusion.

"Did...did you just say he was a *good boy?*" Tank asked as he looked at Peaches and then back at me. "Really?"

I held up a finger.

"Give me a second," I said, focusing on my exuberant hellhound. "Do *not* remove his arm. Or...no extra meat."

<Frank says an ounce of destruction is worth a pound of prevention. If I destroy his hand, I will prevent him from hurting you.>

I don't pretend to understand hellhound logic. Even when it seems to make some kind of sense.

<That is so wrong on so many levels. Don't hurt him...not anymore. Leave his arm attached. I'm serious.>

"Yes," I answered, turning my focus back to the now pale Tank. "Is your arm still attached to your body?"

"Yes," Tank said as sweat started forming on his brow.

"Then he's being a good boy, trust me. Do you want your arm to remain attached?"

"Yes. I'd really prefer my arm attached."

"Are you lead on this team?" I asked. "If not, who is?"

"I'm lead," Tank said with a nod. He was drenched in sweat now. I feared he would soon go into shock from the pain. "Can you tell him to ease up? I can't feel my fingers."

"Sure. Call off your team...now," I said, keeping my voice low. "Unless you want to go from Tank to Lefty."

Tank slowly raised a shaky hand and shook his head.

"Stand down," he said, his voice tight with pain. "I've got this under control."

The team stopped closing in on us.

"Weren't you briefed on—what would you call it—cleared visitors, or something like that?"

"Just started...today," Tank answered through a grimace. "This was my...first shift. Was just about to check the Vetted Visitor Log when you walked in."

"That's it! The Vetted Visitors," I said, relieved he had jogged my memory. "Where is it?"

"Front desk and my phone."

"Where's your phone?"

"Front pocket."

I reached into his pocket and pulled out his phone. I held it while he accessed the page of Vetted Visitors. The first name on the top was mine.

"What's that name at the top?" I asked. "Can you say it out loud?"

"Simon Strong, vetted visitor authorized by Director DeMarco."

"See?" I said. "This has all been a misunderstanding." I glanced at Peaches. "Maybe Monty was onto something with the whole diplomacy thing."

"Mr. Strong, I'm really sorry," Tank said apologetically. "You started singing and acting strange—then I saw the gun, and my reflexes kicked in."

"No, no, I totally get it," I said, returning the phone to his front pocket. "These things happen, believe me."

"Could you, you know, ask your dog, sorry, your hellhound to let go of my arm?" Tank asked. "I can't feel anything now."

"Oh, shit, sorry," I looked down at my awesome hellhound protector. "Let him go, boy."

<No. They still want to hurt you.>

"Excuse me?" I said, glancing behind me quickly. They still looked plenty twitchy. "Tank, you *did* tell them to stand down, right?"

I didn't sense any of the mages spooling energy, but by this point they could have had enough energy stored to blast me to bits several times over, if I recalled Rey's analogy correctly: Mages have the capacity to store energy within, like the bucket heads they are, or something like that. It wasn't an exact recollection, but I knew I was close.

Tank didn't immediately respond. His delay made *me* twitchy.

"Tank? Did you tell your team to stand down?"

"Yes, sir," he replied quickly. "I'd like to keep my arm, sir."

"Good, because Roxanne would kill me if I did anything to destroy her—"

I sensed the orb before it slammed into my back. I managed to rotate my body to avoid the brunt of the impact, and a broken back.

Percussive blasts, how fun.

Percussive blasts were low on the showy energy that Monty used, and high in the kinetic department. It was why I hadn't sensed much of an energy signature. That explained the bouncing mages. I should've known something was up. Most mages don't bounce; at least I'd never seen Monty bounce.

Using percussive blasts only required kinetic energy by the user. (Yes, I had been studying.) The two mages in the back didn't need runes to cast. Just moving their bodies was enough. It was similar to my magic missile, except instead of using life force, they used motion—and it hurt like hell.

The blow punched me across the reception area and into a very solid wall which, rudely, had no give at all. Pandemonium ensued. The lobby, which was still fairly populated as Tank and I conversed, now lost its collective mind.

As I slid down the wall and onto the floor, I wondered why this chaos was called pandemonium. Pandas were slow-moving, gentle bamboo eaters. What was happening in the lobby presently was closer to hellhoundemonium.

It's never a good idea to attack the bondmate of a hell-hound. Never.

Peaches blinked in and out of sight as he pounced on and mangled the security personnel. In a few seconds, the entire security team was incapacitated and in serious need of medical attention. Luckily, we were in one of the best medical facilities on the eastern seaboard.

He reappeared in front of Tank and gave off a low bark which spider-webbed all of the glass in the lobby. Someone had the presence of mind to hit an alarm which locked down the lobby. Klaxons went off and all the doors locked. Red emergency lights flooded the area in an eerie glow. Under the noise, I thought I heard the sound of metal grinding against metal, but, honestly, I couldn't be sure.

I walked over to the now scared shitless Tank and drew Grim Whisper.

"That was not cool, Tank," I said as Peaches growled in agreement. "Not cool at all."

"It wasn't me," Tank pleaded, holding up a hand. "It was the Knockers."

"The who?"

"Knockers," he explained. "That's what we call percussives—Knockers."

"Your Knockers slammed me into a wall, and—you know what? I can't even finish that sentence. You're lead, your team, your responsibilty...your pain."

Peaches growled in agreement again—a little louder this time.

"Wait a second, Mr. Strong," Tank replied nervously. "This is all a misunderstanding, like you said. Remember diplomacy? Let's try that—diplomacy. We can talk this out."

"Funny you say that," I said, looking around. "Every time I try diplomacy, it usually ends up looking like this. Turn off that infernal alarm. You're explaining this to Rox —Director DeMarco."

"Do I have to?"

"Look around, Tank. This lobby went from *Welcome to Haven* to *You have just entered a militarized zone* in the span of a few minutes. Who do you think is to blame for that?"

Tank looked down at Peaches then back at me.

"My team?"

"Good answer. Right answer," I said, holstering Grim Whisper. "When the Director gets here—and she *will* be coming in hot—make sure you inform her that she has a huge pair of vicious knockers."

"What?"

"You may want to rephrase that, but you know what I

mean," I said quickly. "Your team, your responsibility. You didn't have them stand down, your percussives, jumped the gun, and decided I made excellent target practice. A Vetted Visitor, mind you."

The klaxons turned off and I took a moment to collect my thoughts. I looked around and took in the scene. Roxanne was going to be so pissed. The red emergency lights switched off and normal lighting returned. That's when I was able to appreciate the level of damage one hellhound could inflict in a confined space.

The reception area had been transformed into a small warzone. It looked like the walls had taken mortar fire. I stepped close to one of the holes and realized they were about the size of a certain hellhound's head. The front desk had a sizable chunk missing from one corner. The missing section looked vaguely like an enormous bite mark, complete with drool residue.

Several of the tables, which earlier held magazines for visitors, now resembled strange abstract sculptures. Steel shutters had descended over the main entrance and egress points, effectively cutting off the lobby from the building. *That* had been the sound of metal grinding on metal.

The shutters themselves were runed with symbols I couldn't decipher, except to know that trying to break through them would result in massive amounts of pain. Roxanne was really not fooling around. The new security measures were impressively scary. Much like the Director herself.

No one was leaving the lobby under their own power.

After a few moments, the shutters on the stairwell doors slid up with a surge of power. It was a familiar, dangerous, surge of power.

The stairwell doors erupted outward, and more mage security poured into the lobby. Behind the mages, I caught sight of one very angry-looking sorceress making her way to the front of the group.

<Over here, boy. Let's not make them angry—well, angrier.>

<Can I play with them for a little while?>

<No, Roxanne would be upset if you did. If she's upset, she won't make you any meat.>

<I didn't chew the big man's arm off. I'm sure she will make some meat for that. Can you ask her?>

<Yeah, I don't think that's going to get you any meat points. I'm glad you left his arm attached, but she's going to be upset you mangled her security team and redecorated her lobby.>

<I didn't mangle them. They are gently chewed. They all have their arms and legs. That deserves meat.>

<I'll see what I can do. For now, no mangling, gentle or otherwise.>

"What the hell happened here?" Roxanne asked, without raising her voice. That was somehow more fearsome than if she had been yelling at the top of her lungs. "I expect an explanation...now."

No one answered.

The amount of energy coming off of her would have made me mute, too. She sounded calm, but her energy signature said homicidal. I was behind some debris that resembled one of the desks. No, I wasn't hiding—I had just found a good spot to rest after being slammed into a wall. I was engaged in active recovery.

Peaches padded over to the livid Director.

"Peaches?" she said, rubbing his head, much to Tank's surprise. He was also engaged in active recovery behind another pile of debris. Smart man. "Where is Simon?"

My traitorous hellhound padded over to where I sat. Again, I wasn't hiding, I was recovering. Roxanne followed Peaches over.

"Hi, Roxanne," I said with a small wave. "Give me a second. Your knockers launched me into a wall."

"Excuse me?"

THREE

"I mean, never mind," I said, getting slowly to my feet. "Your new security measures are impressive. Scary, but impressive."

"And necessary, it seems," she answered as she surveyed the devastation in the lobby. "Why am I not surprised to see you in the center of this destruction?"

"I can explain," I said. "It's not what it looks—"

She held up a finger and cut me off as she turned to face the now standing Tank. I had to give him credit. Anyone else would have left the lobby running in fear. He stood his ground, trembling in place. The energy Roxanne gave off had a distinct 'obliterating' vibe.

Today she had blasted past annoyed and stepped firmly into anger, just this side of rage. It was an amazing and terrifying thing to experience, due to my proximity to said angry sorceress.

I'd never seen Roxanne truly angry.

Upset, yes, but full-out sorceress on a rampage about to destroy everything and everyone in her path, no. This brief glimpse into her anger made me glad I had never faced her as an enemy. I had enough scary enemies: there was no need to add one more.

"Tank," she said quietly, and he winced. "Explain this...now."

"It was my fault," I said quickly, potentially taking my life into my hands and causing Tank to exhale in semi-relief. At this point it was the equivalent of my jumping on a grenade meant for him. "It was unintentional, really. A misunderstanding."

Roxanne turned to face me again and I saw my life flash in her eyes. It was a brief moment of future agony.

"Really?" she asked, in the same gentle, homicidal tone she used earlier. "Perhaps you should clarify?"

"I walked in, but I didn't know about the new security protocol. Then I opened my jacket." I opened my jacket slightly, showing Roxanne my holster. "He saw my weapon and the security team reacted against what they thought was a threat to Haven."

Roxanne narrowed her eyes at me.

Usually I was a horrible liar, but when lives were on the line—and Roxanne looked like she wanted to erase someone—I could pull off a semi-decent fabrication if it was rooted in some truth.

"Is this true?" Roxanne said, her words clipped with barely contained anger as she turned to Tank. "Is *that* what happened?"

I nodded almost imperceptibly behind Roxanne.

"Yes ma'am," Tank said, quickly, with a wise sense of self-preservation. "I truly apologize for the misunderstanding, Mr. Strong."

"What happened to your arm?" Roxanne asked,

looking at what remained of Tank's jacket, shirt, and the gentle bite marks on his arm gifted to him by my overprotective hellhound. "It's a mess."

"Me again," I said, interrupting. "Or rather"—I glanced down at my sheepish puppy—"Peaches."

My hellhound whined and ducked behind me as Roxanne looked down at him.

"How?" Roxanne asked. "Did you set your hellhound on my security team?"

"Again, another misunderstanding," I said with a small chuckle that died away at her expression. "It's really funny if you think about it."

"I'm practically breathless from the hilarity of this situation...Explain, and make it plausible."

"Well, I thought I was under attack and before I knew it, Peaches had jumped into defense mode," I said. "I managed to stop him before he tore off"—I made a show of looking at Tank's name badge which actually said *Tank* —"Tank's arm, but just barely. Really sorry about that, Tank."

"We're good," Tank said with a dismissive wave. "We aren't really prepped to deal with monst—I mean, hellhounds. These things happen."

"No, they *don't*," Roxanne said, her voice resembling a slab of steel slapping me in the face. "They tend to happen around Tristan and Simon more often than not, but they don't *just happen*. Not around here. You and your team should be prepared for every and any eventuality —*including* hellhounds."

"Yes, ma'am," Tank answered. "This won't happen again."

"Actually—" I started and stopped immediately as

Roxanne gave me a look that said, 'Continue at your own peril'. "Nevermind."

"Go get that arm looked at," Roxanne said to Tank. "I expect a full report on my desk after you're tended to."

"Yes, ma'am. Will do."

Tank left the lobby a little faster than I expected, probably grateful to still be able to move under his own power after that conversation.

Roxanne turned to one of the mage cavalry that had rushed in with her. His name tag said Rogers. Rogers was currently giving me a heaping dose of stink-eye. I ignored him. I had already agreed to take the heat for the destruction.

I wasn't going to lose sleep over some extra mage stink-eye. I'd been glared at by the best. Besides, Rogers was amateur hour; his glare didn't even register as a one on the glare-o-meter. After gods, mortal glares just didn't impress me.

"Rogers, take the rest of the team upstairs and inform the floor staff about what occurred. I'll make certain they receive proper medical attention. Leave some of your team deployed here to secure the lobby."

"Yes, ma'am," Rogers answered, still giving me stinky eyeballs. "Right away, ma'am."

"Simon, with me," Roxanne said. "This way."

"Yes, ma'am," I answered, mocking Rogers, who overheard me and raised his glare to an impressive 1.5 on the glare-o-meter. Better, but not by much. "Where did you find these guys and what's Rogers' deal? He's looking at me like I did this."

"Simon, have you ever considered that your actions

have consequences?" Roxanne asked. "Real-world consequences that impact those around you?"

"All the time," I said, my tone serious. "I have also considered that the consequences of the actions of those around me usually result in blame being directed at me. Unfairly so."

"Unfairly so?" Roxanne asked with a slight smile. It was a smile that said, Okay, let's entertain your fantasy. "Explain."

"Every time something gets annihilated, obliterated, or disintegrated, everyone is looking at me," I said indignantly. "Why? I'm not the one with the energy-manipulating abilities, or the one tossing around orbs of power that blast through almost everything and everyone."

"Do I need to explain it to you, Simon?"

"Please do," I said. "Use non-magical vocabulary, too. It's been a rough morning."

"It's actually quite simple: you present a very clear and imminent threat to your immediate environment."

"Excuse me? What are you talking about?"

"You are bonded to a hellhound," Roxanne said, rubbing Peaches on the head as we walked. "He's adorable *and* fearsome. Leaning more toward the fearsome, I'd say."

<She said I'm adorable and fearsome. Did you hear her?>

<I did. Trying to focus here.>

<If you were adorable and fearsome, you wouldn't need to. Everyone would be focusing on you.>

<That's kind of what she's saying. Now, hush.>

"He can't help it," I said, focusing on Roxanne. "It's part of the package."

"I know," Roxanne said with a nod. "Then there's you. Your energy signature is different now—I'd almost say shifted, but that's impossible, obviously. You've faced formidable opponents, and that leaves a mark. Aside from that, on some visceral level, people pick up on your condition."

"I've been upgraded," I said, remembering Kali's words, "from cursed to marked." I pointed to my forehead. "See? Marked."

Roxanne narrowed her eyes and briefly gave me a look of surprise.

"I see. Marked, indeed," she said. "Then there's *that*—your attitude about this entire thing."

"What entire thing?"

"In the past, you were aware of this world, but not a part of it," Roxanne answered. "Now you are, and you make light of it. Did you know being the 'Marked of Kali' is considered a death sentence in many circles?"

"Does that include any of the circles I currently inhabit?"

"Presently? Yes, most of them. The Marked of Kali was considered a harbinger of death and destruction to be eliminated at the earliest convenience," she answered. "I'm actually surprised we aren't under attack at this very moment."

"Oh, I see some of Monty's humor has been rubbing off on you," I said. "I have to admit, 'marked' sounds much better than cursed, though."

"You are missing the gravity of your situation," Roxanne replied, shaking her head. "The Marked of Kali is a death curse. She has only hastened your demise."

"Good thing she took care of that part first, then," I said, raising a hand before she could continue. "I know. Sometimes, I don't know how I keep it together myself.

Many of the things I've seen, beings I've interacted with or run from, were only hinted at in rumors and stories."

"Anyone else would have been driven mad by now," she said. "Your resilience in light of how you were introduced to this world is remarkable."

"I don't know about that," I answered with a slight smile. "I may have come into all of this with some of my own crazy. I only know that if I don't adjust and deal with it, there are people close to me that will be in danger. I can't afford to lose it—or them."

"I understand," she said. "Well, you wanted to know why much of the blame falls upon you. Now you know."

In classic sorceress fashion, she had answered my question without actually answering my question. I was certain that every magic user went through a class called Obfuscating Answers to Regular Questions 101.

"Not really, but thanks for trying."

We walked over to the elevator banks in silence.

Roxanne pressed her ID card against the far elevator panel, followed by a thumbprint and a retinal scan, activating the Director Only elevator. This was the same elevator that accessed the Detention Area several levels below Haven. She really had beefed up the security. I never recalled the elevators needing several layers of biometrics in the past.

We stepped into the elevator and Roxanne moved to the buttonless panel.

"Top level, please," Roxanne said, stepping close to the panel as a green beam scanned both her eyes.

"Voice and optical recognition confirmed. Welcome, Director DeMarco."

"Whoa, that's a serious security upgrade," I said, stepping back as the elevator slowly rose. "The lobby shutters were a nice touch too. Felt ultra-secure. Just like a bank vault."

"The schism nearly killed him, Simon," Roxanne said after a few moments, her gentle voice sheathed in steel. "It's not safe for him to leave. He's not ready to go out there with you, not yet."

"He's not ready? Or *you're* not ready?"

"Does it matter?" she exploded. "I almost lost him! You're his shieldbearer. You were supposed to watch him."

I was acutely aware that I was in a small space with an emotional and powerful sorceress—emphasis on powerful. I had known this conversation was coming eventually. I just didn't expect it to take place in a moving box with no cover.

I took a deep breath and tried my diplomacy again, hoping for an outcome that was low on the violence and high on the survivability.

"I *did* watch him," I said firmly, but treading carefully. Her thoughts were slightly skewed when it came to Monty. "I watched him sacrifice himself for someone he cares for twice."

"I'm sorry," she said, raising a hand. "It's just that I know he won't stay. I've placed elite magical security and some of the strongest counter-measures I know in place. It's meaningless. He humors me, but I know he can circumvent them, especially now, after the schism. His power has grown considerably."

"How much stronger is he?" I asked, remembering how he'd faced off against Evers even in the midst of his schism. "Dex-level strong?"

"Dex is in a class unto himself," Roxanne answered. "I

don't know many mages as strong as that crazy old man. Tristan is close to being an Archmage. A few more shifts—"

"Are these shifts more schisms?" I asked warily. "More importantly, are they lethal?"

"Not usually."

"Let me clarify...are they lethal to those around Monty? Specifically me."

"A shift is not a schism," Roxanne said. "If he progresses normally, it should happen without much upheaval...or death."

"This is *Monty* we're talking about. Normal and boring he is not," I answered. "If he's this strong, why all the security around him? Is he in danger?"

"No, I told him not to cast. He's just appeasing me, but once he sees you—"

"You think he'll cut and run?"

She gave me a look that said, *Are you serious right now?*

"What do you think?" she asked. "Does he seem like the type to remain locked up in Haven indefinitely?"

"I think you underestimate how much he values and cares about your opinion."

"Values and cares? Yes," Roxanne said. "Follow? Unlikely. In that regard, he's as bad as his uncle. A Montague through and through."

"I don't know," I said, rubbing my chin. "Dex seems to listen to the Morrigan. Maybe you can get her to pay Monty a visit? Convince him to stay put?"

"Are we referring to the same Tristan? Not even *she* could convince him to stay here against his will. She barely manages to keep Dexter clothed."

"I think she likes Dex semi-naked," I said with a wince. "There's an image I won't get rid of anytime soon."

"Tristan has his own motivations. He may hear what I have to say, but it's unlikely he will listen."

"It's Monty. You know him. He's stubborn and thick-headed. You tell him not to cast and he'll listen most of the time, unless he sees those he cares about in danger."

I remained silent for a few moments to let my words sink in.

"He should have never cast on the skywalk," she said. "Evers knew he would."

"She probably did," I said. "The fact that it was booby-trapped wouldn't have made any difference to him. Nothing would've stopped him. You were in danger, and that's all that mattered to him in that moment: your safety."

"I know," she said. "He can be so...."

She threw her hands up in the air, exasperated.

"Impossibly difficult," I said with a nod. "I know. But he cares for you deeply. You know that."

"I know," she said. "He views you as his family. Did you know you were the only one he wanted admitted the first day? He's impossible."

"He's Monty. Comes with the territory. How is he? Really?"

"I'm...concerned," Roxanne said as the elevator doors whispered open. "The schism has left...traces."

"Traces?" I asked, worried. "What does that mean, traces?"

Magic users were notorious for their skill in under-stating situations. What I saw as major devastation to property, Monty saw as urban renovation. The fact that Roxanne admitted she was concerned was the equivalent of the sorceress running around the room with her hair on fire.

My heart may have skipped a beat or three.

"Come see me after you visit," she said, placing a hand on my shoulder. "I was just there and I'm sure he would like some space from my mothering. We can discuss it then."

"Okay," I said with a sudden knot in my stomach. "I'll do that. What room is he in?"

"731, far end of the hall, to the left," she said, pointing behind me as we reached the top floor and exited the elevator. "It's the only patient room on this level. I had it converted from a conference room, so as to monitor his condition and recovery. My office is on the other side of the floor."

"That's convenient. How many offices are on this floor?"

"Besides mine, none."

"So, it's just your office and his room?"

"Considering my responsibilities here, it was the only way I could ensure he received the care he needed after a schism," she explained. "Very few physicians are competently trained in dealing with the after-effects of one."

"And you are?"

"One of the few on the entire eastern seaboard," Roxanne said with a nod. "It's a specific body of knowledge. His recovery will take some time, and he will exhibit uncharacteristic quirks during the process."

"Quirks which require close supervision, it seems."

"Quirks which require isolation, for his safety," she

answered. "As I mentioned earlier, he is not ready to leave, even if he thinks otherwise."

"I see," I said, looking down the corridor to where Monty was impriso—I mean, where Monty was getting expert medical care. "I'm sure he's enjoying the extra level of care you're providing."

She gave me a withering glare.

"This is Tristan," she said dryly. "He absolutely hates it. In any case, you should have no trouble getting past the security on this level. I briefed them myself."

"How soon should I expect the orbs of destruction after meeting them?"

"These are professionals, not easily prone to surprise," Roxanne answered, glancing at Peaches. "Just remember what I said about your presence and tread carefully. The security detail on this floor is on high alert."

"Because of Monty's quirks?" I asked. "I mean, how bad are these quirks? Has he started drinking coffee?"

"Initially, they manifested as random obliteration circles all around his room."

"Oh," I said, having second thoughts about my visit. "Maybe I should come back when he's more quirk-free?"

"It should be safe," Roxanne said. "I placed the nullifying runes myself. Besides, what's the worst that can happen? The circles won't kill you. You may suffer excruciating agony and wish death many times over, but they won't *kill* you."

"Well if that's not incentive, I don't know what is."

"Go see him," she said quietly. "He needs to see someone besides me. Just don't irk the security team. They are a bit skittish these days."

"Can't see why," I said as Peaches bumped my knee and

nearly shoved me into the nearby wall. "Oh, I don't want to trouble you, but does the kitchen have some extra sausage for my bottomless hellhound?"

Roxanne gestured and materialized a large sausage for Peaches. She stepped close and fed it to him, then bent over and whispered something I couldn't make out in his ear before walking away.

"Come see me after your visit with Tristan. I have information you need."

She walked off and headed to her office. I understood her concern, but she wasn't going to keep Monty in Haven for long with these methods, no matter how powerful she was.

I was pretty certain Monty was stronger than Roxanne. He was also a wise mage who knew better than to piss her off in her hospital by trying to escape. It's not like she couldn't locate him if she wanted to. Staying put was the smart play here, but it wouldn't last.

I rubbed my hellhound's head and started heading in the other direction, towards Monty's cell—I mean, room.

<What did she tell you?>

<She said she was making me a sausage because I didn't rip off the big man's arm. Then she said something about how I'm much more photogenerous than you are and that the lobby is filled with cameras. She knows what I did. What did I do?>

<The word is photogenic. You redecorated her lobby single-houndedly. That's what you did.>

<Is that good?>

I looked down the corridor Roxanne had taken to her office. Like I said—impressive and scary.

<Not usually. C'mon, let's go see Monty.>

FOUR

In order to get to Monty's room, we had to cross a gauntlet of some of the scariest sorcerers I had ever seen.

Even before the squad of sorcerers, I noticed the nullifying runes etched into the floor and walls, slowly pulsing from deep reds to bright blues. Roxanne wasn't kidding when she said she had counter-measures in place. This area was beyond secure. The runes gave off so much energy that the security detail on the floor felt like window dressing.

They weren't.

The security team stood some distance from Monty's door. I figured the runes would affect them too, which was why they were remaining just this side of the runed area, outside of the null zone.

It reminded me of the set up in the Randy Rump. As a neutral location, casting was strongly discouraged inside its walls. This was reinforced by the nullifying runes strategically placed around the property, both inside and out.

Much to Jimmy's distress, it hadn't stopped the regular

destruction of the place, but the last batch of runes that had been inscribed at the Rump had been scary strong. If anyone managed to cast through them, nullifying runes were the least of anyone's concerns.

I visually scanned the security team quickly and processed the information they provided. At first glance, there were four sorcerers with serious energy signatures. Any one of them would've been a handful. All four of them together as a team sent the message loud and clear: *Attack this level and die a quick and painful death.*

Roxanne wasn't fooling around.

At first, I thought the message was for someone who had realized they no longer wished to live and figured that the best way to end it all was to stroll up to this level, looking for Monty. It took me a few seconds, and then I realized this was Roxanne's way of sending Monty a not-so-subtle message.

You will be discharged when I think you're good and ready, not one second before.

It would have been touching, if it weren't a bit scary.

I knew Roxanne cared deeply for Monty, I just hadn't realized she cared four-insanely-strong-sorcerers deep. It was a nice gesture, I guess, for magic users. Ultimately, it was futile. I could sense the undercurrent of power that was Monty's energy signature, beneath the nullifying runes. If I wasn't a mage and could sense him, I was certain the security team knew they were outclassed. Monty's signature replied to Roxanne's not-so-subtle message.

I'm staying here because I choose to, not because I have to.

His energy signature dwarfed the power of the four sorcerers combined. If he really wanted to, Monty could stroll out of here, and all they could do, was hold the door for him as he left. His power had increased from certain badass to scary kickass.

Even though this security detail wasn't in the same league as Monty, they still looked plenty intimidating. They weren't slouches—they just weren't strong enough to deal with a determined Monty.

It reminded me of the glimpse of power Dex had shown me recently. It was on a scale of: *You should give up now, lay down, and die.* And that was without Nemain, that scary mace-axe of his. I now had an idea of what the Morrigan saw in him and why he had never joined the Ten.

Dex and the Morrigan were both more than slightly unhinged, and were made for each other.

I realized that Dex wielded so much power that his very presence was a threat. I shook myself out of my thoughts, refocused on the security team and approached slowly, keeping my hands in sight. I didn't want a repeat of the destruction tango that had happened downstairs.

Somehow, I knew I would walk away with more than just a few bumps and bruises, if it came to that. Peaches would have to go lethal, which meant they would react in kind. In the end, it would spiral into a messy and bloody nuclear option. It was too early for nuclear options, and I hadn't had any coffee.

Even though this team was smaller than the lobby and reception squad, these were heavy-hitters, and I wasn't Monty. One of the energy signatures was off the charts and I actually paused in my approach. The one who had focused my attention was the tall, burly man standing closest to me and effectively barring my path.

Actually, he was wide enough to bar anyone's path and

comfortably take up all the remaining space in the corridor. It never crossed my mind that some sorcerers trained their bodies as well as their minds.

My image of them was always of the stereotypical bookworm studying in a dusty library, practicing how to cast, and learning arcane finger wiggles. Clearly, I was mistaken here. This sorcerer looked like he bench-pressed the library after studying in it.

They all wore rune-inscribed combat armor, but I could tell from the way he stood and the look in his eyes that the first sorcerer had seen action. Deadly action.

Time to break out the diplomacy.

"Good morning, Mr. Strong," the sorcerer closest to me said. His voice was a deep baritone that reverberated in the corridor. "Visiting Mr. Montague?"

"I'd like to," I said, looking up into his face. He stood at least six inches taller than me. The full beard gave him a rogue lumberjack look. "You are?"

"Elias Pirn," he said, holding out a massive hand about the size of my head. "I'm lead security here. If you need anything, don't hesitate to ask."

I gave his hand a firm shake and nodded to the rest of the group. They all returned the nod and then went back to standing relaxed, but alert. Elias and his team were dangerous. They made Tank and the group downstairs look like the novice B-team. Up here, I was dealing with the professional A-team.

The lethal A-team.

"Thank you for keeping him safe," I said. "I'm sure he's been a royal pain in the ass."

Two of the sorcerers exchanged glances and smiles.

"Nothing we can't handle," Elias said quickly, shutting

down the smiles with a look. "We've guarded...challenging clients in the past. Mr. Montague is not much of a problem, once you get to know him."

"You must have a different Montague in there then," I said with a small laugh. "I need to bring my hell—er, my very large canine-like partner with. That okay?"

"If he's on this floor, Director DeMarco approved it," Elias answered. "Not an issue with us, unless he starts destroying property. Hellhounds aren't known for their delicate natures. Has he been fed in the last hour?"

"A few minutes ago," I said, impressed. "You know about hellhounds?"

"I've never met a puppy, but yes," Elias answered, glancing down at Peaches with a raised eyebrow. "Forces of nature and damn near impossible to stop."

"That sounds about right," I said, rubbing my hellhound's head. "But Peaches is an above-average hellhound."

"You've come across many hellhounds, then?" Elias asked, still looking down at my own superbly behaved hellhound. "Did you say Peaches?"

"Just one other, his dad," I said. "Yes, his name is Peaches."

"He seems okay at this size; it's when they get supersized that they become truly dangerous," Elias replied, looking at me. "Not a situation I want to revisit in my life ever again. At least not without an ample amount of RPGs. Know what I mean?"

It was a subtle, not-so-subtle message: *Keep your hellhound under control or we will.*

"They can be a handful," I said with a chuckle that never reached my eyes. "Peaches is an awesome hellhound.

He'll behave, and I'd never let any harm come to him. Not while I'm breathing. Know what *I* mean?"

"I'm glad we see eye to eye on things," Elias said, stepping to one side. "We aren't equipped to deal with a hellhound level of property damage."

"Property destruction is so not his thing. Now, sausages—well, he loses his mind for those."

<I don't lose my mind. I just think meat is the most important thing.>

<More important than your bondmate?>

Silence.

<Really?>

<I'm thinking. I would say it's close. Does my bondmate have meat?>

<Good to see my importance is conditional on how much meat I can carry.>

<How much meat can you carry?>

<Whatever I can carry is never enough for a certain black-hole hellhound I know.>

<Too much is never enough, when it comes to meat.>

Elias gave me a nod and a tight smile, motioning to the door at the far end of the corridor.

"Right that way, Mr. Strong," Elias said. "I'm sure Mr. Montague will be glad to see you."

I walked past the four sorcerers and into the null zone. The shift in energy prickled against my skin, as I pushed on the door.

Nothing happened.

"Apologies," Elias said, walking into the null zone. With a gesture, he placed an orange-glowing hand on the door, unlocking it. "The locks are runically enhanced for safety. They default to being locked."

"Are you saying Monty is locked in?" I felt the anger rise within. "Why is he locked in?"

"Monty?" Elias asked, giving me a look. "Mr. Montague?"

"Yes, Mr. Montague. You have him locked in for his safety?"

"For *his* safety?" Elias asked. "You misunderstand. The locks on the door are for *our* safety, not his."

"Oh," I said, chagrined. "I thought you were keeping him here against—"

"Have a good visit," Elias said, cutting me off and moving out of the null zone. "Please don't agitate him. That would be...unpleasant for everyone involved."

It wasn't lost on me that Elias could cast while standing next to me...in the null zone.

It was a subtle show of force that said: *We can control your access, and we aren't scared of your hellhound. Keep it frosty, and you can leave here in one piece. Bring the heat, and we will burn you down.*

Roxanne wasn't kidding with these four.

I gave Elias a brief nod and pushed the door open, stepping into Monty's room.

I paused to catch my breath at the sheer scope of the room. Roxanne had spared no expense renovating the space into...I wanted to say a patient suite, but it was closer to a patient wing. A very upscale patient wing for just one pris—patient.

Palatial didn't begin to describe it. I felt like I had stepped into a high-end furniture showroom. The room was easily three to four times larger than any normal hospital room. There was enough space to fit four more beds and still have room left over for something small, like a jacuzzi or a bus.

An Eames sofa sat along one side of the room. Behind it, was a series of three large, dark rosewood Smania bookcases filled with books. Opposite the sofa, and across the large Persian center rug, sat a medium-sized desk from the same Italian craftsmanship as the bookcases, with a pile of books spread out across its surface. All of the books on the table were open to different sections. Sitting on the desk was a large notepad with Monty's handwriting on the page.

The bed was an oversized, industrial behemoth. It looked like someone had seen a hospital bed and created one for an ogre or a giant. I turned back and looked at the door, which was definitely too small for the bed to pass through, and shook my head.

Monty sat in the enormous bed with his laptop and looked up as I entered. A small smile crossed his lips as he closed his computer. His hair was in the usual Monty style —just this side of unkempt. He held a teacup and took a small sip as I crossed the expanse that was his room. His face was slightly drawn but had good color. He looked like a somewhat thinner version of his usual self.

Peaches gave Monty a low rumble. Monty returned the greeting with a nod. My hellhound did a few circles, plopped down on the rug next to the bed, and a few moments later, I heard the low snore. I looked around the room once again, took off my jacket and placed it on one of the several chairs around the desk.

"The next time I need some downtime," I said, pulling another chair to the bed and turning it so the back faced Monty, before sitting. "I'm going to ask Roxanne to save me this room. Do I have to make a reservation to get this room?"

"Roxanne has gone a bit overboard," Monty said, glancing around the room. "She wanted to make sure I was comfortable."

"This has crossed comfortable and stepped right into decadent," I said. "Can I sit on the Eames?"

"I wouldn't," Monty answered. "She doesn't even want me to sit on it and supposedly it was for my comfort."

"Ah, okay, house rules then."

"Precisely."

"It pains me to see you suffering so," I said, looking around again. "How *do* you get through your days in this room? It must be sheer torture."

"It's good to see you, Simon," Monty said. "Have you come to rescue me?"

"Rescue you?" I asked, incredulous. "You don't look like you need rescuing. In fact, I think I'm moving in. Can I get a bed like yours?"

"Roxanne may have an opinion about that," Monty said. "She was reluctant to admit you to my Vetted Visitors list. Something about you being a negative influence on my recovery."

"Me? A negative influence on you? Seriously?"

"Boggles the imagination, I know," Monty replied. "You are a paragon of virtue and positivity."

"Damn straight I am," I said. "You're looking good—thin, but good. Is Roxanne not feeding you?"

"Of course she's feeding me."

"Are you sure? Maybe she's planning on keeping you too weak to leave." I looked around nervously. "Can she hear us? The room is amazing, but a gilded—"

"A gilded cage is still a cage," Monty said. "Her intentions are in the right place, but—"

"You're not?"

"Precisely," he said, putting down his cup. "Your arms? Are those scars?"

I looked down at the jagged crisscrossed lines that decorated my arms. It was Evers' parting gift to me before she died. She gifted me with a lattice of pain...a reminder that even immortals could die.

"Evers was using the same kind of blade the Lucent had. I'm told the scars will fade eventually as my body deals with them."

"She held a kamikira?" Monty asked pensively. "That was unexpected. Those blades are extremely rare."

"And extremely sharp," I said, holding up a forearm. "By the way, where did Roxanne find Paul Bunyan the sorcerer and his team? He comes across as pretty powerful."

"Did you antagonize him?"

"Funny, he asked me not to agitate you, as if you were easily agitated," I said. "Imagine you, agitated. You are the calmest mage I know."

"Is that a yes?"

"Why would I antagonize him? I'm just here to visit my good friend who nearly lost his mind. Hey"—I pointed to the walls of the room—"these walls, are they made of rubber?"

"Elias and his team," Monty began, ignoring my rubber-wall statement, "are a highly trained sorcerer security force. Angering them would be unwise."

"We almost got off on the wrong foot when I thought they were locking you in," I said. "Then I used diplomacy."

"Oh no," Monty said, concerned. "How many casualties?"

"None...on this floor."

"On this floor?" Monty asked warily. "What do you mean, 'on this floor'? How many floors have you visited today?"

"Well, we had a slight misunderstanding in the lobby. Nothing major. I got knocked up. Then Peaches gently mangled a few of the team; well, most of the team. There may have been some minor destruction—nothing that can't be fixed with some sheetrock and a fresh coat of paint—but it wasn't our fault. They started it."

"You got knocked around?" Monty asked. "Who started what?"

"Oh right," I said. "They have percussive mages downstairs with twitchy fingers. Hit me with some blasts, bounced me off a wall, then it all went to hell...hound."

"You contained the damage to the lobby?"

"Totally," I said with a nod. "Elias Bunyan and his crew look potentially lethal. Didn't want to chance another misunderstanding. Really flexed my diplomacy up here. Did you know he could cast in the null area of the floor? Heavy hitter."

Monty pinched the bridge of his nose.

"Please make a concerted effort to avoid the sorcerers on this level. Roxanne would be highly displeased if we injured them. They are only here to watch me, not to risk their lives."

"I figured from the energy signatures that Roxanne was serious about keeping you put," I said, giving him a long look. "How are you?"

"Bored out of my mind," he said. "If I don't leave soon, I'll be forced to take drastic measures."

"Drastic measures?" I asked, concerned. "Like?"

"Relax, Simon. I suffered a schism, not a psychotic break."

"Aren't those one and the same?" I asked. "You were full-on Darth Monty there for a moment. *Follow me and die.*"

"At no point did I utter the words: 'Follow me and die'."

"True, but that was the intent, the spirit of the statement. Like I said, major Darthness."

"There was no Darthness at work. The schism merely affected me more than I anticipated," Monty said. "I'm still dealing with some of the aftereffects, but it is under control."

"Roxanne feels like you should leave here later rather than sooner," I said. "She feels you were also a little too close to Darth Monty the last time we faced each other."

"I seem to recall saving you the last time we were together," Monty said with a semi-smile, "as you were trying to face an extremely homicidal Evers on your own."

"I had that situation completely handled and under control."

"As the scars on your arms attest," Monty answered after taking another sip of tea. "A few more minutes and she would have reduced you to ribbons of immortality."

"She was beyond fringe," I admitted. "Thanks for coming back. It was looking dicey there for a moment. She was serious about eliminating magic...and you."

"She wasn't the first and she won't be the last," Monty

said. "There are large factions that believe the world would be better off if magic never existed."

"What happened? Why was she so determined to reduce you to a memory?"

"My past is filled with acts that I will answer for at some point in my lifetime," Monty said. "I own these acts and would do them again if the need arose. We were in a war to save this plane…to save humanity. I committed atrocities I'd prefer not revisiting."

"And Evers?"

"She was a willing subordinate who became a victim, sadly. At the time, there was no other choice. I thought she had perished."

"She was very much non-perished."

"I'm aware," Monty said. "My concern is about her activities since the war. She may have set certain events in motion."

"That doesn't sound ominous at all."

"So far, nothing has reared its unpleasant head to attack us or eliminate…well, everything," Monty said, somewhat upbeat. "That, in itself, is good news. Rest assured, there are more like her out there."

"I've met a few," I said. "I'd like to not meet any more. Anyway, thanks, really. You didn't have to come back, but you did."

"You're welcome," Monty said. "I'm sure you would've done the same for me."

"I don't know," I said, shaking my head in mock seriousness. "Do you have any more super powerful psychos coming for you?"

"I have plenty of enemies," Monty said, narrowing his eyes at me. "Anything is possible. Now, tell me why you're here, and please don't insult my intelligence by saying this is just a regular visit."

"That's all this is," I lied. "I wanted to make sure you were still the cheerful mage I know."

"I'm a mage—we don't do cheerful, and you lie atrociously," Monty said, leaning back. "This must be serious if you were willing to brave the wrath of Roxanne by coming here. She's still quite upset with my schism and, for some reason, lays some of the blame on you."

"Imagine that, considering *you* were the one who cast when *you* weren't supposed to," I said. "Yet *I* get some of the blame."

"I think she just enjoys torturing you. Also there is the whole *guilt by association* theory working against you."

"So I'm learning," I said. "How did you know?"

"Your energy signature," Monty said with a hand wave, "while straightened out, which I can assume was Kali's handiwork, is all over the place. You're agitated; tell me why."

I looked down at my arms, but surprisingly I couldn't see my own energy signature.

"Has that always been the case?" I asked, still looking at my arms. "You can read my signature?"

"I'm a mage; I can see almost anyone's energy signature, unless they are deliberately trying to mask it," he answered. "Now, stop stalling and share."

"Ramirez got a call," I said. "For me."

"Did he finally upgrade to a real phone?" Monty asked. "Is this cause for celebration? Since when does he relay your personal messages?"

"He doesn't. This was a special call."

"Special enough to warrant a call from the Director of

the NYTF," Monty said. "I'm listening."

"It was from Shadow Company, specifically Douglas."

Monty's expression darkened.

"The same Shadow Company that doesn't officially exist?"

"The one and the same."

"Peter Douglas is a person of no small influence," Monty said. "For him to personally call Ramirez speaks volumes."

"I figured he wanted to keep the circle of information small."

"Which only lends this call more weight. What did Ramirez say?"

"I tried to convince him that digging into this was a bad idea," I said. "But this is Angel—"

"You may as well have told him to dig deeper."

I nodded.

"They gave him minimal information," I said. "Enough to be convincing. Asked for me by name and gave him some pertinent info about my past."

"How much did Ramirez uncover?"

"He knows I was a dead-eye," I said. "Don't think they told him much more than that."

"If he keeps digging, they'll consider him a liability," Monty said. "Groups like Shadow Company don't like liabilities."

"I explained as much to Angel. Douglas was flexing."

"I see," Monty said, his voice clipped. "I take it this wasn't a social call."

"Not even remotely," I said. "They want to meet."

"What did you say?"

"I didn't. I came here first."

FIVE

"It sounds urgent," Monty said, getting out of bed. "Did you call them back?"

"Not yet," I said. "Wait, what are you doing?"

"How long do you have before the number becomes inoperative?" Monty asked, pulling out his suit from the closet. "What does it *look* like I'm doing?"

"Signing my death warrant with Roxanne?" I said. "No way is she going to let you leave. Can you even cast safely?"

"The most dangerous weapon a battle mage possesses is his mind," Monty answered, tapping his temple. "How many times must I demonstrate this to you?"

"You just suffered a schism. Isn't that kind of serious in the mage world? Doesn't your brain need a break? I know mine does."

"A schism, when severe, is a cause for concern, but I've mostly recovered from my episode," Monty answered. "Barring some insignificant side effects, I'm good as new."

"Insignificant side effects, like?"

"Nothing major," Monty said. "Possible miscasts, orbs

being stronger than intended—that sort of thing. Nothing serious."

"That all sounded serious."

"Nothing to be overly concerned about," Monty said. "I'm practically fully recovered."

"Does Roxanne share this opinion?" I asked, looking around. "Judging from the security teams downstairs *and* upstairs, the runes on this floor creating a null zone, plus the fact that your room is a glorified cell, I'd say she disagrees with your assessment."

"Roxanne has always worried about my well-being, sometimes overly so."

"You didn't answer my question. Can you cast or is the tri-state area in danger when you start your little finger wiggling?"

"I don't do finger wiggling, and you are aware I possess other methods of attack besides my orbs?"

"That's what I'm scared of," I said. "Next thing I know, you're going to pull out your crybabies and wreak havoc all over the place."

"The Sorrows," Monty corrected. "Yes, I do use them, among other methods at my disposal. I don't seem to recall hearing any complaints on their use when Evers was bent on testing your immortality."

"I'm not complaining, it's just that—"

"Yes?" Monty asked. "You don't hear me mentioning your siphoning dark blade of destruction, do you?"

"That's because my blade has the sense to keep quiet," I snapped. "Your blades keen, wail, or do that moaning thing. It's disturbing."

"What's this about? They've never disturbed you before," Monty said. "It's 'wail,' by the way."

"Okay, listen," I said. "The truth is, I haven't fully recovered from Dex's screaming mace-axe. Could you not use your moaning blades for at least two or three years? I'd really appreciate it, thanks."

"My uncle used Nemain on you? That is quite the privilege. He only wields that when he's serious."

"Oh, he was serious, trust me. Seriously trying to scare me to death."

"You must tell me why, and how that went. Did you know the Morrigan herself cursed that weapon? It's quite lethal. Drives whoever uses it mad with prolonged use. Typical of her curses."

"That actually explains so much about Dex," I said. "How often has he used it?"

"Not very, like I said; he must think highly of you to unleash Nemain," Monty said with a slight smile. "He doesn't just whip out his weapon for anyone. Either he was quite upset or terribly concerned."

"I'd say a mix of both," I answered. "He was busy defending the gate he had created to the Golden Circle, and wanted to make sure I was ready to bring you back."

"The fact that he sent you, no offense intended, is surprising," Monty said. "I was in the midst of a schism. If I had lost control, I could have harmed you, or worse."

"None taken. Dex is full of surprises," I said. "Most of them scary and heart-stopping."

"Indeed," Monty said. "I suppose it makes sense, you being my shieldbearer."

"Not just yours," I said. "Kali gave me an upgrade."

"Upgrade? Is that code for another curse?"

"Do your squinty thing, you'll see. Apparently it's easy to see now."

"Really?" Monty said, narrowing his eyes at me. "I saw your signature had been unraveled, but I didn't notice... Oh, I'd say that is a considerable upgrade, yes."

"She said I'm now the Marked of Kali," I said. "It's suppose to warn off enemies."

"Really? Because this mark of hers will only signal that you are a target to be eliminated. Your potential power has increased significantly."

"I know," I said. "Not exactly the benefit I was expecting."

"You knew this and still accepted the mark?"

"She told me this *after* giving me the mark," I said. "Not like I had much of a choice. Besides, what do you suggest I should've done? Hey, Kali, goddess of death and destruction, possessor of a short temper, no thanks on the new mark? I'm good, thanks."

"That would have been a bad idea," Monty answered. "She's not known for her pleasant disposition."

"You think?" I said. "Anyway, I've had enough of screaming and sobbing blades to last me several lifetimes. Keep your crybabies sheathed for the time being, at least until my post-traumatic sword distress eases up."

"It's simply fascinating Dex would use that weapon on you," Monty replied. "The fact that you survived facing it is astounding. My uncle, when using that blade, is known as the—"

"Harbinger, I know," I finished. "The Harbinger of Destruction."

Monty nodded.

"He's infamous with that thing. The mere mention of his name would send hardened soldiers into a panic. Scores of men would flee before him—those who weren't driven mad by fear, of course."

"Of course. So glad your uncle unleashing his screaming, madness-inducing death axe on me has become the highlight of your day," I said, pointing to the bed. "Can you get back in bed?"

"Out of the question," Monty answered, putting on his jacket and straightening out his sleeves. "You must address this business with Douglas and the Shadow Company. For that, you will need assistance. Competent assistance. Now, how much time?"

"If Roxanne finds out you're trying to esca—I mean, discharge yourself—I would say exactly ten seconds after she finds out."

"It's good to see you haven't acquired a proper sense of humor in my absence. How long?"

"Monty, look," I said, holding up a hand. "I really appreciate the gesture. I do. But this is a horrible idea. Have you even tried casting since the schism? For all you know, your orbs could explode in your face, or crater the city."

"My casting is fine," Monty said, extending a hand and forming a brilliant white orb the size of a baseball. I had to look away from it or risk being blinded. The next moment, it was gone. "As you can see."

"Barely. What the hell was that?" I asked, trying to focus after being slightly blinded by the intensity of the orb. "I didn't even see a finger wiggle."

The next moment I heard a small knock at the door.

"Because there wasn't any," Monty said, looking at the door. "That will be Elias."

"What the hell, Monty?" I asked. "Since when are you

creating orbs without finger wiggles? And why is Paul Bunyan knocking at the door?"

"Elias is under strict orders to monitor any casting coming from this room," Monty answered as he headed to the door. "Roxanne is a bit nervous about my new strength level."

"No shit. *I'm* a bit nervous about your new strength level. What? Are you harnessing the power of the sun now?"

"Preposterous," Monty said. "That was only a small nullifier."

"Only a small nullifier? Designed to do what?"

"Eradicate the use of most magic on this level," Monty answered matter-of-factly. "It was completely harmless unless you were wielding energy. Your new mark is completely unaffected."

"Harmless? Even I know enough to know that small orb was a magic nuke. Are you insane? You just nullified magic on this level. No wonder Roxanne is monitoring this room."

"These melodramatics don't suit you," he said dismissively. "Like I said, it was a small nullifier and I had it completely under control. It needed to be done."

Another knock on the door, this time a little louder.

"You realize we are standing in a null zone and that this floor is covered in runes to prevent exactly what you just did?"

"I'm aware," he answered, holding up a finger. "One second. If I don't address this, Elias gets bothered."

"Elias gets bothered?" I asked incredulously. "What happens when Elias gets bothered?"

"He lets his imagination get the better of him," Monty answered. "He's still young."

"Somehow Elias doesn't seem like the type to overreact. What happened last time he unleashed his imagination?"

"Well, last time, we had to replace the door after Elias blasted it to bits in a fit of overprotective exuberance. There was debris everywhere. That door is made of runed ironwood; Roxanne was not pleased."

"I can't imagine why."

He answered me by holding up his finger again. A wave of orange energy raced across the surface of the door as it clicked open. Monty opened the door, which was currently filled with one concerned-looking lumberjack sorcerer.

"Good morning, Elias," Monty said in a congenial voice as he looked up at the towering man. "Is something amiss?"

"Hello, Mr. Montague," Elias answered as he glanced in and around the room. I could tell they had played this game before. "You know the rules. Director DeMarco wants no casting from this room, you know that."

"I'm aware," Monty said with a slight nod. "I was just demonstrating a cast for my associate, Simon."

"Is he a mage?" Elias asked, glancing in my direction. "My files say he isn't."

"Files?" I asked. "What files? Since when are there—?"

"Not in the least," Monty said, interrupting me. "Simon is what I would call an anomaly. I was making a point."

"A point?" Elias asked warily. "Would it be possible to make your points without spiking the energy levels on the floor?"

"My apologies," Monty said. "I wasn't aware my orb would have that effect. Are you unharmed?"

"Unharmed and neutralized," Elias said, narrowing his eyes at Monty. "You cast a nullifier again, didn't you? Are you planning another excursion? You know how she gets when you go AWOL."

"I have no idea what you're referring to," Monty answered with a straight face. "I was merely showing Simon that the schism had left my abilities intact and unaffected—enhanced, even."

"Of course," Elias answered. "You realize it makes my team nervous when you blast through the nullifying runes like that. You could see how we would think it was an attack, especially when it leaves us defenseless? Then we can't protect you."

"I wasn't aware I *needed* protecting."

"Mr. Montague," Elias said with practiced calm. "If you nullify the floor, we can't do our jobs effectively. If we can't do our jobs, Director DeMarco gets...Well, let's just say she's not happy. You want to keep her happy, don't you?"

"Absolutely," Monty said. "Once again, my deepest apologies if I've caused you and the team any discomfort. I'm sure your abilities will return shortly."

"Please refrain from any more casting or unsanctioned outings," Elias said. "Any kind of casting, enhanced or otherwise."

Monty actually paused and looked up at the ceiling, all the while nodding slowly.

"I'll give it a thorough consideration," Monty said after a few seconds. "Will there be anything else?"

"Nothing else," Elias answered. "Let's keep the casting to a minimum, as in zero. Can you do that?"

"Of course," Monty said. "No rogue casting from me at all."

"Thank you, Mr. Montague," Elias said, then turned and stopped mid-stride before turning back. "That is one sharp suit."

"Oh, this? It's nothing," Monty said, looking down at his suit. "Just an old suit. One of my favorites I like to wear. Really more of a house suit. Something to lounge and relax in."

"*That* is a runed, bespoke Zegna," Elias answered. "It's something. A very powerful something, designed to protect you and multiply your natural abilities."

"You do know your suits," Monty answered. "I've always considered it a mark of proper upbringing to know your clothes and tea."

"I do," Elias said, narrowing his eyes again at Monty. "Are you planning on going somewhere? Maybe take a short walk around the city? Obliterate a building or two?"

I almost lost it then, but managed to keep a straight face. It was clear Monty's reputation was known to Elias.

"Absolutely not." Monty feigned surprise. "Director DeMarco would never hear of it. I'm under strict instructions to remain within the walls of Haven until such a time as the Director deems it safe for me to venture forth."

Elias actually sighed in relief.

"Thank you, Mr. Montague," Elias said. "Have a good afternoon. I'll be right outside if you need anything."

"Thank you, Elias," Monty said and closed the door before turning to me. "He means well, but he's a bit high-strung. Obliterate a building or two, really?"

"Seems like he knows you pretty well, actually." I said.

"Have you been going out for walks or random acts of destruction?"

"Absolutely not," Monty said. "I've had matters to attend to. Things I couldn't do while confined to this room."

"Right, I'm sure there's a building in need of dire renovation somewhere in the city," I said. "It's just waiting for you to put it out of its misery."

"Rubbish," Monty said, waving my words away. "Every bit of destruction I've caused has been in service to this city and its populace. It was absolutely necessary."

"I know a few agencies that would disagree with that statement," I said. "Is Elias going to be okay?"

"Without a doubt," Monty said. "As I mentioned earlier, he has the best of intentions, but is a bit excitable."

"You're going to give him a heart attack, really," I said, grabbing my jacket off the chair where it hung. "Listen, I'm glad you're feeling better and even leveled up to wiggle-less casting. For the record, the mini-sun you just created was amazing and scary as hell. Can you not do that again...ever?"

"It was a small demonstration to let you know I'm fine."

"That's just it," I countered. "The Monty I know wouldn't do that. I think you still need to recover. "

"Do you, now?" Monty said. "Refresh my memory. How many schisms have you dealt with?"

"Outside of yours?"

"Hmm?" he said with a nod. "Outside of mine, yes."

"None—and no, I'm not a mage," I said before he could remind me. "I also know enough to know that if you leave this room, we'll have Bunyan and his crew in addition to an extremely heated Roxanne after us...mostly me. Pass."

"You're missing the point, Simon," Monty said. "Why did I cast the nullifier?"

"You mean besides giving me a minor heart attack and burning my retinas?"

"Yes, obviously. Think."

It took a few seconds. My synapses were still dealing with the fact that Monty was able to cast without a gesture and the fact that Elias, a pretty kickass sorcerer, was actually scared of the mage he was tasked with watching.

"You bought us time," I said after a few seconds. "If their abilities are nullified they can't sense if you're gone... Wait, no, you shouldn't be going anywhere. What about Roxanne? She's not nullified."

"Roxanne is"—he looked up for a moment—"in her office," he said after a few seconds. "Her office is the most secure room in this entire building including the Detention Area. I should know, as I secured it myself."

"You can sense where she is? Even through the null zone?"

"Yes," he said. "The runes of this null zone are strong, but easily circumvented when you know how."

"Roxanne is going to lose her mind if she finds you gone, you know this, right?"

"I'll deal with Roxanne," Monty said. "As for Elias, he won't even know I'm gone until it's too late. Now, tell me how much time before you need to make that call?"

"Twenty minutes on the outside."

"Excellent, plenty of time to do what we need to do."

"Need to do?" I asked, confused. "What do we need to do?"

"We need to get travel insurance," Monty said as he began gesturing. "It's for our safety."

"Travel insurance? What are you talking about? Shadow Company is in the city."

"Yes, but their targets aren't," Monty said. "I have an idea what your friends at Shadow Company want. It's not pleasant or located in our city."

"How could you possibly?" I asked, my voice growing serious. "And, for the record, they aren't my friends."

"No, they aren't," he agreed with a nod. "That's why we need travel insurance. Get ready."

"Get ready?" I asked. "For what? You're not making any sense."

A large, green teleportation circle appeared on the floor in front of us. My stomach clenched reflexively at the sight.

"One more thing," Monty said, looking around the room. He gestured and a small golden orb floated over to the bed, hovering there for a few seconds before fading from sight. "Now we can go."

"That"—I pointed to the bed—"feels like your energy signature. How?"

"I've been practicing," Monty said as he stepped over to the circle. "Are you coming? Or do you want to be here when Elias and his team check in on why you've been in here so long, only to find you've absconded with their charge?"

"What? There's no way they're going to think I kidnapped you out of a null zone."

"True," Monty said. "Elias knows you're not a mage but

Roxanne will be livid and place the blame squarely on your shoulders—*shieldbearer*."

"Roxanne is so going to kill us," I said, staring and pointing in the direction of the orb that disappeared. It still read like Monty's energy signature. "Will they sense that?"

"They're supposed to," Monty answered. "It should read like I'm in bed."

"And when they realize you aren't in bed, but AWOL? Then what?"

"We'll be long gone before they realize that. Ready?"

"If I say no, will you get back into bed?"

"No," he answered with a slight smile. "You need to make a call and we're running out of time. Let's go."

I stepped into the circle next to Monty and waited for Peaches to saunter in next to me. He padded over quietly and gave me a low chuff.

<The angry man smells good. Do you think he can make me some meat?>

<He may smell good, but he's acting strange. Let's wait on the meat>

<You act strange all the time. I'm still part of your pack, even if you are strange.>

I was getting an assessment on *my* strangeness from a plane-walking, laser-beam-shooting, sonic- barrier-breaking, virtually indestructible hellhound. I shook my head in disbelief.

"I'm so going to regret this," I said as the circle began to glow. "I'm going to make sure Roxanne kills you first."

"Will never happen," Monty answered with one last gesture. "I'll inform her you came in and convinced me of a dire emergency that absolutely, positively needed my presence. How could I refuse?"

"You wouldn't dare, would you?"

"I would," he said with a devious smile. "Who do you think she would believe?"

I was about to answer when the circle flashed green and the room disappeared.

SIX

We appeared in the subway.

Specifically, we appeared in the tracks of some unused portion of the subway, judging from the debris and trash I noticed scattered all over the tracks. The hot sauna-like feel of the city's underbelly washed over me, accompanied by the assaulting aroma of old trash and vermin—Eau de Rot.

"This is where you needed to escape to?" I asked, taking in our surroundings. "You needed to leave the comfort of Haven for this?"

"Appearances can be deceptive," Monty answered, looking around and getting his bearings. "This place may look rundown and abandoned—"

"Because it *is* rundown and abandoned...and filthy. Why are we down here?"

"I told you, insurance," Monty answered.

"Yes, you mentioned that," I said. "Insurance from what? Being able to smell properly for the next few months?"

"The smell will pass," Monty said. "This is essential." He pointed ahead. "That way."

Peaches shook his head at the smell and padded silently next to me. I couldn't blame him; wherever we were, it had been abandoned long ago. I heard the distant sounds of the subway and looked up and down the tracks for the telltale lights of oncoming trains. Everything was dark, indicating that this section of the subway was no longer active.

"If you needed a ride, I could have gotten the Dark Goat," I said, looking around. "Where are we? I don't recognize this part."

"This is an old abandoned stretch of track between Penn Station and Grand Central Terminal," Monty said, peering into the dim light. "No one really knows about its existence any longer. The entry points have been sealed to the public, and maintenance doesn't visit often, unless there's an emergency."

"Let me guess: there's never an emergency on this section of track."

"It would seem that this section of track has escaped most of the normal wear and tear plaguing the city's Metropolitan Transit System."

"A plague is what we'll catch if we stay down here too long," I said. "This travel insurance you mentioned—what exactly are we getting insured against?"

"I'll explain later," Monty said, moving forward. "I do hope I have the right track. It would appear no one has been down here in some time."

"I can tell," I said, gazing at the small mountains of trash everywhere. "This is where you want to get travel insurance? Where are we supposed to be going? The Great Dumpster below the city?"

"Some place more dangerous than that," Monty answered, picking his way around the trash. "Shadow Company has been quite busy since you were retired from their ranks. They have a singular purpose these days. A purpose very few are aware of."

"Except you, it seems," I said, trying to follow his gaze as he walked. "What are you looking for?"

"Not a what, but a who, although *what* may also apply," he said. "No one really knows their origins."

"Whose origins?" I said, concerned he really was losing it. "What are you talking about?"

Monty stared at me for a few seconds before walking farther down the tracks.

"I want to assure you, I'm in my full capacities," Monty said as he walked into the darkness. "As I mentioned earlier, I'm still dealing with some of the effects of the schism, but I'm fine."

"These effects you keep mentioning, can you elaborate on what they are exactly?" I asked. "You were a little on the vague side earlier."

"Nothing too serious, really. Enhanced ability, adaptation and regulation of increased power levels. A slight deficiency in mental acuity as I grow accustomed to the knowledge the schism unleashed."

"A slight deficiency?"

"Nothing to worry about."

"Now I'm worried."

"It's a minor side effect, and it will pass as I assimilate the information."

"All of that sounds serious, like 'you should be in Haven

under magical supervision', kind of serious," I said, concerned. "Monty, we need to go back to Haven—preferably before Roxanne unleashes Paul Bunyan on us. You need to be resting."

"No," Monty said, turning to face me. "The best recovery for my condition is to keep my mind occupied, not sitting in Haven until Roxanne deems it safe for me to step outside."

"Is it?" I asked, keeping my voice calm. "Standing in a dirty subway is part of your recovery?"

"Roxanne means well, but she is operating emotionally, not as a magical professional," Monty answered. "She cares, and it impacts how she reacts."

"A magical professional? Are you certain the schism didn't screw with your mind?"

"Of course it did," Monty admitted. "I'm not saying it didn't. I'm saying that I can deal with its effects, and can function despite what I experienced."

"Roxanne just doesn't want to see you get hurt; none of us do."

"I'm fine," Monty said. "You need to trust me on this."

"I do. It's just that I remember your Darth moment. It wasn't pretty. It looked and felt like you had lost control."

"So much so that I was still able to restrain myself from attacking you, then managed to assist and intervene on your behalf when you were about to be skewered by Evers. I'd say I managed it well, wouldn't you? My state of mind is fine."

He did have a point. If it hadn't been for him coming back, Evers would have sliced me into little Simon pieces with that blade of hers. He may have been slightly off, but he was still mostly Monty.

Mostly.

"It's been my experience that those who have to assure others of their state of mind," I said, "are usually entering batshit crazy territory." I looked around. "Tell me, Monty, are we entering batshit country?"

"Not in the least," he said, pointing ahead again. "Trust me, we need to do this and then you can make your call. We have a good fifteen minutes, correct?"

"Yes, give or take a few seconds. Though I doubt I'll get any reception down here at the Twilight Zone station."

"We'll relocate somewhere better suited for your call," Monty said and started walking again. "It should be just a little farther."

"Would be great to know where *exactly* we're going."

"This way," he said, leading me down the tracks to a figure I could barely make out, hunched over in the darkness. "Let me do the talking."

"You want to have a conversation with a homeless person?" I asked. "Of course, why would I want to interrupt such an important conversation? Please go chat."

I motioned with my hand for him to keep going.

"Precisely," Monty said as we approached the old woman. When we were close, he crouched down and faced the figure. "Hello, Grandmother."

SEVEN

"Mage," the old woman said, waving her cane in his direction. "You've grown."

"You've grown?" I said under my breath as I kept my distance. "How long have you known her?"

Monty gave me a look that said *shut it*, so I shut it and kept quiet—until she turned to face me. She smiled when she saw me and waved me closer with her cane. She could have been anyone's grandmother, actually. I realized Monty used the title to refer to her age, not his actual relation to her. This was an old, bordering on ancient, woman wrapped in too many layers to be comfortable in the heat of the subway.

The wrinkles on her face were pronounced and she had achieved that state where her skin looked more like worn leather than actual skin. Despite all that, her gaze was soft and welcoming. I felt safe around her. Even though the amount of power she radiated was immense, I didn't feel threatened by it.

Her energy signature was a warm blanket on a cold day,

a cup of hot coffee during a winter storm, and I could swear I smelled freshly baked chocolate chip cookies.

"Kali's Chosen. Come let me look at you. Let me look at you both," she said, her voice sounding surprisingly young for someone who appeared to be just this side of a thousand. "Step closer. There is nothing to fear here."

Monty stepped closer, but I hesitated. At this point, I was pretty sure that whoever sat huddled in front of us wasn't human. It could have been me, or the fact that her eyes were giving off a soft, golden glow.

"Who are you?" I asked as I took a step forward. "What are you?"

"Simon," Monty hissed under his breath. "A bit of decorum would be appropriate at this moment."

"Rubbish," she said. "He has asked the right question. The long explanation would hurt your brain; the short explanation is that I'm a Transporter."

"You're like FedEx or UPS?"

She laughed as Monty glared at me.

"What?" I asked. "She said she was a transporter."

"Not quite like that," she said. "I transport locations to you, instead of the other way around."

"What? How can you transport locations? Is that even possible?"

"Transporters are similar to the most advanced tele-porters in our reality," Monty said, entering lecturing mode. "They don't teleport, exactly; they shift."

"They shift? Like a mage shift in power level?"

"No, completely different," Monty continued. "This is a shift along the dimensions of space-time. Rather than teleporting you where you want to go, a Transporter warps time, space, and gravity around you so that the place you wanted to go ends up aligned to your location."

"That sounds like severe gastrointestinal distress for me."

"Not in the least," Monty said. "Aside from your new energy signature helping you, when transported, you are aligned."

"Aligned to what?" I asked.

"Good question," the Transporter chimed in, but Monty had entered full lecture mode and couldn't be stopped. "Once aligned, she will give you the equivalent of a runic kick and send you down the bridge she created."

"So she's not teleporting but creating space-time bridges? Wormholes?"

"That's an oversimplification, but the concept is similar."

"Isn't that what mages do with their teleportation circles?"

Monty shook his head.

"No mage in history has been able to teleport using a Transporter's method," Monty answered. "This is why we are here."

"We're here so you can give a dissertation on the difference between transporting and teleporting?" I asked. "I could've called Ziller and had him melt my brain for that, *without* visiting an abandoned subway."

"We're here," Monty answered with a barely contained sigh, "to procure a shift for each of us."

"Excuse me? A shift where?"

"Do you know what you ask?" the Transporter said. "I will need to read you."

"Wait a second," I said, holding up a hand. "Let's slow down for a moment. Where are we shifting exactly?"

"We'll be shifting back."

"Right, because that makes perfect sense," I said. "What's this about *reading* us?"

"In order to shift us properly, she needs to read our runic signatures," Monty answered. "The shift we need requires a deeper reading. She needs to be able to locate us wherever we are."

"That doesn't sound so bad," I admitted. "This is like, what, a deep scan?"

"Something like that," Monty said. "Except your deepest emotions will be exposed and raw. It's not pleasant."

"So, let me see if I get this straight," I said, taking a step back. "You want me to let this old"—I then decided to err on the side of not pissing off some supernatural being of space-time and of staying alive—"this elderly being do a runic scan on me and expose my deepest emotions, just so she can be some kind of runic GPS system in case we have to shift back from some place we haven't gone? That about right?"

"It's missing some of the details, but yes, it's accurate."

"Oh, is that all?" I asked. "That's simple...No. Let me be extra clear...Hell no."

"Simon, you don't understand," Monty answered. "I know what Shadow Company wants you for."

"How? How could *you*?" I asked, upset. "I've been off their radar for years. I can guess what they want, but I haven't been in direct contact with them for some time."

"They're hunting dragons," Monty said quietly. "I received information about this some time ago, before we went after your vampire. Other matters seemed more pressing at the time."

"Dragons?" I asked. "They must be looking to exit life. Why would they need me?"

"You tell me," Monty said. "Did the call sound urgent?"

"It wasn't a call to catch up, that's for sure. The call was deliberate. They wanted me to know."

Monty nodded.

"They wanted you to know they can reach out and touch not only you, but those close to you."

"Violently if needed," I said. "Shadow Company doesn't do invitations or suggestions. If I don't make this meet, they will convince me it was a mistake."

Monty turned to glance at the Transporter.

"Sounds like you need insurance, don't you think?"

"Is this going to hurt?" I asked. "It's too early for agony, and I haven't had my coffee."

"Not in the way you think," Monty said. "You'll be fine."

"Those sound like famous last words."

EIGHT

"Do you have something for me?" the Transporter asked.

"Why would I have anything for her?" I asked, confused. "I didn't even know we were coming down here."

"She's addressing me," Monty said and gestured. "Will this be sufficient?"

A large brown and gold box appeared in his hand. It was wrapped with a red ribbon that easily came undone as the Transporter removed it. I could tell it had some heft to it, as he needed both hands to hold it in front of the Transporter. She clapped her hands together like a small child and took the box from Monty.

She opened it slowly and took a deep breath, inhaling the aroma of the contents. Even I could smell what it was...chocolate. Not just any chocolate; this was the most chocolate-smelling chocolate I had ever smelled in my life.

"What is that?" I asked as I did my best to keep from drooling. "More importantly, can I have some?"

"That is a box of Teuscher Select chocolates. Dolf is

known as the best chocolatier in the world," Monty answered. "This box is their special Aztec blend of cacao, not available to the public. Dolf makes these boxes exclusively for the mage sects. The answer to your second question is no, you can't. This is her payment."

The Transporter squealed with delight as she took a small piece of chocolate out of the box and ate it. She took out another small piece and held it, as the box disappeared into her coat somewhere. It moved too fast for me to follow.

"You're paying for our insurance in chocolate?" I asked, incredulous. "Seriously?"

"Yes," Monty said with a short nod. "I don't make the rules. Transporters expect chocolate as their preferred form of payment. The more difficult the request, the higher caliber chocolate needed."

"So I just can't give her a Snickers and expect a shift?"

"Precisely," Monty said. "That would be viewed as an insult. She would probably shift you to Antarctica."

"Ouch."

"Without clothing."

"Whoa, she takes her chocolate seriously," I said. "I'll keep that in mind if I ever need a chocoshift."

The Transporter still held the small piece of chocolate in her hand. At this rate it was going to be a chocolate mess if she didn't eat it soon. She turned to me and held out the small piece of chocolate.

"Bloody hell," Monty said under his breath. "This is...unprecedented."

"Is she offering me a piece of chocolate?"

"What does it look like?" Monty asked, semi-exasperated and completely flustered. "I'd suggest you take it."

I extended a hand and she placed the piece of chocolate in my hand. I looked down at the chocolate confused.

"What do I do now?" I said. "Is there a Transporter chocolate protocol?"

"You eat it," she said with a chuckle. "It will make the next part easier."

Monty gave me a look that said, *Eat the chocolate...now*.

I quickly put the piece of chocolate in my mouth. The flavors exploded across my tongue and overwhelmed my senses. It was absolutely the best chocolate I had ever tasted. The Transporter came over to me and nodded.

"Good, isn't it?" she asked.

"The absolute best," I answered around the flavor explosion in my mouth. "Is it always this good?"

"Not always," she answered with a small wink. "I may have added a little something to make it special. Now, hold still."

"Hold still?"

"This will be over before you know it," she said with a nod, and then put a finger to her lips. "Ready?"

"Ready? For what?"

The Transporter slowly removed the finger from her lips, pulled her hand back, and formed a fist. It seemed to be happening in slow motion. I turned to look at Monty, who nodded at me.

"Brace yourself," he said. At least I thought that was what he said—his words were stretched out and distorted, sounding more like, "Brayyyce yourrrsellf."

The Transporter's fist began to glow with golden light and I found myself transfixed by the energy coming from her hand. I still tasted the chocolate in my mouth and wondered at how that could be. It was a small piece; it shouldn't have lasted this long.

I was about to ask Monty, when the Transporter slammed me in the chest with her glowing fist. A rush of emotions washed over me. It ran the gamut from grief to elation and back to grief in the span of milliseconds.

Every happy memory flooded my brain followed by every moment of sadness. This was chased away by moments of rage, anger, and regret. One moment I was laughing with joy; the next, tears of anguish were streaming down my face.

As soon as it began, it was over. I felt drained, spent and in need of a long nap.

"I have him," she said as I staggered back. I would've fallen if Monty hadn't grabbed me by the arm. "Your signature is known to me, mage. Do you wish another reading?"

"No, Grandmother," Monty said. "My mental state is a bit...fragile at the moment. One of your readings would be contraindicated."

She nodded.

"You have stepped into darkness. It pulls at you. Have you balanced?"

"Yes," Monty said after a pause. "Yes, I have."

"Very well," she said. "Remember, there is always the cost."

"I shall."

"The scion of Cerberus is to be read?" she asked, glancing down at Peaches.

"Yes, he possesses abilities of planewalking, but not powerful enough to transport us to where we will need to go."

"Understood," she said, and placed a hand on Peaches'

head. "He is still young, and bonded to Kali's Chosen. This is a good bond."

Peaches rumbled as his eyes began to glow. A moment later, he barked, shattering most of the concrete around us. We stood untouched in the epicenter of his sonic blast. The Transporter patted Peaches on the head.

"I have him," she said. "I will be able to bring you all back safely. Do you know the request?"

Monty let me go and I stood unsteadily on my own. He traced a violet rune I had never seen in the air and the Transporter nodded.

"Thank you, Grandmother," Monty said, forming a large, green teleportation circle beneath us. "I am in your debt."

"Your payment covers your debt," she said. "Come visit me when you are finished. We will see if you have truly found balance."

"I shall," Monty said, gently maneuvering me into the circle. "May your paths always be clear."

"May your casts be ever true," she replied.

"We're ready," Monty said.

"Not yet," she answered, "but you will be."

The last thing I saw was her reaching again into the large box which floated gently in front of her. She reached in and pulled out another piece of chocolate. With a smile and another wink, she waved an arm in our direction.

The subway twisted and disappeared.

NINE

"Make the call," Monty said when I opened my eyes. "You have very little time."

I had five minutes left before the number Ramirez gave me would be useless. I pulled out my phone and looked around. It took a few moments for me to realize we were standing in the main room of an empty Randy Rump.

"Why are we—?" I asked, looking around. "Where's Jimmy?"

Monty pointed to the phone in my hand and made a speaking gesture, insisting I get on with it. I saw him pull out his phone as he stepped away.

I dialed the number and waited for the call to connect.

Three rings later, a gruff voice answered.

"Strong, I thought I was going to have to convince you further."

It was Peter 'Pitbull' Douglas.

The voice brought back a flood of memories. Douglas was the commander of Shadow Company. He was an ex-military officer who believed the means, no matter how horrific, justified the ends. He was the primary reason I had been "asked" to leave Shadow Company.

We didn't exactly see eye to eye on who deserved death. I drew the line at non-combatants; he drew the line where he damned well pleased, and I had crossed it one time too many.

"Douglas," I said, keeping my voice neutral. "Convince me for what?"

"We have a mission," he growled, his voice a rough baritone of glass and sandpaper. "We need one more."

"*You* have a mission, I don't."

"This one is off the books," Douglas continued, ignoring my answer. "FODS from the top."

FODS stood for 'Fully Operational Disavowal Status'. It meant that Shadow Company could do whatever it needed to do to complete the mission, except get caught doing it. If discovered, they would be disavowed—basically, abandoned.

If this mission came from the top, it usually meant someone or something powerful needed to be eliminated. With Shadow Company, it was usually someone non-human.

"All Company missions are off the books," I said warily. "What makes this one special?"

"The targets, or specifically *the* target," Douglas answered. "Balfour."

"What's a balfour?"

I noticed Monty had turned in my direction at the mention of the name. His expression was one of concern, mixed with curiosity.

"Not what, who," Douglas said, gruffly. "That's as much

as I'm willing to share over this line. Not that I don't trust you..."

"You don't."

"Damn straight I don't. Let's meet to discuss the details."

"Pass," I said, actually shaking my head. "I'm not Shadow Company. Not anymore."

Douglas gave me a short, rough chuckle. I could practically see the unlit cigar in his mouth as he shifted the phone around.

"Bullshit," he replied, calmly. "Once Shadow Company, always Shadow Company. You're part of the family. Besides, I'm not the one asking."

"Who is?" I asked. "Who wants an incompetent, trembly handed, blind dead-eye on a FODS mission?"

I wasn't holding a grudge, but I still remembered Douglas' words when I was asked to leave Shadow Company. They'd stung then, and they stung now.

"Rott is," Douglas said after a long pause. "I was against calling you in on this, but George insisted. Says you owe him and you're the best dead-eye he knows."

"Fuck you," I said, the words thick in my throat. "It's one thing to go through all the cloak and dagger shit—contacting Ramirez, the limited use phone, and the rest. I get you can't help yourself, but using George's name to justify your actions is sad...A sad and desperate joke, that no one finds funny."

I was about to hang up when another voice came over the phone.

"It's not a joke," the voice said. "You're the best man for this job."

George Rott.

"You're dead," I said in shock. "You were taken apart by an entropy bomb. I was there. Who is this?"

"It's me," George said. "You saw an explosion that took out the Kragzimik, yes. I thought I was dead, too, except I landed several blocks away—barely alive. Somehow, the synthetic entropy bomb altered me."

"Impossible," I said, barely above a whisper.

For a few seconds the synapses in my brain forgot how to fire. George had been torn apart with the Kragzimik. I had seen the explosion.

"Improbable," Rott said. "Not impossible. I'll explain it when we meet. I need your help, Dead-Eye. Balfour is a major threat."

"I don't even know who this Balfour is, much less what kind of threat he poses."

"He's a dragon," Rott said, with barely masked rage. "That should be enough."

"It's not," I said. "Look, I'm sorry about—"

"I'm going to hand the phone to Douglas now," Rott said, cutting me off. "I expect to see you tonight."

"I'm retired."

"Not according to Rott," Douglas continued on the phone. "Says you've been active since you left us. Teamed up with some Brit and taking down major threats. A dragon, last I heard."

My head was still reeling from learning Rott was alive. How did he survive?

"I didn't leave you. I was asked to leave."

"Now, I'm asking you to return. It's only one mission, and then we wipe the slate clean. After this, if you want to completely turn your back on us, your family, after all we did for you, feel free."

"How do I know that's really Rott doing the asking?"

"He said you'd ask that. He said we should meet where he lost Cass—where *you* lost Cass."

I remained silent for a few seconds and controlled my breathing. The words were deliberate, designed to do the most damage to maximally push my buttons.

They worked.

"Fine. When?"

"Tonight, 2300. Bring your Brit. I'll make the introductions and brief you on the mission then. Glad to have you aboard."

"I haven't agreed to anything yet."

"Yes, you have," Douglas said. "You need to make this right. This is your chance to do so."

He hung up the call.

Monty looked at me, his expression serious.

"He mentioned Cassandra," I said, keeping my voice low as I looked at my phone. "Rott asked for me."

"Rott perished in the entropy blast that killed the Kragzimik."

"Apparently it didn't stick," I said, still slightly shocked. "I just spoke to him, or someone who sounded just like him. Could he have survived?"

Monty rubbed his chin.

"I suppose if the Kragzimik was powerful enough, he could have formed a cocoon of energy around his body. Rott was in proximity when the blast went off, but..."

"Are you saying there was a chance he could have survived?"

"Slight, but yes. There were several variables at play that night," Monty replied. "The entropy bomb was synthetic, keyed to Rott's life force...The Kragzimik was a considerably powerful threat...And don't forget Salao, the demigod—any one of those or a combination could've played a role in Rott surviving the blast."

"He still blames me for Cassandra."

"Her death was *not* your fault," he said. "Cassandra understood the risks and danger."

"I should have kept her farther back, out of the action," I said. "She would've been safe then."

"Unlikely," Monty said. "Slif would have hunted her down in any case. She was not about to let us walk away from that conflict. What did Douglas want?"

"It's a mission. Shadow Company," I said. "Rott requested me specifically. The target is a Balfour. What kind of name is that?"

"A dangerous one. Are you certain he said Balfour?"

"Positive. They want to meet tonight, same place where Cassandra died."

"They're hunting dragons."

"Didn't sound plural. Rott said this Balfour is a dragon."

"Rott requested you specifically. Ever since Cassandra, he's been obsessed. I thought with his demise this would be put to rest."

"He sounded slightly off, said the entropy bomb altered him," I said. "Maybe it's not really Rott?"

"Even if it isn't entirely Rott, there's enough of him to request you for this mission."

"If they want me for this mission I'm going to go with: I'm bait and they're leaning toward hostile."

"You think you're a target?" Monty asked. "Why?"

"My last mission with Shadow Company," I said. "I

disobeyed a direct order. Derailed the mission, the target escaped. Got myself bounced out."

"I see. And now they want you back?"

"Offering redemption, it seems," I said. "One last mission to set things right and finally put things to rest."

"Sounds more like it may be an opportunity to put *you* to rest," Monty said. "Have they kept track of you since you left?"

I nodded.

"Seems like it. They know about you, too. Douglas said you should come with."

"To my recollection, there are no mages in this group."

"None. Shadow Company is too twitchy to run with mages," I said. "They don't trust magic users."

"Yet requested my presence?"

"Yes, Rott has been keeping tabs on us, apparently."

"This seems off," Monty said. "Why now?"

"Who is this Balfour?"

"No one to be trifled with," Monty said, serious. "We want to stay as far away from him as possible."

"If he's the target, my guess is that they have a small window of opportunity to get to him, and want me there."

"This is unwise. Facing dragons is no trifling matter," Monty said, shaking his head. "Their power is several orders of magnitude above most mages, including my own."

"I know."

"What happens if you refuse?"

"Depends on who's really doing the asking," I said. "He says it's Rott. If I say no to George, that would be bad. If it's Douglas? Well, he was never overly stable. If I turn him down, it could go south in a hurry."

"I see," Monty said. "You really need to upgrade your circle of friends."

"They're *not* my friends," I said, my voice hard. "Not even close. To them, I'm expendable. Everyone who stands in their way is. Shadow Company is a dysfunctional family that discards those Douglas thinks are useless."

"Is that why they asked you to leave?" Monty asked. "He thought you useless?"

"He asked me to leave because I dared to defy him," I said, the words spilling out. "I was young, and naive, but I wasn't a blind follower. He expects, no, *demands* complete compliance and blind devotion. Does that sound like me?"

"Not in the least," Monty said. "Apologies, I didn't mean to pry."

"No apologies needed," I said, waving his words away. "Just not one of my favorite subjects."

"Understood," Monty said. "We all carry the luggage of our youth."

"Baggage, but it still works," I said with a tight smile, turning when I heard the footsteps. "Sounds like Jimmy... plus one. Plus one very large one?"

Jimmy the Cleaver came into the main room, followed by—I didn't know exactly what he was being followed by. It looked like an ogre crossed with something worse, if that was even possible. It carried several large boxes of meats and cases of beer with room to spare for a small SUV in its arms. I let my hand drift to Grim Whisper, wondering if even entropy rounds would stop the enormous creature.

Jimmy smiled when he saw us, his expression shifting to one of alarm when he saw my hand moving to my weapon.

"No need for that," Jimmy said, stepping behind the counter and pulling out an enormous titanium bowl with a large letter P on it. "This...is Grohn."

"Fascinating," Monty said, looking up at the large creature. "You've befriended an ogre hybrid?"

"He works here now," Jimmy said, taking the cases of beer. "He came highly recommended. Put all that over there, Grohn, thanks."

The large creature placed the cases gently on the floor, surprising me as it sorted the meats from the beers. I didn't think ogres were capable of fine motor skills that didn't involve removing a head from its shoulders. Thankfully, he didn't have the patented ogre B.O., sparing me the melting of my lungs. He smelled vaguely of cut grass and wood. For a few seconds, I was transported to the forest after a hard rain. The floor shuddering under my feet snapped me back to reality.

"By whom?" I asked, taking a step back to take in the entire Grohn image. "The last village he destroyed?"

"Simon..." Monty said, shaking his head slightly. "Do not anger the large ogre hybrid in an enclosed space. A large, null, enclosed space, I might add."

"Good point," I said. "Sorry, just not used to seeing an ogre in action without running for my life in the process."

"Give me a second," Jimmy said. "I'll take care of your pup before getting your usual."

Grohn looked like an ogre on steroids. He was larger than any ogre I had ever had the displeasure of facing. He towered over Jimmy and dwarfed Monty and me. Peaches vibrated in place as he stared at Jimmy, oblivious to the huge wall of ugly creature that crouched several feet from us, putting supplies away.

If Peaches was only thinking about meat, this Grohn creature couldn't have been too bad. On the other hand, my hellhound had a singular focus when it came to meat and Jimmy was currently filling his bowl with premium pastrami.

<The bear man is getting me meat.>

<How do you know it's for you?> I teased. *<Could be for that big guy, Grohn.>*

<The large tree man would never eat out of my bowl.>

<Can you smell the large tree man? Is he okay?>

Peaches sniffed the air and chuffed.

<The large man is good. He smells like trees and my meat. The bear man is getting meat for me.>

<Yes, yes he is. Behave. Once he's done, you can go over and devour.>

<The bear man is a good man.>

<Don't forget to say thank you.>

So much for my 'easily-distracted-by-the-scent-of pastrami' hellhound threat detector. If any of our enemies ever weaponized pastrami we were in deep trouble.

"Since when do you hire muscle for the Rump?" I said, looking at Grohn. "And by muscle, I mean the very large wall of ogre currently occupying all of the space in here."

Jimmy looked at me and laughed.

"Since you two roam the streets freely?" he said. "Thank you for the runework, by the way, Tristan. It's been ultra-effective."

"My pleasure," Monty said. "Any incidents?"

"Not since the runes and Grohn here," Jimmy said, glancing over at the large ogre-like creature. "Things have calmed down somewhat."

"I can imagine," I said. "Is he an ogre?"

"Ask him yourself," Jimmy said. "He understands you. Need to get some more things out of storage. In the meantime, let your hellhound snack. Be right back."

I glanced down at Peaches, who gave me the utmost set of puppy-dog eyes followed by a tiny whine, and a ferocious fang-filled hellhound grin.

<*We really do need to work on your smile. Go. Don't mangle the bowl.*>

Peaches bounded off toward his bowl and promptly set himself to devouring mode as the pastrami disappeared into his gaping maw.

Jimmy glanced down at Peaches with a nod, smiled, then headed to the back room, leaving us alone with Grohn.

I turned to the massive creature staring intently at me. Every cell in my body wanted to draw my gun, shoot first, run across the street, and then ask questions. I deliberately dropped my hands and shook them out.

"Right, what could possibly go wrong with this scenario?" I said, mostly to myself. "Hello, Grohn."

"Hello, Mr. Strong," Grohn said, his voice reverberating around us. "Welcome to the Randy Rump."

"You know who I am?"

Grohn nodded as he sorted more of the crates.

"Mr. Jim told me about you and showed me pictures," Grohn said. "He said you like to break things and I should stop you if you break the Rump."

"*I* like to break things?" I said, glancing at Monty, who had suddenly taken an intense interest in the view outside the window. "He said *I* break things?"

"Yes," Grohn answered with a smile. "Don't worry. I like to break things, too."

"Can I ask you a question?" I said. "I don't mean to be rude."

Grohn looked at me and nodded as he placed some of the crates aside.

"A first time for everything," Monty said, heading to a table as Jimmy reappeared with his arms full of some more meats and supplies. "Some tea, James?"

"The usual?"

"Yes, please," Monty said with a nod, settling into a chair. "It would be much appreciated."

"What are you, Grohn?" I asked, keeping my voice low. "I've met ogres before; usually they're angry and want to rip me to pieces. You're unlike any ogre I've seen."

Grohn nodded again.

"I'm a trollgre," Grohn said. "Half ogre, half troll. We are very rare."

"And very dangerous," Jimmy said, from behind the counter. "You need anything, Simon? Coffee?"

"Yes, Deathwish me please, with extreme caffeine intent. Thank you," I said, moving over to the table Monty occupied. Grohn stepped over a moment later. "A trollgre. No wonder you haven't had any incidents lately. It's nice to meet you, Grohn. I hope I never have to find out how dangerous you are."

"One massive heart attack and herbal royalty coming right up," Jimmy said from behind the counter as he prepared our drinks. "Grohn's only dangerous if we're attacked."

"All are welcome to the Randy Rump, as long as they behave," Grohn said. "If they don't, Mr. Jim said I can break them."

Jimmy gave me a smile from behind the counter. I could tell he was enjoying himself.

"Makes sense," I said, extending a hand. "I promise not to break the Randy Rump."

Grohn took my hand in his and shook it slowly. My hand was dwarfed by the immense trollgre.

"We still have to unload the rest of the truck," Jimmy said. "Before you go on back, why don't you share some of your wisdom with our guests?"

"Can I?" Grohn asked with anticipation. "I would like that."

"Sure," Jimmy assured him, staring at me. "They would love it. Especially Simon."

Grohn turned to me and captured my complete attention—like I had a choice.

"Remember when air was free at the gas station?" Grohn asked. "Remember?"

"Um, sure," I said, unsure of where this was going. "That was long ago, though."

"Well, now, its $1.50," Grohn said. "Do you know why?"

"Not really, no," I answered, still slightly confused. "Do you?"

Grohn nodded vigorously.

"Inflation!" Grohn bellowed with a wide smile that rivaled Peaches' grin of friendliness. It was a fearsome sight to behold, and my hand moved reflexively to my gun before I realized he was smiling at me. "Inflation!"

It took me a few seconds. Then, inwardly, because I still enjoyed breathing and the small comforts of life, like keeping my limbs attached, I groaned, realizing where he'd gotten his name.

I returned the smile as best as I could, fighting the

limbic part of my brain that was yelling at me to kill it with fire immediately before he bit off my head.

"That was excellent and profound, Grohn," Jimmy said with a wicked smile, patting Grohn's shoulder. "Why don't you go finish unloading the supplies? That way we can be ready for tonight's guests."

"Yes, Mr. Jim," Grohn said, glancing at me with another heart-stopping smile before lumbering off. "Inflation."

"You could have warned me," I said as Jimmy donned an apron that read I'm Unbearable. "That was so bad. I can't believe you encourage him."

"Yes, it's horrible, but no one dares tell him that to his face," Jimmy said, looking back over his shoulder to make sure Grohn was out of earshot. "The last person who tried had to be carried out of here. He takes his moments of wisdom seriously. My advice? Smile and thank him."

I rubbed my face as Jimmy brought my coffee and Monty's tea. The aroma of the Deathwish was spectacular and jolted my brain into a heightened state of awareness. I kept my flask of javambrosia in my pocket. I wasn't in the mood to taste colors and see sounds, so the coffee would be enough.

"I'll remember to do that," I said. "I have a situation, and maybe you can provide some insight."

Jimmy's expression darkened immediately as he crossed his massive arms.

"Does this *situation* in any way, shape, or form involve blowing the Rump to bits?" Jimmy asked, suddenly serious. "If so, I'm going to need you to take your beverages to go."

"Not at all, I hope."

"You *hope?*" Jimmy said, narrowing his eyes at me. "What exactly is this *situation*?"

Jimmy grabbed a chair from a nearby table, pulling it close, and sat on it with the back of the chair facing us.

"What do you know about dragons in the city?" I asked. "The old powerful ones."

Jimmy gave me a hard look and then sighed.

"You do not want to go messing with dragons, Simon," Jimmy said. "No offense, but neither of you are powerful enough, together or alone, to deal with one mature dragon. Not even with your pup, amazing as he is."

"None taken," Monty said, raising his tea cup before taking a sip. "I try to avoid dealing with pure magical beings capable of unleashing untold destructive fury upon my person. This is"—Monty pointed at me—"his situation, not mine. I'm actually on hiatus and recovering."

"Recovering?" Jimmy asked, raising an eyebrow. "From what?"

"He had a small run in with a being wishing to unleash untold magical fury upon his and my person," I said, glancing at Monty, who just happened to be focused on the window next to us again. "That, and he went through a schism."

"Whoa," Jimmy said, staring at Monty. "Shouldn't you be in Haven or some medical facility? I hear schisms are serious for mages. Are you okay?"

"I am perfectly fine."

"We all know what fine stands for," I said. "Anyway, despite the better judgment of medical and magical professionals, he checked himself out."

"You're out here against Roxanne's wishes?" Jimmy asked, surprised. "You enjoy living dangerously."

"Tell him why," Monty said, taking another sip. "Don't give him half the story."

"I've been contacted by some…dangerous individuals," I said, trying to avoid mentioning names. I didn't want anything to blow back on Jimmy or the Rump. "Monty thinks they want my help in hunting dragons. Specifically, a dragon."

"This dragon have a name?"

I momentarily debated sharing the name with Jimmy. Despite the number of times the Rump had been redecorated, Jimmy had always welcomed us to his place. I didn't want to ruin that goodwill. If I didn't tell him, he'd hold it against me, and this was Peaches' second favorite pastrami place, after Ezra's.

I doubted he would cut off Peaches. No one risked pissing off a hellhound like that, not even a werebear, but I wasn't taking any chances.

"Balfour. They said his name is Balfour."

"Are you sure?" Jimmy asked, his expression grave. "Did they mention a first name?"

"First name?" I asked. "I thought that was the first name."

"Balfour is the enclave name," Jimmy shared. "The Balfour and Obouros Enclaves are ancient and dangerous. Not groups you want to tangle with."

"They're going after this Balfour," I said. "I don't know why."

"No one hunts dragons anymore," Jimmy said. "You're talking hundreds of years ago and nowhere near this continent. What makes you think they want to hunt dragons?"

"I don't, Monty does," I said. "I think they want to meet me to tie up some loose ends."

"Loose ends? Meaning you?" Jimmy asked. "You really have a knack for pissing people off, don't you?"

"It's a gift," I said with a mock bow. "I just wanted to know if there were any dragons actually living in the city, not visiting for a holiday of mayhem and destruction. I know it's far-fetched, but this will put the myth to rest, and then I can focus on preventing these individuals from trying to take me out."

"These individuals, are they magic users?"

"No, they are a group of highly specialized and trained assassins," I said. "It was a group I belonged to a lifetime ago."

"What do they specialize in?"

I paused.

"Jimmy, I don't want to involve you in anything that can come back and burn you," I said. "If they thought I was mentioning them to you, you would be in danger."

"So don't mention them," Jimmy said. "What do they specialize in?"

"Hunting beings of magic—"

"And killing them?" Jimmy asked, the anger creeping into his voice. "They kill magic beings?"

"Yes," I said. "They believe they are ridding the world of evil. I know it's twisted and wrong, but they have the support of some very powerful people."

"Are they hunting *you* now?"

"Why would they hunt me?" I asked. "I'm not...Shit."

"Finally, it dawns," Monty said, waving a hand. "Are you certain Evers didn't smash a stone into your cranium?"

"She tried, several times," I said, as the realization hit. "This could be a bait and switch."

"With you being the bait," Monty said. "They use the

guilt card, which you're obviously still susceptible to, present you with a clandestine mission which is par for the course for the group, then serve you up as the prime target. Have you forgotten Slif?"

"She's pretty hard to forget," I said. "You think they're playing both sides?"

"It's what I would do," Monty said. "The dragons get revenge for Slif—I can assure you they haven't forgotten, either—Rott gets revenge for Cassandra's death, which you're still being blamed for, and everyone gets a happy ending."

"Except me."

"Well, there is that."

"I thought I was being low key. Staying off the radar."

"Low key?" Jimmy said. "You're bonded to a hellhound—which, if the rumors are true, can grow larger than Grohn. You roam the streets with a powerful mage. You take on beings of magic who want to destroy you both, while you inflict severe property damage to the city. I'd say that makes you a being worth hunting, wouldn't you?"

"Indeed," Monty said, before taking another sip. "I wonder if there's a substantial bounty on your head? It would explain much."

"Not helping," I said. "Why would they hunt me? It doesn't make sense."

"If only to stop depreciating property values in the city," Monty said. "You really should rein in your destructive tendencies."

I glared at him.

I tried to punch holes in Jimmy's argument, but couldn't. If Shadow Company had been keeping tabs on me ever since Cassandra died, they had plenty of material to prove I was no longer normal.

"We need to prepare for tonight," I said. "There's a good chance I'm walking into a set up. I'm pretty sure dragons have been gone from the city for decades at this point, if not centuries."

"Well," Jimmy said, "that's not exactly true."

"What? What are you saying? Dragons are in the city?"

"Not exactly *in* the city," Jimmy said, looking away. "More like close by."

"Can you be a bit more vague?"

"I hear there's a large enclave of dragons accessible from the city, if you know where to look, which I don't," Jimmy said. "I do hear rumors, though. Don't recommend it, since it will probably be a one-way trip. It seems they can be reached and still maintain a small, but influential presence in the city."

I saw a flatbed roll up to the front of the Rump. On the back sat the Dark Goat. Robert got out and stepped inside the shop, clipboard in hand.

"I took the liberty of having Cecil transport the vehicle to us," Monty said, standing and walking over to Robert. I waved and he nodded back, fear clearly etched on his face. "One moment."

I turned to Jimmy.

"Where and how?"

"I can't tell you," Jimmy said. "I'm a werebear, not a dragon. Even if I did know, I wouldn't tell you."

"What? Why?"

"For several reasons. You would try and go there. You would then bring your special brand of destruction to their realm. Then, they would squash you before coming here and doing the same to me."

"You're scared of them?"

"No, not scared. I have a healthy respect for creatures that don't wield magic," Jimmy said, his voice firm. "They *are* magic. Unlike you, I understand what I'm facing. I'm not operating on some irrational fear. This is a very rational and—"

"You're a werebear, how can you be scared?"

"Having power doesn't make you invincible or invulnerable," Jimmy replied with a sigh. "Don't do this, Simon. This is one time you need to walk away."

"I can't," I said. "There are some things I need to set straight, some debts that need to be repaid."

"No debt is worth your life," Jimmy said, getting up from his chair. "Go deal with this group of yours, but trust me, you do not want to get involved with dragons, especially not the Balfour Enclave. I have to get ready for the evening rush. You're welcome to stay as long as you don't blow anything up."

Monty came back to the table, a look of concern on his face.

"We have a problem."

TEN

"What kind of problem?" I asked. "Why does Robert look like he's ready to bolt at any moment?"

"Could be it has something to do with your vehicle, but I doubt it," Monty said, glancing at Robert, who had returned to the truck to offload the Dark Goat. "That is not the problem."

"Wait, are you saying we have another problem beside the fact that I have to go see Douglas?" I asked, glancing around Monty to the fearful Robert. I waved, but he just ignored me. "What's his deal?"

"All SuNaTran personnel have been instructed not to engage with you for the time being," Monty said, raising a hand when he saw my expression. "Hold on, it's not their fault. This directive comes from Cecil ,and it's for their safety."

"I'm a menace now? Is that it? Why would Cecil do this?"

Monty raised an eyebrow at me.

"Fine—I mean, I know *why*, but why? He's had plenty

of opportunity to blacklist me in the past," I said, offended. "I noticed he hasn't blacklisted you. Robert had no problem speaking to you."

Robert stepped into the Rump, handing Monty a clipboard and pen. He glanced my way and barely nodded, doing his best to ignore me.

"This issue may have something to do with your friends—associates—whom you conversed with earlier," Monty said, taking the clipboard from Robert and signing it. Robert wordlessly tipped his hat to the both of us and practically dashed out of the Randy Rump and back to his truck before speeding off. "He moves quite fast for someone his age."

"He almost broke an ankle trying to get away. What's going on?" I asked, confused. "I know the Dark Goat gives off some serious creepy vibes, but this is Robert. He should be used to it by now."

"James, may we use the back room?" Monty asked, looking at Jimmy. "We have a delicate matter to discuss."

"You can use my office," Jimmy said, pointing to his office before ducking down behind the large counter to organize more supplies. "You know the sequence. Backroom is currently being set up. I have some Dark Council people using the space later tonight for some meeting of theirs."

"Thank you," Monty said, leading the way to the office. "We shall be brief, no more than ten to twenty minutes."

"All yours," Jimmy replied with a grunt as he moved one of the crates of beer. "Don't break anything."

"Wouldn't dream of it," Monty said.

"Wasn't talking to you, Tristan," Jimmy said, glancing my way. "Remember what I said, Simon. Walk away."

"Would if I could, but I can't," I said, following Monty to the back.

Monty approached the office.

This door, even though it wasn't as strong as the back-room door, was still impressive. It stood eight feet tall and half as wide, making it easy for the werebear to enter his office without stooping.

I could tell Monty had reinforced some of the runes. Not that I could make out what they meant, but they just felt different, stronger than before.

"You changed the runes?"

"Enhanced them, yes," Monty said as he activated the sequence that opened the door. "You can sense the difference?"

"They feel stronger—scarier and stronger."

The door and frame were made of Australian Buloke ironwood, one of the hardest woods on the planet. I narrowed my eyes and saw that it, too, was magically inscribed with new runes on every inch of its surface.

Most of the runes on the door were indecipherable. The few I did understand scared the hell out of me. Jimmy had asked Monty to increase the configurations and Monty had gone to town.

Before, if anyone tried to use this door without knowing the sequence, they were in for a world of pain. Now, with the new runes, trying this door without knowing the sequence would leave the victim in a pile of dust before they knew what hit them.

"I'm impressed you can sense the difference," Monty said, opening the door and stepping into Jimmy's office. "It means your sensitivity is growing."

"I've always been in touch with my sensitive side," I

said, still looking at the runes on the door. "How did you manage to enhance proto-runes?"

"The same way anyone improves at anything—practice." Monty glanced over at the faintly glowing runes. "I do admit it was dicey there for a few moments. Nearly disintegrated this place a few times."

"Wait—Jimmy tells me not to break anything, but trusts you to enhance the destructo-runes on his door?"

"Doors," Monty corrected. "I needed to do the protorunes on both doors: this and the main door. That one took some work. In any case, we aren't here to discuss my runework, impressive as it may be."

"How strong are you now, exactly?"

"Irrelevant," Monty said, waving my words away. "If you recall, I called Cecil earlier to get your vehicle delivered. He shared some disturbing news."

I held my hands up in surrender.

"I haven't destroyed any vehicle and I don't think the Dark Goat *can* be destroyed. Whatever he's saying I did —wasn't me."

"You do realize that not everyone who knows you thinks you are a source of mayhem and destruction," Monty said. "Some actually think it's you *and* your creature."

"Hilarious, really," I said. "I'm going to go on vacation and let everyone see what a menace you two are. If it's not about the vehicles, then...?"

"This has to do with something—someone—else."

"Who?" I asked, actually concerned because we were having this discussion in a secure office inside a neutral zone. It meant either Monty was taking major precautions, or worse, he was scared of something. "What's going on?"

"Cecil was instructed to deliver a particular vehicle tomorrow night."

"Since when does Cecil give you his delivery schedule, and what does that have to do with telling his people I suddenly have the black plague?"

"Every few decades, Cecil delivers a special vehicle. The 1939 Duesenberg Coupe Simone Midnight Ghost."

He paused to let the words sink in.

"That piece of automotive art was never found after the war," I said in almost a whisper. "There's only one of them, and it was lost."

"Not lost, hidden and kept hidden, even to this day," Monty said. "Except for rare occasions when its owner requests it."

"I thought Cecil owned the 'Duezy'—and why is this relevant?"

"Cecil owns *a* 1939 Duesenberg Coupe Simone Midnight Ghost."

"You're saying there's two of them?"

"This Simone Midnight Ghost is owned by one Magnus M. Balfour," Monty said. "Cecil informed me that he will be delivering this vehicle to a location downtown tomorrow night."

"Magnus M. Balfour?" I asked. "There is no way this is a coincidence."

"I was just informed that Slif belonged to a very prominent dragon enclave, one of the most powerful in this country. Would you like to guess what her last name was?"

"Please tell me it was something generic, like Slif Smith?"

Monty just stared at me and shook his head.

"Balfour? Her name was Slif Balfour?"

"It's not a proper surname, but she belonged to the Balfour Enclave."

"Of course, this Magnus is just paying the city a visit?" I asked hopefully. "Coming to take in the sights and do the tourist thing?"

"After he instructed Cecil where to deliver his automobile, he expressed a desire to meet the individual who ended his enclave sister's life—a particular Simon Strong."

"Bloody hell," I said as Monty raised an eyebrow. "Seriously?"

"It has been my experience that dragons lack an appropriate sense of humor," Monty said. "He is aware of you and your actions regarding Slif."

"How are *you* not part of that equation?" I asked in disbelief. "I mean, yes, I was the one who was dragonploded and I was the one that buried Ebonsoul in her neck, and...Oh, shit."

"Well, I admit, I did provide the orb," Monty said matter-of-factly. "However, *you* provided everything else."

"No wonder Cecil is acting like I'm toxic waste," I said. "How strong is this Magnus Balfour? And for the record, what kind of name is Magnus M. Balfour?"

"An old one. He is the leader of the Balfour Enclave of dragons," Monty said. "I highly doubt it's an honorary position. I'm fairly certain this 'mission' we are being briefed on tonight involves Magnus and his imminent demise."

"Shadow Company is going to try and kill a dragon enclave leader? Is that even possible?"

"They're going to try and fail, killing you in the process," Monty said. "That's my best guess. Especially if Rott is part of this plan."

"If this Magnus is holding a grudge, why not just take me out directly?" I asked. "If he's as powerful as he sounds, he can dust me without much effort."

"Politics and optics, I'm sure," Monty said. "You're just a human to Magnus; to take direct action against you would be beneath him. But if you were to be part of an operation to kill him...?"

"He would be free to wipe me out without a second thought. Without repercussions."

"Self-defense will carry more weight than, 'This was the insignificant human scum who managed to kill my sister with only a blade.'"

"I'm noticing how you left out the enormous orb of destruction you supplied."

"Insignificant details," Monty replied, his expression serious. "If this is the case, this would be the ideal time to decline this mission and meeting. I don't know if Kali's curse will allow you to survive a dragon attack."

"You know I can't walk away," I said. "I need to see this through to the end."

"Why?" Monty said. "You owe these men no allegiance. If anything, they are trying to eliminate you."

"If Rott is alive, I need to make things right with him and end this."

"What if what he's after is your life?"

"He's going to find taking my life difficult."

"It won't stop him from trying, especially if he's trying to balance the scales of Cassandra's death with your own. He will never stop."

"Then I'll have to stop him."

ELEVEN

"Jimmy doesn't know how to find dragons," I said. "Although he makes a solid argument against my locating them. Do you know?"

"Why would he know?" Monty asked. "He's not a dragon."

"I just figured he's part of the supernatural community," I said. "Maybe he had an address?"

"You do realize *you're* part of the same community now?"

"I'm only partially supernatural. The rest of me is entirely natural, without the super."

Monty just stared at me for a few seconds.

"The workings of your brain are truly indecipherable," Monty said as we left the office. "His being a werebear doesn't mean he's a fount of information. Dragons are wealthy, old, powerful, and invisible. James wouldn't be privy to that kind of information."

"Invisible as in hard to see?"

"Invisible as in operating behind the scenes," Monty

said. "They have two major enclaves in the city, the Balfour and Obouros—or, at least they had. They have been dormant for some time now."

"For a moment I thought you were going to say the Capulets and the...hey?"

"No relation at all," Monty said. "I do believe my uncle had words with William's use of the family name. Apparently it was cleared with the elders of the time. Poetic license or some such."

"Dex knew Billy Shakes? I'm impressed," I said. "Actually, that explains a few things."

"Do I even want to know?" Monty asked. "Forget I asked. The point is that dragons prefer to remain quiescent, hidden, and behind the scenes, pulling strings and influencing events from the shadows."

"Slif didn't seem all that inactive when she was trying to kill us," I said. "Why haven't I heard of the dragon enclaves before all of this?"

"Did you forget the part about being invisible?" Monty asked. "They take great pains to remain in the background, shunning all kinds of attention."

"Which means Jimmy can't share what he doesn't know," I said. "Are you saying Slif and Kraggy were outliers?"

"Quite," Monty said with a nod. "In any case, even if James knew, I doubt he could divulge that information."

"Why not? Would they hit him with some kind of mute cast? Or maybe something that creates spontaneous amnesia? Then he would forget every time he was asked."

"On occasion, I wish I could suffer from acute, spontaneous amnesia, usually every time you come up with these ideas," Monty said. "The reason he wouldn't share is because dragons are notoriously homicidal about their privacy. They would come back and reduce this establishment—and James—to atoms for sharing their location."

"So, what then?" I asked. "It's not like we can google 'dragon enclave NYC.' How do we locate them?"

"There is a method, but we will have to see an Auer," Monty replied. "Which will complicate things considerably."

"Who do we need to see in an hour? Do we have enough time?"

"Not 'see someone in an hour', we need to go *see* an Auer."

"Right, that makes perfect sense," I said. "What's an Auer? Don't you dare say a measurement of time."

"The closest approximation would be a type of archive. She is a guardian of information."

"You mean we're going to go see a glorified librarian?"

"Whatever you do, if you enjoy a functioning mind, do not call her a 'glorified librarian'. She is an Auer, or *The* Auer. Do not address her as anything else, at your own risk."

"She sounds dangerous," I said. "For once, can't we go see someone harmless? Someone like the barista of scrumptious coffee who will drown us in caffeinated goodness if she feels insulted? Why is it every time we go see one of your people, the chances of obliteration escalate?"

"My people?" Monty asked. "What do you mean, *my people*?"

"You know," I said, with some finger wiggles. "The magey/sorcerer types. So far, they've all been dangerous, deadly, or unpredictably homicidal."

"Because mages and their ilk *are* dangerous, deadly, and

unpredictably homicidal," Monty said, pinching the bridge of his nose. "The world *you* are now part of can and will kill you, or at the very least try to, repeatedly. Although, you visiting the Auer should be safe."

"Oh, you're saying this Auer is harmless?"

Peaches padded over to where we stood. I was surprised he was capable of any movement after devouring his enormous bowl of pastrami. Monty glanced down at my partially sated hellhound.

"Not exactly," Monty said, stepping to the side to allow my hellhound passage. "She's probably as harmless as your creature."

I looked at my—harmless—hellhound, and he looked back at me with a serious dose of puppy dog eyes. The effect was lessened a bit by the red glow.

"You realize it may be time to put your creature on a diet of some sort," Monty continued, having avoided a dislocated hip from an accidental collision. "He's looking a little rotund around the middle."

"He doesn't like the 'D' word," I said, lowering my voice. "Says I'm trying to punish him when I bring it up."

"He could stand to lose a few pounds."

"He could," I said, glancing at Peaches. "He just ate the equivalent of a small cow in pastrami. I don't know if I could put him on a di—modified eating program."

"Why ever not?" Monty asked. "If he continues on this course he won't fit through normal doorways, much less the car."

"I tried and Ezra shut me down," I said, patting my wonderful hellhound on the head. "Said he's still growing and needs all the food he can get."

"At this rate," Monty said, approaching Jimmy, "we're going to need a bus to transport him."

"I just need to exercise him more," I said. "Hellhounds have boundless energy. I just need to channel it."

"You could always let him and Grohn play," Jimmy volunteered. "I'm sure it would help him burn off some excess energy."

I stared at Jimmy.

"Where exactly do you suggest this 'play' take place?" I asked, looking around. "Here at the Rump?"

"Are you insane?" Jimmy said, glaring at me. "They would destroy it. I know just the place—when you have some time, bring your pup."

We thanked Jimmy for the tea and coffee and stepped outside. The Dark Goat greeted us with a wave of menace that radiated outward in every direction for several dozen feet.

"Whatever runes Cecil used on the Dark Goat, maybe I could have him place some of the same on a jacket?"

"You want Cecil to rune a jacket that causes fear and repulsion in a radius around its location?"

"That way it would make my life easier," I reasoned. "When something comes to pound on my mage partner, they will stay away from me. That way I avoid the poundage."

"Or it may have the inverse effect and make you a target, just like being the Marked of Kali does. In fact, it may even multiply the effect of the mark, attracting some insanely formidable enemies to your location."

"Shit," I said, opening the door for my slow-moving hellhound. He bounded into the Dark Goat, occupied the entire backseat in a sprawltastic way, rocking the car as he settled in. Monty just stared and shook his head. "Do you think the Mark is that bad?"

"I think we're going to need to visit Cecil soon to redo the suspension on this car," Monty said, getting into the Dark Goat. "The mark Kali graced you with inherently acts as a deterrent."

"That's a good thing, right? Deterrent is good."

"Inherently, yes. As you grow in power, you will attract powerful enemies," Monty added. "Like attracts like and in this case, whatever you attract will most likely try to obliterate you."

"Without even getting to know me first?"

"Killing the Marked of Kali is a high honor," Monty said. "If a challenger manages to accomplish the task, it's rumored Kali will favor them with riches and glory."

"So, I'm basically a walking, breathing lottery ticket for some enemy wanting to take me out."

"Well, I wouldn't put it so crudely, but yes. If someone manages to vanquish you, they will gain substantial notoriety, vast material wealth, and power. It's quite enticing, actually."

"Thanks for the morale boost," I said, placing my hand on the dash and starting the Dark Goat with a roar. "Why would she do that? I was perfectly fine being the Chosen of Kali—well, not fine, but you know what I mean."

Monty nodded.

"If I were you, I'd ask her," he said. "She may even answer you."

I shuddered at the thought of "visiting" Kali again.

"Hard pass," I said. "Have you met Kali? Fun times it is not. Maybe I can just live as a hermit in the office. Maybe just stay in Dex's room for the duration?"

"As an option, that sounds unlikely," Monty said. "Eventually they will find you as your power increases. The beings seeking you out will be stronger, able to locate you wherever you are, this plane or another."

"Maybe there's such a thing as mark camouflage? Something to mask it for a specific amount time, like two or three centuries?"

"Perhaps the Auer may have some information," Monty said. "We need to head to Queens."

"Queens?" I said, as we headed away from the Randy Rump. "Really?"

"Yes, specifically Flushing Meadows Park, the site of the last World's Fair in New York City," Monty said. "The Auer resides in a reinforced structure within the park. Do you know how to get there?"

"Do you know where the Thames is?"

"Don't be ridiculous, of course I know—"

"Rhetorical," I said, cutting him off. "Of course I know where Flushing Meadows is. I was born and raised in this city."

Monty reached over and pressed his hand on the decorative mound above the dash. A medium-sized screen, about eight inches wide, rose into view several seconds later.

"What the...? How long has that been there?"

"Since we received the new vehicle. Didn't you read the manual?"

"There's a manual?"

"Of course there's a manual," Monty said, as he pressed buttons on the touch screen, bringing up different displays until he located what he was looking for: the GPS system.

"We have GPS, really?" I asked, surprised. "Does it only work for this plane, or is it interplanar?"

"Interplanar?" Monty asked. "Have you been imbibing too much of your flask? No GPS could be functionally interplanar. This works for this plane only."

"That's pretty amazing."

"Is this your first experience with GPS?" Monty asked, as he kept manipulating the display. "It's actually old technology. Even *I* know about it."

"That humor of yours is practically Saharan," I said. "Of course I've heard of GPS. I just didn't expect this much tech in the Dark Goat."

"Every SuNaTran vehicle is equipped this way. How do you think Cecil locates this vehicle to bring it to us? Divination?"

"I thought it was some kind of runic tracking beacon, or something like that."

"I'm sure he could devise something like that, but Cecil is not a mage. Besides, why use runes when he has technology?"

Monty pressed a few more buttons, zooming out and then back in until he located Flushing Meadows. A few more presses and he had managed to input a route to the park from our location using the navigation system.

"You know, you're pretty tech savvy for a mage senior citizen."

"It's a common misconception that science is the antithesis of magic. Those who would balk at my use of runes and manipulation of energy have no issue channeling electricity through metal and plastic boxes, which they then use to communicate across the planet."

"Well...when you put it that way, it sounds—"

"It sounds like magic," Monty said, still looking at the display. "According to the GPS we need to cross the Ed Koch Bridge."

"No, wrong."

"It says so right here." Monty pointed at the map. "This is the Ed—"

"No one calls it the Ed Koch anything. That is the 59th Street Bridge, or in a pinch, the Queensboro Bridge—never the Ed Koch, ever. The same way the Triboro will forever be the Triboro Bridge and not the RFK anything."

"I had no idea this was such a sensitive subject," Monty said. "I stand corrected. For having such thick skins, New Yorkers can be quite sensitive."

"We're territorial that way," I said. "It would be like me calling the Tower Bridge the London Bridge, which would be—"

"Incorrect," Monty said with an edge to his voice. "It is not and has never been called the London Bridge."

"Good thing you aren't sensitive about the subject," I said with a small smile. "What is the name of the river it crosses, again? The Windy Twisty River?"

"You know full well it's the Thames."

"Right," I said. "Now you know why it's called the 59th Street Bridge."

"You've made your point."

I nodded, satisfied that I had won the minor skirmish in upholding the naming of my city's landmarks.

"What else does that display show?"

"I'd suggest you read the manual first," Monty said, still arranging some of the settings. "I thought you never used it because you were a purist and refused to accept this much technology in your vintage vehicle."

"You mean the same vintage vehicle covered in death runes that make it an indestructible mobile menace? That vintage vehicle?" I asked. "The one we added suicide doors to so we could accommodate a certain sprawlificent hellhound?"

"Well, there is that," Monty admitted. "The manual is quite informative. When you have time, I recommend perusing it."

"Did you study it?"

"Yes, of course."

"Then I'm good," I said. "At least one of us has the information."

"I don't even know why I try sometimes."

"Wait, do we have machine guns, oil slicks or nitrous oxide?"

"You are confusing this vehicle with a particular fictional Aston Martin driven by a British spy," Monty said. "There are no armaments on this vehicle that I know of. One could argue this vehicle is a weapon unto itself."

"Good point. The runes of death are enough to creep anyone out. That, plus being indestructible, is plenty."

"More than enough, I would say."

"I think I'm going to have to read the manual," I said, swerving around traffic heading to the bridge. "Maybe there's an eject button?"

"It's a solid roof," Monty said, glancing upward. "An eject button would lead to a broken neck."

"I'll double check for one when I read the manual," I said. "Can you go into more detail about this Auer person?"

"She is an archivist of sorts," Monty said as we sped uptown. "Her site is similar to Professor Ziller's library, except, unlike Ziller, she exists in a fixed point of time and space. The knowledge contained within her archive spans most of human history."

"So, she's the ultimate encyclopedia?"

"No, she possesses more information than any encyclopedia can ever hope to contain," Monty said. "Her ability as an Auer allows her to assimilate and compile the sum total of human knowledge."

"Is she even human? Wouldn't that much information destroy anyone's mind?"

"She is decidedly not human, she's an Auer. They are specifically trained to manage the amount of information they encounter."

"They? There's more than one?"

"Archives? Yes," Monty said. "Auers are rare. I only know of this one."

"What makes her different from Ziller's living library?"

"Professor Ziller and his library have a very specific focus—all things magical," Monty replied. "If we need an obscure rune or a special cast, then Ziller is perfect. If we need information on how to find dragons in this city, we need to speak to the Auer."

"Are we putting her in danger?" I asked, concerned. "You said dragons would get pissed if anyone revealed their location."

"I did," Monty replied. "The Auer is not just anyone. The dragons may be formidable, but I doubt they would engage her in battle, much less attempt to attack the fortified location that is her compound."

"All the dragons I've met have been beyond unhinged," I said. "Is there any way to keep this meeting secret?"

"The park is large and no one knows we're going to see

her," Monty said. "I'd say this is about as stealthy as we can be without taking extreme measures in our approach."

"You do realize Flushing Meadows is enormous? I don't seem to recall any fortresses in the park. Where exactly is she located?"

"She's not exactly *in* the park. Beneath it would be more appropriate," Monty answered. "She is in a compound beneath the Unisphere. Very few know of its existence."

"She's under the Unisphere?"

"In a specifically designed structure, yes," Monty said. "Access to her location will be difficult. You can imagine her safety is a priority."

"Who would want to threaten a super librarian?"

"Knowledge is power," Monty said. "She is a mage and a repository of knowledge. What could you do with information about anything and everything whenever you need it?"

"I have that now," I said, swerving around traffic. "It's called the internet. Hello? Welcome to the twenty-first century?"

"The Auer is different. Not only does she possess information," Monty said, "she can also see probabilities with that information. This makes her powerful and dangerous."

"She can see the future?"

"No. She's an Auer, not an oracle, although I'm pretty certain the oracles of history were most likely Auers," Monty corrected. "With her information, which is vast, she can predict outcomes with fairly accurate certainty."

"And she's a mage? What kind of mage? A bibliomancer?"

"Bibliomancy is using books for divination," Monty said. "What her discipline allows her to do is control, transfer, and remove information. The closest comparison would be an informaticist."

"Sounds like hype," I said. "What is she going to do if confronted with an enemy, throw books at them?"

"Her abilities are subtle and incredibly powerful," Monty said, shaking his head. "Imagine confronting a mage that could instantly erase your memory, or your knowledge of language? Or worse, implant false memories and knowledge in your mind?"

"Holy hell, that is dangerous," I said, pulling onto the 59th Street Bridge into Queens. "She could stop most mages in their tracks."

"The greatest danger to the Auer comes from humans."

"Humans? What threat could they be? She's super powerful."

"Her ability does not work against the non-magical," Monty said. "Anyone with a weapon could end her life, as long as they were normal. She would be exposed and vulnerable."

"And an easy target," I said.

"Which is why Auers are sequestered, away from society," Monty said, looking out over the East River as we crossed the bridge. "She makes everyone around her nervous and uncomfortable, and with good reason."

"Are you sure we need to go see her?" I asked, suddenly not a fan of meeting this Auer person. "We can send her an email. Wouldn't that be easier, and more importantly, less explosive?"

"No," Monty replied. "This whole situation with Shadow Company seems deeper than it appears. We need to go into this meeting with as much information as possible, especially if they are targeting the Balfours. That means seeing the Auer."

We had several hours before we were scheduled to meet Douglas and the rest of Shadow Company. I agreed it was important to go into the meeting armed with as much information as we could acquire—but meeting some mind-melting mage to get this information wasn't exactly my idea of a great plan.

TWELVE

We arrived in Flushing Meadows Park forty-five minutes later.

Normally, vehicles weren't allowed into the area of the park we needed to get to. Our NYTF credentials and the threatening menace flowing from the Dark Goat made it easier to approach the Unisphere.

I parked the Dark Goat near the Arthur Ashe Stadium entrance and looked down the long, picturesque, tree-lined road to where the Unisphere sat. The road was wide enough to double as a four-lane highway and ended at the large, stainless steel replica of the Earth which sat in the center of an enormous circular reflecting pool.

It was early evening; the sun hadn't quite set, but was on its way. The sky was cast in a spectrum of oranges and pinks, and I could hear the laughter of children carry over to where we parked. The area was still occupied by families and park goers looking to enjoy a day away from the concrete and steel of the city by spending a few moments among the trees and grass of the park.

"We can't drive over there," I said, pointing down the road. "Even with our creds, they don't like cars driving in such a highly populated area."

We stepped out of the Dark Goat. I opened the suicide door for my hellhound, Sprawler McSprawl, as he bounded out of the car. I placed a hand on the roof and locked it as a wave of dark orange energy raced across its surface. The Dark Goat rocked for a few seconds before settling into stillness. I glanced at Peaches and shook my head.

"That, and we don't work for the city's Parks Department," Monty added, following my gaze to Peaches and then at the long road ahead. "This will be a good opportunity to exercise your creature."

"Sure, because nothing says calm, enjoyable evening at the park like a hellhound running around scaring the population half to death," I said, shaking my head. "Besides, you know he's just going to ask for meat after this short walk. I swear he's bottomless."

"True, his presence can be a little off-putting," Monty admitted. "Perhaps keeping him closer to you would prevent a panic."

"You think?" I said, looking down the road. "Where is this place?"

It wasn't like Monty to suggest Peaches go on a romp through a populated park. I figured his lapse in judgment was a side-effect of the schism. I'd have to keep an eye on him just in case he suggested something completely off-base, like wholesale destruction of the city to resolve the Shadow Company situation.

"The entrance is at the Unisphere," Monty said, peering down the road. "There will be several security measures in place before we can access the structure itself."

"What do you mean at the Unisphere? It's just a large empty globe and a big reflecting pool. I don't recall there being any structure near there large enough to house an ultra-library."

"Under the reflecting pool," Monty said, "sits the Auer's Archive. Access is granted at the inverted tripod that's holding up the globe. It's an ingenious design."

"Is this archive physical? Like Ziller's?"

"Yes, why?"

"Why aren't these archives digitized?" I asked. "I understand the magical books being physical, but the ones about mundane things should be digital. Would certainly take up less space. It would eliminate the need for a book batcave."

"Who said it wasn't?" Monty said. "Part of the archive is certainly modern. There are parts that are not, and some are redundant sources of information. Physical books do not require electricity to power them."

"Good point," I said with a nod. "Physical books can't be hacked, either."

"Correct. In any case, stay alert," Monty said. "I'm certain our presence has not gone unnoticed."

"Stay alert?" I said, looking around. "What? We're going to be attacked by rogue book thieves?"

Monty glared at me.

"You fail to see the danger because you are not seeing the larger picture," he said. "Expand your thought process and re-examine the current situation."

He walked off, heading down the road to the Unisphere.

"Next, you'll tell me to free my mind, Morpheus."

"That would presume you had one to free," Monty shot back. "Don't dawdle. This process is somewhat extensive and we are tight on time."

"Damn," I said, patting my jacket as I caught up to him. "I left my library card at home. Are you sure she will see me?"

"Do you actively practice this thing you call humor?"

"It's part of the package. Impressive, right?"

"If I were you, I'd return the package and ask for a refund."

"Oh, the drollarity," I said. "Seriously, though, how much security are we going to face?"

"A substantial amount," Monty said, pointing ahead of us. "Observe."

Four men and three women were walking our way. They were dressed in black suits that almost rivaled Monty's Zegna flair. I could tell each and every one of the suits was a runed affair. Mages were such fashion divas, really. The energy signature they possessed was staggering to say the least.

"Whoa," I said, opening my jacket to allow me access to Grim Whisper, just in case things got extra magey. "Who is that?"

"The Archive Guard," Monty said. "Whatever you do, don't draw your weapon or make any sudden movements."

"Got it," I said, looking at the Guard. "They look serious. How did they know we were here?"

"Sophisticated runic sensing devices situated throughout the property," Monty said, without looking at me. "They were aware of our presence the moment we stepped into the park."

"This Guard is strong," I said, sensing their energy signatures. "Right up there with Paul Bunyan and your sorcerer security team at Haven."

"Possibly stronger," Monty said. "They are the first line of defense for the Auer. To become an Archive Guard is no small feat. Many die in the attempt. Do not antagonize them."

"Right, I'm not really looking to fight The Magnificent Seven here," I said under my breath as the Archive Guard approached and spread out. "I'll let you do the talking. Go, unleash that diplomacy."

"That is my intent," Monty said, taking a few more steps forward and stopping ahead of me. "Stay close, but try to look less menacing. Whatever you do, do not allow your creature to smile. They'll think it wants to eat them."

I let my arms hang by my side as I patted Peaches' immense head.

<Sit, boy. These people are just security. They're protecting a place we need to visit.>

<Can I bite them?>

<No, we need to get inside this place without a fight.>

<I'm not going to fight, just bite. Maybe a small chew?>

<No biting or chewing of any kind. Let's just let Monty talk to them. If they attack, then you can bite them.>

<If I bite them, they can't attack. Frank says it's better to be pre-empty and attack first. I haven't eaten in so long, I feel empty. If I attack, will they have sausage?>

<It's preemptive, and no, they don't have sausage. Do not attack them unless they attack us first, no matter what Frank says.>

<Are you saying Frank is wrong?>

<On so many levels.>

<How many levels? Frank doesn't like to jump around much. His legs are too small.>

<What I'm saying is: I'm your bondmate, Frank isn't. No biting unless I say so.>

<Can the angry man make some meat later?>

<As long as you behave, I don't see why not.>

Four of the Archive Guard stopped walking and remained some distance away. The remaining three closed the distance with the two on either side stopping about half way between the four rear guard and Monty, letting who I assumed to be the leader approach us alone.

Their formation and situational awareness were excellent. These were trained mages, and it showed.

As they spread out, they made sure each of the Guard had a clear line of sight on Monty and me, without endangering one another. They were relaxed and alert. Their training was top notch, which meant they were a threat to be taken seriously.

"Who's that?" I asked under my breath as the center mage approached. "She feels dangerous."

"Because she is," Monty said, keeping his focus on the woman. "She is the Captain of the Guard."

Monty stepped forward a few steps as the Captain of the Guard approached. She was tall, dark, and menacing. Her tanned skin contrasted nicely with the rose-colored blouse she wore under the basic, black-on-black mage funeral ensemble. She had what I liked to call "tuning fork" energy.

The very air around her vibrated with the promise of violence. Everything about her was measured and under control, but beneath that layer of calm poise, I sensed the potential obliteration she could unleash.

I made sure to keep my hand away from Grim Whisper.

It wasn't what I'd expected. Actually, I hadn't known what to expect. I mean, these mages guarded a library. How dangerous could they be? If the energy signature of the leader was any indicator, they were dangerous enough.

"Tristan Montague, to what do we owe this pleasure?" the woman said with a melodic voice that carried a slight accent. "You haven't been here in ages. Critical studies in your last year at the Circle, if I recall?"

"Roma, the pleasure is all mine," Monty said with a slight nod which Roma returned. "We need to see her."

THIRTEEN

"I see," Roma said, glancing my way quickly. "All three of you?"

"Yes, it's urgent."

"Does she know you're coming?"

"No, this is all rather spur of the moment."

Roma's eyes narrowed.

"You know she doesn't do 'spur of the moment', ever."

"It can't be helped," Monty said. "We are somewhat pressed for time and need information."

Roma made a slight gesture and the air around us became thick. The sounds of the park, which were clear a moment earlier, became muffled. She had created a sphere of silence around us with barely a finger twitch.

"Information?" Roma asked. "What information?"

"We need the location of the Balfour Enclave," Monty said. "We have reason to believe they are being targeted."

"Who would dare target the Balfours?" Roma asked. "That would be suicidal."

"Shadow Company," I said from behind Monty. "Usually, they are suicidal."

"Simon Strong," Roma said, giving me the once over. She lingered a little longer this time. I wanted to think it was my irresistible attractiveness that gave her pause, but judging from her expression of mild irritation, I doubted it. "A pleasure to make your acquaintance. I am Roma, Captain of the Archive Guard. Tell me why a clandestine organization, like Shadow Company, would target one of the two most powerful dragon enclaves in existence?"

"A pleasure," I said with a nod. "One of the leaders of Shadow Company lost his daughter to a dragon, Slif."

"Cassandra Rott, yes."

"You knew?" I said, opening my eyes wider in surprise. "How?"

"We are an archive," Roma said. "It is our business to know. Information is the most precious currency in the world, Marked of Kali."

"Whoa, now that's just creepy," I said, staring at her. "How long did you know that?"

"The moment I saw the mark upon you. Observation is just another way to gather information," Roma said with a small smile, before turning to Monty. "Tristan, why are you here? What does this have to do with either of you, or a hellhound?"

"Simon once belonged to—"

"Shadow Company, yes, we know," Roma finished, crossing her arms. "Archive?"

"My apologies. Of course," Monty continued. "They have requested his presence in their next mission."

"Which is?"

"You don't know?" I asked. "I'm surprised."

Monty gave me a sideways glare.

"What? She knows everything else, I figured she knew this, too."

"We are not psychics, nor can we see the future," Roma said. "We possess information of what has occurred, not what *will* occur."

I raised a hand in surrender.

"My mistake," I said. "I just figured—"

"Deny the request," Roma said with finality. "Tell them you can't join them on this mission. It sounds ill-formed and suicidal."

"I can't."

"Can't or won't?"

"Both," I said. "I'm partially responsible for Cassandra's death, and I need to stop them. Hunting dragons sounds like a bad idea for everyone all around, don't you think?"

"The events that led to Cassandra's death were out of your control and always were," Roma said. "She was going to die the moment she encountered Slif, whether you intervened or not."

"You can't possibly know that," I said. "There were too many factors involved. If I had kept her back, away from the action—"

"She would have died later," Roma said, softly. "It was out of your hands."

"No, no it wasn't," I countered, keeping my anger in check. "It was my call, and she died because of it."

Roma just stared at me in silence for a few moments.

"You cannot change the past," Roma said. "However, hunting dragons could destabilize the delicate balance between the two major enclaves. If the Balfour weakens, the Obouros would seize the opportunity to strike. That would be...catastrophic."

"Exactly. I'd like to prevent the catastrophe," I said. "Can we go see the Auer person now?"

"You? No. You're not even a mage," she said, turning her attention to Monty again. "To see her, you would need—"

"A formal audience," Monty said, shaking out his hands. "I agree."

Roma raised an eyebrow and smiled in typical mage style. I knew this was bad. It was one of those smiles that said: *There will be pain in ample doses for everyone here —prepare.*

"Monty? Can we discuss...?"

"A formal audience?" Roma asked and moved a hand. Two of the four mages from the back stepped forward and walked behind us. We were effectively surrounded by a cabal of librarian mages. Yes, I had been studying. "Are you certain?"

"Yes," Monty said. "Will you grant me passage?"

"You know the way to gain passage, better than most," Roma said. "If you are successful, you, Mr. Strong, and his bondmate will be granted passage. Do you need time to prepare?"

"One moment," Monty said, raising a finger. "I need to clarify some things with my associate."

"Of course," Roma said. "You have five minutes, or your request is null and void."

"Thank you," Monty said with a slight nod as he approached me.

"Why is it never simple with mages?" I asked. "Let me guess, gaining passage is some crazy fight to the death?"

"Don't be ridiculous," Monty said, waving my words away. "It's not that kind of battle."

"It is a *battle* though, right?"

"Well, yes. A duel."

"Is there a potential for a lethal outcome?"

"Everything has its risks. You know this," Monty argued. "Merely crossing the street—"

"Nope," I said, raising a finger. "Wrong. If I'm crossing the street alone, there is zero risk. Do you know why?"

"No, please enlighten me," Monty said with a small sigh. "I can hardly contain my curiosity."

"Because if I see a truck barreling down the street, I do *not* cross the street," I said loud enough for Roma to hear as I looked around Monty. She deliberately ignored me. "A mage would be gauging what would happen if they unleashed several orbs at the right moment to deflect the truck from crushing them. *That* is the difference."

"Your logic makes for fascinating study, truly," Monty said. "Now let me explain what will happen next, here in reality. Not in Simonworld."

"Explain away," I said, squinting my eyes and giving him my best Clint glint. "I'm listening."

"Do you need a restroom? Because we hardly have that kind of time."

"Oh, ha, ha," I said, waving him on. "Explain the duel."

"The six mages around us will create an impenetrable alternate temporal plane," Monty said. "Hence their positioning. Roma and I will engage in the duel, while discussing theorems."

"Excuse me? You're dueling and taking a quiz at the same time?"

"That's an oversimplification, but, yes, that is an apt description," Monty said. "It's part of the process."

"What are we doing?" I asked, motioning to Peaches and myself. "Dodging orbs? Is this like a tag-team type of duel? You tag me in when you get tired?"

"Absolutely not," Monty said, pointing behind me to one of the mages. "You will be standing over there, next to that mage. This is not a duel to the death. I have to neutralize her ability to cast before she does the same to me."

"While answering questions?"

"Yes, while answering questions," Monty repeated. "Have you lost the basic comprehension of language?"

"Just being clear. How are you going to negate her abilities? You're not a negomancer," I said, then paused. "Wait, *are* you a negomancer now? Did the schism upgrade your abilities to your final form?"

"Final form? No, I have not acquired the ability to use negomancy," Monty snapped. "Focus—I said neutralize, not negate. I have to create a situation where she cannot cast, before she can do the same thing to me."

"Why does that sound dangerous?"

"Because, it *potentially* it is," Monty said. "I have to predict and outthink what she will do, while preventing her from doing the same to me."

"While answering questions," I repeated. "Am I the only one that sees this as insane? Just call the Auer and make an appointment."

"Yes, you are the only one. This is how it's done and has always been done," Monty said, pulling on a sleeve. "Think of it as mage chess."

"Do you get to ask her questions?"

"Why would I need to ask her questions?" Monty said with a sigh. "I'm the one needing a formal audience, not her."

"What kind of questions is she asking?"

"Anything and everything related to being a mage and my studies."

"Well, I just thought it would be fair if you got to ask your own questions."

"Are you still under the impression that life is fair?"

"Touché. Why not just play regular, non-lethal chess?" I asked. "The chances of death by explosion are close to zero; although you're mages so there's always a possibility. Besides, the last time I checked you don't have to answer questions while playing chess, unlike this duel of yours."

"I don't create the rules here, I just follow them."

"Since when?"

"Since we need to see the Auer and she would be displeased if I didn't."

"Oh, let's not piss off the mind-melting Auer," I said. "Good plan. Can you take Roma?"

"The last time we did this, she trounced me soundly," Monty said, glancing over his shoulder at Roma. "She's an exceptional strategist, and I was still studying in the Golden Circle at the time. I have improved somewhat since then."

"I hope so. She doesn't look like a slouch in the kick-ass mage department," I said. "Are you sure it's only going to be brain-melting mage questions? If I shoot her, I can even things out a bit. She can't ask too many questions if she's wounded. I can wing her. It'll be just a flesh wound."

Monty stared at me.

"If you shoot her, the six mages around us will consider

it an unprovoked attack," he said, turning to walk back to Roma. "They, in turn, will immediately attempt to blast us into submission or death, whichever comes first."

"That would be bad."

"Quite," Monty said as he walked away. "Stay back, don't draw your weapons or unleash your creature, and we should be fine."

I took a few steps forward.

"Does she know about your schism?" I asked, keeping my voice low. "Maybe you should let her know you're a bit fragile right now."

"Fragile?" Monty shot back, keeping his voice just as low. "I am not *fragile*. Now, step back. Duels tend to be somewhat chaotic."

"Are you ready?" Roma asked, as Monty approached her. "Do I need to reacquaint you with the rules?"

"They are still fresh in my mind from last time, thank you," Monty said. "I'm ready."

"I haven't had a duel in quite some time," Roma said. "I'm going to enjoy this. Do you acknowledge that you enter into this duel of your own free will and without any coercion?"

"I do."

"Do you understand and agree that once the duel has begun, every question posed must be met with a satisfactory answer?"

"I am aware, yes, and agree."

"Do you understand that any damage or pain suffered as a result of our duel is with the full knowledge of the risks involved? Do you accept?"

"I do," Monty said. "I will abide by the rules of this duel and accept the outcome, whatever it may be."

"Sounds like that fine print that needs to be examined in every contract," I said, then raised a hand in surrender at Monty's expression. "Just pointing it out. Don't want to be surprised by any hidden clauses."

"Over there," Monty said, pointing at the mage behind me. "Do not interfere."

"Wouldn't dream of it," I said. "If she pulps you, I'm not the one telling Roxanne, just FYI."

"I'm ready," Monty said, scowling at me before turning back to Roma.

"Excellent," Roma replied, looking at one of the mages surrounding us. "Begin."

Each of the mages outstretched their arms to the side. Blue energy beams flowed from their fingers, connecting them. Once they were all connected, the park disappeared from view and they spread out even farther, giving Monty and Roma an expansive dueling arena in the center.

I moved back to the edge, next to my designated mage. I was about to comment on how amazing this all was when I noticed the mage next to me seemed to be in a trance. His eyes were covered in the same blue energy that flowed from his fingers, his expression vacant as he turned his face upward.

I looked around and each of the six mages were doing the same thing. In order to create this time arena for the duel, it appeared they needed to check out from this reality. Something about this made me nervous, but I trusted Monty—and like he said, we needed to see the Auer.

He needed to beat Roma, and he needed to do it fast.

FOURTEEN

Roma traced a rune in the air and unleashed a golden lattice which raced at Monty. The lattice was easily five feet across, and looked like it was going to envelop Monty when he gestured, bisecting the golden energy with a thin, violet beam of his own.

The two halves of the lattice sailed by him as he traced a rune.

"Explain Ziller's basic theorem of multi-planar travel," Roma said, tracing another rune, "as it relates to temporal teleportation within a singular plane."

I knew the words she used were English; they just didn't make sense, except for teleportation, and all that did was make my stomach clench.

Monty unleashed a flurry of golden runic symbols in her direction. Roma had formed a small orb of blue energy in her hand as Monty's runes raced her way.

"Ziller's theorem posits that teleportation within a singular plane must conform to the laws of interplanar travel," Monty said with a gesture as the runes he sent closed in on the strangely calm Roma.

"Which are?" Roma said as she sidestepped the runes and released the orb from her hand. "The first two laws, please."

Her orb began rotating until it picked up speed. The rotation acted like a siphon, sucking in the symbols Monty had unleashed at Roma. It flashed with golden light for a few seconds until all of Monty's runes were gone.

The orb floated lazily by Roma's head as she smiled.

"The first law being the law of permeability—all matter is permeable and subject to transposition."

Roma nodded her head and tapped the orb with a finger.

"The second?" she asked as the orb raced at Monty. "Please don't hold back. You know I won't."

Monty slashed a hand downward, creating a shield. The orb bounced off of it and sailed into the distance. A few seconds later, Monty's shield began disintegrating.

"You used my runes to create a matter disruptor," Monty said, glancing at his shield. "Impressive."

"No less than your runes of transport," Roma said, forming three more blue orbs around her. "What was the destination? The Arctic?"

"Bahamas," Monty said. "I imagine you're due some time off."

"Nice of you," Roma said, moving a hand, setting the orbs in motion around her. "Second law?"

"The law of permanence—all teleported matter will observe and retain its original state of mass, irrespective of teleportation."

"Excellent," Roma said with a nod. "The next question will be somewhat...difficult. Are you ready?"

"Yes," Monty said confidently. "Ask."

At this point, even I was feeling confident. Monty was a runicpedia when it came to all things mystical and such. I was pretty sure that even the fictional Doctor Strange would call on Monty, if he needed assistance on a particular rune or cast. If Roma thought she was going to stump Monty by Zillerfrying his brain, she was in for a rude surprise. That big brain of his was Ziller-proof.

Monty began tracing more runes as Roma nodded. The blue orbs floating around her head crackled with white energy. Roma traced a short set of runes, charging the air around us with power.

"In all the time you've known Roxanne DeMarco, not once have you verbally expressed your feelings for her. Why not?"

Oh shit.

"I beg your pardon?" Monty asked, pausing, clearly taken off-guard mid-rune. "What did you say?"

The three orbs around Roma raced at Monty, followed by a smiling Roma who had materialized a blue blade of energy in her hand. Monty backpedaled, reaching for one of the Sorrows sheathed invisibly behind him.

A soft wail escaped the blade as he drew it, barely managing to parry Roma's thrust as she closed the distance. One of the orbs punched into his opposite arm throwing him off-balance. Monty rotated with the blow, slicing the remaining orbs with a diagonal slash. He grimaced with pain as he rolled his shoulder, stepping to the side, and blading his body to Roma.

I took a step forward and felt a hand rest upon my shoulder.

Another mage appeared next to me. She had stepped out of the blue beam connecting the six mages who were forming the battle arena.

"You can't," she said. "If you interfere, the Auer will not grant him, or you, passage. He must answer the questions posed to him. Those are the rules."

"Your rules suck," I said. "That last question was a low blow."

The mage nodded.

"Yet it's pertinent isn't it?" the mage said. "He refuses to address that situation. The attack by Evers was personal. Tristan is an accomplished mage from a powerful family and yet for all that power, he was—is—vulnerable."

"Who are you again?" I said, turning to the woman. "Do you know Monty?"

"Yes," the woman said. "I've known him his entire life. My apologies—my name is Jean." She extended a hand, which I took. "A pleasure to meet you."

I looked at the woman, assessing if she was a threat.

Jean was nearly as tall as Monty, and wore the same type of mage suit as the Archive Guard, but in dark blue, and hers looked extra comfortable. Her salt-and-pepper hair was cut short and her face was open and friendly, except for her eyes. Behind her silver-rimmed glasses, her eyes radiated a deep, dark power as she observed the duel taking place in front of us.

"I'm Simon and this is—"

"Peaches," Jean said, looking down at my hellhound, and risking a hand by patting him on the head softly. "I know, your bondmate, and most excellent hellhound."

"You're her aren't you? The Auer?"

Jean smiled with a small nod.

"I'd say you're acclimating to this world nicely," Jean said. "Now, if you could only manage to pause for a few seconds before letting your words get you into a world of trouble, your life would be somewhat easier."

"I think I've been doing okay, considering," I said in my defense. "I wasn't exactly eased into this world; more like shoved...violently."

A small chuckle escaped Jean as she slowly shook her head.

"What do you think of that last question?" she asked. "Too personal?"

"Totally off-limits," I said. "I thought this was a mage duel? He wasn't expecting that at all. Monty is kind of touchy about the whole 'Roxanne' subject."

"Indeed," Jean said. "That is why Roma asked it; we need to know if he is still suffering the effects of the schism. He was always impetuous and quick to anger. He can't afford that now. The stakes are so much higher."

I looked back to the duel and saw Monty adequately handling Roma's multiple attacks. I could tell she knew her way around a blade. Monty was parrying and avoiding her attacks, but he wasn't exactly sailing through this duel.

"She's good," I said, concerned as a swarm of orbs pounded into Monty's chest. "Scary good."

"Yes, she is," Jean said. "Fortunately, this isn't a duel to the death. He allowed the last question to unsettle him and has lost a crucial advantage. If he's not careful, she will end this soon."

"Why, though?" I asked. "I mean the entire duel. Couldn't he have just made an appointment to see you?"

"No," Jean said, her tone serious. "To obtain a formal audience with the Auer, with me, requires knowledge, primarily of oneself. He needs to confront this aspect of himself, or the next time—and there will be a next time—someone close to him is in harm's way, he will falter or act irrationally."

"Monty doesn't do irrational," I said, focused on the duel. "Have you met him? He's the closest thing to a Vulcan I've ever met."

"Are you certain?" Jean asked. "He knew Haven was runed with security measures, many of which he had personally put in place, and yet he cast anyway."

"Roxanne was in danger."

"Afterward, in Kali's domain, when *you* were in danger, the rational thing would have been to rely on his blades, yet he cast—again."

"Those were special edition Rakshasas," I countered. "They don't play nice with others on a good day. Kali is all kinds of twisted with those things."

I looked around, just in case. The last thing I needed was a visit from Kali.

Jean nodded.

"Later, when you were losing your fight to Evers—"

"Not losing," I interrupted. "It was a strategic withdrawal. I was regrouping to catch my breath."

"Of course," Jean placated. "It wasn't like she was wielding a god-killing blade designed to end your existence, nor had you suffered multiple wounds at her hand."

"Fine, I was losing," I said with a low growl. "Evers was trying to shred me."

"And succeeding," Jean said. "Yet, Tristan returned to help you, risking his life in the process."

"Those were extenuating circumstances," I said. "Evers wanted to end me, Monty, and *magic*. She wasn't exactly firing on all pistons. She and Monty had a past during the war. Whatever had happened to her, left her angry, broken, and looking for vengeance."

"While all that may be true, I just provided you with several instances of Tristan acting irrationally. The last thing he can afford to do is lose control."

"A mage losing control is a bad thing," I said as Monty slid back, and side stopped another barrage of Roma's orbs. He slashed his hand in the air again and created another shield, deflecting Roma's orbs. Instead of standing behind the shield, he stepped through it, catching Roma off-guard. "Whoa, that was unexpected."

Roma stepped back, surprised at Monty's move. He thrust forward with the Sorrows while unleashing a small barrage of five golden orbs. Jean raised her eyebrow and nodded.

"This will be over soon," Jean said. "He created a golden star. Tristan has truly become formidable. Roma is in for a surprise. She is not facing the Golden Circle student from decades ago."

Roma parried Monty's thrust as the small orbs punched through her defenses. Each golden orb slammed into one of her limbs, the last one impacting her forehead, whipping her head back.

Roma recovered instantly, but it was too late. Monty gestured and beams of golden light connected the small orbs, forming a pentagon, freezing Roma in place, arms and legs apart, standing as if she was about to do a cartwheel.

"A golden star?" Roma asked, immobile as she looked

down. "Well done, but you know the rules. The question must be answered, or the formal audience will be denied."

Jean put a hand on my shoulder again.

"This is the real duel," she said, keeping her voice low and her eyes on Monty. "Will he dare confront himself?"

I followed her gaze, wondering the same thing.

FIFTEEN

Monty stood still.

"The answer, Tristan," Roma said still immobile. "Reply, or forfeit the audience."

From his expression, I could tell he was upset. There were certain topics he avoided, and then there was the topic of Roxanne. Bringing that up was like running through a minefield, blindfolded, at night. You didn't know how far you'd get before something was blasted off, but it was guaranteed.

"I've known Roxanne for many years," Monty said. "She knows how I feel about her."

"Does she?"

"Yes. I've risked my life for her, more than once."

Roma smiled and gestured, disappearing the golden star. Monty raised an eyebrow, clearly impressed.

"That's not the same as expressing it," Roma replied, taking a few steps forward. "You were willing to risk bodily harm on the skywalk at Haven, even when you suspected it was a trap."

"She was in danger."

"It's a simple question, Tristan. Why not?"

"The last person I expressed my affection for was taken from me," Monty said, his expression hard. "It will not happen again."

"What happened to your mother is not your fault," Roma said, gently. "You were a child."

"What happened to his mother?" I asked under my breath. "He's never shared that."

"That is for him to share with you," Jean said. "Ask him one day."

"I don't see how my response to this question is pertinent to the matter at hand," Monty replied, turning to Jean. "You, of all people, know the answer to that question."

"I'm not the one who needs to know it," Jean said. "The rules stand for a reason. Answer or forfeit the audience."

Monty stared hard at the Auer. For a brief second, I thought he was going to turn around and walk back to the Dark Goat. A flash of anger flitted across his face—but then he took a deep breath and let it out.

"Fear," Monty said after a moment. "I will not risk losing her. Expressing my feelings or emotions will cause her to alter her behavior. This in turn can expose her to danger she will not be prepared to face."

"You underestimate her abilities," Roma said. "Roxanne is a powerful sorceress."

"I have never underestimated her abilities," Monty said, still looking at the Auer. "Words have power. You feel she is my vulnerability? Yes, she is. So is my uncle; so is Simon. Anyone close to me"—he glanced at me

—"anyone within the very intentional small circle of my family is at risk. I will protect them from those who would attack. If need be, I will unleash my complete wrath and tear this plane asunder to keep them safe, but I will not subject them to undue danger. Being close to me is enough."

"You feel that justifies keeping your feelings from Roxanne?" Roma asked. "You don't think she needs to hear the words?"

"Yes it does, and no she doesn't," Monty said. "She knows my feelings, and that is all that matters. No words can convey the depth of my emotion for her. And I believe that now, in accordance with the rules of the duel, I have answered the question posed. The matter is closed."

Monty crossed his arms and stared at the Auer. Roma looked like she still had more to say, but the Auer shook her head. Roma nodded and motioned with one hand. The blue beams of the Archive Guard shifted to a deep green. The Auer turned and started walking.

"This way, please," Jean said. "You have your audience."

We followed her into the green beam. One moment we were in the park, and the next we were in a large lounge area surrounded by immense, rune-inscribed wooden bookcases. I looked around, taking in the area. The book cases were easily forty feet tall and twice as wide. They were arranged in rows that seemed never ending. I walked to one end of the closest bookcase and saw more rows.

The lounge area was a series of small desks, large sofas, a few wingback chairs, and a counter holding fresh fruits and water. It was a well-lit area, brighter than the surrounding space. When I looked down the rows of bookcases I noticed other pockets of light spaced out every thirty bookcases or so: small oases of rest in the desert of books we stood in.

"How big is this place?" I asked, looking around again. "This can't all be on this plane. Really, why haven't you gone digital? You could probably fit the bulk of this information on a few Fugakus and call it a day."

"This is my reception area," Jean said. "Information storage is several levels below us. We have a total of ten-thousand Orions which can exceed one thousand exaflops to process the several million exabytes contained within them."

"Impossible," I said, awestruck. "Something that fast hasn't even been created."

"I know," the Auer said. "Rest assured, we have several, and most of the information you see contained within these books has been duplicated electronically. But we aren't here to discuss the Archive's computing power and storage, are we?"

She motioned for us to take a seat. She sat in one of the wingback chairs and waited.

"No," I said, "I need to find dragons, specifically the Balfour Enclave."

"Are you looking to test the power of Kali's curse?"

"No," I said, about to explain, but stopping myself. "Wait, do you know why?"

"What do you think?"

"I think you already know," I said. "Roma said you can't see the future, but you know what has already happened. You know about my conversation with Shadow Company and why they called."

"I do," Jean said with a nod. "Do you?"

"According to Douglas, they need my help," I said.

"Rott wants vengeance and Douglas wants—I don't know what Douglas wants. This is not a usual Shadow Company mission, or at least it wasn't when I was there."

"You sound uncertain, why?"

"Rott was dead, and now he's not," I said. "I'm not one to talk about people not dying—in fact, I should be the last person discussing this—but something is off about Rott still being among the living."

"His presence makes you uneasy?"

"I left uneasy the moment I heard his voice," I said. "It freaks me the hell out."

"Tristan, your thoughts?"

Monty was deep in thought as he sat in one of the other wingback chairs. He held his steepled hands in front of his face and looked off into the distance before answering.

"Rott's motivations are simple to understand, at least on the surface," Monty said. "He blames Simon for the loss he suffered and wishes to exact some measure of vengeance on both the dragons who killed his daughter, and the person he feels responsible for her death."

"Except he's supposed to be dead," I said. "He blew himself up with an entropy bomb. I saw him."

"You saw an explosion, we both did," Monty replied. "We never saw what happened to his body."

"What body? How could there be a body after an entropy bomb goes off?" I asked. "The Kragzimik was torn apart and turned into atoms. I'm supposed to believe Rott survived *that* blast? No way."

"What about Douglas?" the Auer asked. "What are his motivations?"

"Unknown," Monty said. "It's evident he dislikes

Simon, but is not above using guilt tactics to manipulate him. I don't understand his motivation, and that concerns me."

"As it should," Jean said. "Like Roma mentioned, I'm not omniscient, nor can I foretell the future. I can predict outcomes based on past events, but all that is, is an educated guess."

"The present is formed in the past, and the present shapes the future," Monty said. "Except when it doesn't."

"Precisely, or rather imprecisely, put," Jean said. "Simon, if I give you this information, will you still meet with Shadow Company?"

"Yes," I said. "I need to close this part of my past."

"And if I don't?"

"I still have to do this," I said. "Shadow Company doesn't know how to take no for an answer. The next time they contact me, it won't be polite. You don't know these people; the first knock is soft, the second time they use C4."

"I'm somewhat familiar with their methods," Jean said with a smile. "It comes with the position."

"Oh, damn," I said, realizing she probably knew more about Shadow Company than I would ever know. "Sorry, I keep forgetting..."

"Are you putting yourself in danger by providing this information?" Monty asked. "I'm certain we can try another method if this act endangers you."

"You could try," Jean said, "but you won't find the location you need before your meeting tonight."

"Not without your resources, no," Monty agreed. "I respect your power and ability, but I,—we—have no wish to cause you..."

"What he's trying to say," I interrupted, "is that we don't want your helping us to come back and bite you in the ass. What if the dragons get pissed because you revealed their location?"

"Simon," Monty began, "this is the Auer. A modicum of respect is warranted."

"Exactly," I said, focusing on Jean, "She's the Auer. I bet she's heard curse words we haven't even discovered, right? Can you share some?"

The Auer chuckled as she stood.

"Follow me, please," she said and started walking down one of the rows of bookcases. "I have a formidable Archive Guard and am not without my own defenses. If the dragons wish to pay me a visit of violence, they will not be disappointed."

"How would they even know?" I asked as we walked by several bookcases. "It's not like we're going to tell them."

"Yes, you will."

I stared at the Auer for a few seconds.

"No, we won't," I said, letting the anger seep into my words. "That's not who we are, especially if we know it would endanger you."

"Be that as it may," Jean said, "you will reveal where you obtained your information. I will make certain of it."

At this point I could barely follow what she was talking about. I remained silent for all of three seconds out of respect.

"What do you mean?" I blurted suddenly as we kept walking. "You want them to come here and roast you? Have you faced a dragon? They're nice until they want to barbecue you to ash."

She stopped walking and pointed down one of the bookcases.

"You let me worry about that," Jean said, placing a hand on my shoulder. "Remember, dragons, like any other powerful being of magic, only respect one thing..."

"Power," I finished. "They respect power."

"Correct," she said. "You need to go to the Balfour TINY and speak to Gant. Tell him, and only him, that Magnus would like a word. He will facilitate the rest."

"The tiny what?" I asked. "Are we shrinking now?"

"The TINY is where you're going to need to go."

"We need to go tiny? Am I the only one not understanding here?"

"Yes," Monty said. "Let her finish."

"There you will meet Gant. You will speak to him."

"Are we looking at another duel?" I asked. "Just want to know what to expect."

"You're dealing with dragons," Auer said. "Expect the unexpected. Be wary. When they place an arm around your shoulder to befriend you, always look for the concealed dagger. Do not trust them. Always remember that, to them, you are insignificant—a tool to be used and discarded. If Magnus wants to meet the slayer of his enclave sister, it is only to determine how best to remove you from existence."

"That's a cheerful thought. Thanks for that."

"You're welcome," Jean said, then turned to Monty. "As for you, stop being such a mage. Get over yourself. Go tell that woman how you feel, before you lose the opportunity."

I had never seen Monty turn that particular shade of

red before. He struggled for a few seconds to find the words, before composing himself.

"Thank you," he said with a slight nod. "I will certainly take that into consideration."

"You do that," the Auer said, pointing again. "That will take you back to your vehicle. Once there, you will have the location you need. Come visit me when you're not pressed for time."

"We will," Monty said and headed down the row book-cases. "Thank you, again."

I watched him take a few steps and then disappear in a blue flash.

"Is that a teleportation bookcase?" I asked warily, eyeing the bookcase. "I'm not a big fan of teleportation. Maybe I could just go back the way we came?"

The Auer laughed.

"Your bonds are reconciled; teleportation should not be an issue for you, unless you make it one," she said, gently pushing me by the shoulder. "One more thing: please be vigilant with Tristan."

"What? Why?"

"I accepted his answer to the duel question because that is what he believes," the Auer said. "That doesn't mean it's the truth. You need to find out the true answer."

"This is Monty you're talking about," I said. "I think I'd rather take my chances fighting the dragons —unarmed."

"You underestimate your power," the Auer said, as a soft blue glow flashed across her eyes. "You are a shieldbearer."

"I know. It means I have to keep him safe."

"Yes, but that is not your *only* function," the Auer said,

tapping my chest. "Did no one inform you? A shieldbearer does not only protect his charge; he protects all those around him. Your ability is warding, like the first light of dawn after a night of darkness and death. The same must be said for your presence."

"That is completely unclear," I said.

"Right now it is, yes," she said, continuing the gentle not-so gentle shove out of her library. "It won't always be. Get to Tristan's truth and it will begin to make sense."

I was about to answer when she gave me one last shove.

The world disappeared in a blue flash. When I could see again, I was standing next to the Dark Goat. Monty and my hellhound were already inside. My stomach rumbled, but surprisingly, that was the extent of my discomfort.

I jumped into the Dark Goat, and started the engine, revving it for a second before letting it settle into its familiar purr.

"Did she give you the information?" Monty asked.

I was about to say no, when the location of the Balfour meeting place became clear in my mind. It was the kind of memory that lingered, like some odd deja vu. I knew exactly where we needed to go.

"Yes," I said with a nod. We still had several hours before our meet tonight. "I know exactly where it is."

Monty nodded as I put the car in gear and sped off.

SIXTEEN

We crossed over the 59th Street Bridge and headed back downtown.

The Balfour TINY was a three-story brownstone located at 135 West Broadway, in the heart of Tribeca. I parked the Dark Goat and stood outside the pink building, looking at the facade.

"It's pink," I said as Monty got out. I held the door for my hellhound, Sprawler DeSprawl, as he stretched his way out of the car. "This building is...very pink."

I placed a hand on the roof of the Dark Goat and locked it.

"I believe the color is called rose," Monty said, stepping to the door of the restaurant located on the ground floor. "This is a pastel shade in the pink family."

"Thank you, Mr. Pantone," I said, staring at him. "I'll stick with pink."

"Are you certain this is the place?"

"What do you mean am I certain? Didn't she tell you, too?"

"If she had, why would I ask?"

"Good point," I said, nodding and searching my memory. "This is the place, but I don't think we're going to find any Balfours here. I mean, it has charm, but upscale this is not."

"Let's not be fooled by appearances," Monty said. "For all intents and purposes, you and your creature look like an average man and his dog. We both know that is far from the truth."

"Yes, we are both way above average," I said, patting Peaches' head. "It's actually not that hard to see."

"I'd say one of you is above average in ability, and the other, above average in his capacity to induce migraines," Monty said. "I'll leave you to figure out which is which."

"I've never heard of this place before," I said, looking around the entrance. Everything was turned off and the restaurant looked closed for business. "What kind of name is TINY?"

"A small one," Monty said, moving to the door and locating a barely visible rune. "Here."

"Was that mage humor?" I asked. "Because that almost sounded droll. Did the schism activate your inner comedian?"

"I don't even know the meaning of the word," Monty said, pressing a sequence of runes. "TINY stands for Temporal Interstitial Neutral Yard. Think of the Randy Rump as a portal to another location—that is what a TINY is. This one happens to lead to the Balfour Enclave. There."

The runes on the door flashed with orange light for a half a second before disappearing. The lock mechanism unlocked with an audible *click* as Monty pushed the door.

We stepped into a large dining area, complete with fireplace. A large bar dominated one side of the floor. Several people were seated there, enjoying drinks and engaging in conversation. The main dining area was filled with small round tables.

Patrons sat at the tables, most of them couples. The first thing that made me realize this place was different was the lack of attention. No one gave us a second glance. Everyone was completely immersed in their conversations.

I could understand not looking at Monty or me, but ignoring a hellhound? It took me a few seconds to adjust to the feeling of normalcy. Monty motioned to the bar with his chin.

The bartender was a short man, broad around the shoulders, who looked like he spent plenty of time in the gym. Actually, he looked like he spent plenty of time lifting the gym. He was cleaning a glass with a large chamois.

"How can I help you?" the man asked, his voice gruff.

"Earl Grey and coffee, black and potent for my associate," Monty said looking around the place as I took the stool next to him. "We're looking for someone."

"Aren't we all?" the bartender said as he prepared our drinks. "This someone have a name?"

"Gant," I said. "Heard of him?"

The energy of the room shifted slightly. What I took for a lack of attention earlier was actually a subtle shift in the attention of the room. Not everyone was watching us, but those who were were trying to be subtle about it and failing.

The bartender placed the cups of tea and coffee in front of us. The coffee smelled amazing, and was nearly

Deathwish level. Monty's tea smelled like it always smelled —something close to boiled grass.

Monty hummed in approval as he let his cup sit a moment longer. I took a sip from my cup and felt the initial jolt as my coffee cracked its knuckles and hit me in the jaw with a right cross of coffee goodness.

I stared at the bartender in surprise as he nodded in my direction.

"I know, it's *that* good," he said. "Special house blend. What do you want with this Gant?"

"Sorry, but we were instructed to only speak to him," I said. "No offense."

"None taken," the bartender said. "People who ask for me usually shoot first, then get to the questions. This is a nice change."

"You're Gant?" I asked incredulous. "Seriously?"

"What were you expecting?"

"I don't know exactly," I said. "With a name like Gant —tall, dark, and dangerous?"

"Two out of three isn't bad," Gant said, smiling and winked. "I happen to be height challenged. On the plus side, being this tall means it's easier to kneecap the idiots who equate my height with a lack of intelligence."

"A pleasure to meet you, Gant," Monty said. "The tea is exquisite."

"At your service," Gant said with a short nod. "Now, how can I help you?"

I had no way of proving or disproving this was the Gant we needed to speak to. For all I knew, he could be trying to get information out of the two clueless tourists who managed to walk into his place.

It was thin, but possible. I looked at Monty who nodded.

"I hear Magnus would like a word with me."

Gant's expression changed immediately at the mention of Magnus. He narrowed his eyes at me and nodded.

"You're on the wrong floor," he said curtly before pressing his hand to a section of the bar. A second later, runes on the corner of the bar he had touched glowed a deep red then faded to nothing. "Third floor. Now."

Gant pointed to a set of stairs at the other end of the bar. I glanced over and saw that each of the stairs was covered in softly glowing orange runes.

"Now?" I asked, grabbing my cup of coffee delight. "Can I just finish...?"

"No. Now," Gant said. "Make sure to take the stairs and don't speak to anyone here. Go. Now."

Gant stepped to the other end of the bar and went to the back. Monty placed a hand on my forearm and shook his head.

"Let's go," Monty said, leaving his tea and heading for the stairs. "It would be prudent to head upstairs now. Most of these patrons only appear to be human."

I looked around the restaurant. We now had the attention of several of the tables. Some of the looks were disinterested, but a few looked angry. None of them were welcoming.

"Good idea," I said, following Monty. "Let's go, boy."

Peaches stayed close to me as we climbed the stairs and let out a low rumble as we left the ground floor. The second floor was only a bar—no tables for sitting, just stools in front of a long, L-shaped bar. Sitting at the bar was one person who glanced our way, then ignored us as we kept climbing.

The energy signature on the second floor was impressive. The person read like a sorcerer, but more. We kept climbing and came to a large rune-covered door. Gant opened it from the inside and motioned for us to come in.

The third floor seemed reserved for private events. It was arranged as a lounge with large sofas and comfortable chairs spread out around the floor. A small bar sat on one side of the space, with another large wooden door dominating the opposite wall. The floors were the same wood as the doors and covered in runes.

The space felt familiar, like the Randy Rump.

"This is a neutral zone?" I asked taking in the space when I smelled the coffee from downstairs. I focused on the small bar and saw my mug waiting for me. "That my coffee?"

Gant nodded.

"This level is part of the Balfour estate," Gant said heading to the bar. "You said Magnus wants a word with you?"

"Yes," I said, before taking another sip of coffee heaven. "Can I get a bag of this to go?"

"You can't drink more than that," Gant said. "Not unless you're a dragon."

"Are you a dragon?" I asked. "You certainly seem to get along well with them."

"No, I'm not," Gant said, narrowing his eyes at me. "For the record, no one gets along well with dragons. You either follow their instructions or suffer their wrath. There's no in between with them." He narrowed his eyes at me. "You're not exactly human, but you're not a dragon, either. What are you?"

"Complicated," I said. "I'm not a dragon, at least not the last time I checked."

"Only way you can drink that"—he pointed to my mug—"and survive, is to have some dragon in you. So, I'm going to ask again, who are you?"

"My name is Simon Strong," I said. "This is—"

"I know who *he* is," Gant said. "Mage Montague, responsible for the regular destruction of buildings in this city."

Monty narrowed his eyes at Gant but remained silent.

"Finally," I said, throwing up a hand. "Someone who speaks the truth."

"I didn't say he blew up the city alone," Gant replied. "You're just as dangerous to property as he is, especially with your hound."

"I'm just as dangerous?" I said, offended. "How is it that I can be just as dangerous as a mage who considers blowing up buildings just another Tuesday? This makes no sense."

Monty glanced at me, ignoring my rant.

"You are a gatekeeper," Monty said, looking around. "This is...?"

"I'm the Head Gatekeeper," Gant said. "This place is the entrance to the Balfour estate on this plane," Gant said. "At least one of them. Magnus will be here shortly."

"Magnus?" I asked, alarmed as my focus returned to Gant. "The dragon Magnus?"

"Do you know another Magnus?" Gant asked. "Relax. If you were here with the intent to do harm, the stairs would've stopped you. If he says he wants to talk, he wants to talk. At least until you piss him off."

"Talking is good, as long as you can walk away from the conversation."

"Trust me," Gant said, "if he wanted you dead, you wouldn't have gotten past the first floor."

"The patrons on the first floor?" Monty asked. "Are they all...?"

"Dragons? Yes," Gant said. "Some of them are part of the Balfour Enclave, but most of them are looking to join. They come here to be seen in the right place at the right time, by the right people."

"Who was the man on the second floor?" I asked. "He was drinking alone."

"Basic black, looked angry, felt powerful?"

I nodded.

"Looked like he was having a bad day."

"That's Rell," Gant said. "Balfour lead enforcer. He's not having a bad day, he's having a bad century. If you value keeping your limbs attached to your body, stay away from him."

"Copy that," I said. "Stay away from the angry, limb-ripping dragon."

"That puppy of yours trained?" Gant asked, looking down at Peaches. "Our hellhound insurance is basic and doesn't cover extensive property damage."

"There's such a thing as hellhound insurance?"

"There is, and it's pricey," Gant said. "Keep him under control. I don't feel like renovating this place. Too damn expensive."

"He's trained and well-behaved, mostly," I said,

glancing at my amazing hellhound. "You have any sausage in this place?"

"You don't carry meat with you?" Gant asked. "How long since he fed?"

<It feels like forever.>

<It has not been forever. You ate at the bearman's place. A little while ago.>

<Forever ago.>

"Not that long ago," I said. "About two hours."

"Two hours?" Gant said. "You realize hellhound puppies are eating machines?"

"It has come up once or twice," I said. "That, and he has a black hole for a stomach."

"He's not a dog," Gant said. "Hellhounds have insane metabolisms. Two hours will feel like a lifetime for him. Let me see what I can scrounge up."

Gant crouched down behind the bar and resurfaced a few minutes later with a large metal bowl filled with sausage.

"Is that regular aluminum?" I asked, looking down at the bowl.

"No, this bowl is carbon steel," Gant said. "Aluminum wouldn't last ten seconds with this puppy."

"Thanks, really, but you don't have to go through all..."

"This isn't for your benefit," Gant interrupted, setting the bowl in front of Peaches. "If you let him get too hungry, that would be a bad thing. For you, and more importantly, for me and my place."

Peaches gave me the imploring puppy-dog eyes. I nodded and he proceeded to vacuum in the sausages. Each time, it never ceased to amaze. I really was beginning to think his stomach existed in another plane.

"I thought you said this was the Balfour's place?"

"This place is a TINY," Gant said, crouching down again, out of sight. "You know what that is?"

"Yes, kind of a portal that leads to another place."

"Exactly," Gant said. "This place is like the front door to a larger place located elsewhere. In this case, the Balfour Estate, which is not on this plane. As Head Gatekeeper, I select the location of transition, while Magnus makes the bridge."

"Isn't that a bit complicated?" I asked. "I mean, wouldn't it just be easier to have a place on this plane?"

"Last time they tried that, someone tried to kill an enclave leader," Gant said. "Needless to say, there were plenty of unhappy dragons ready to rip through one another. Magnus came up with this solution."

"It's complicated and clunky."

"It's supposed to be," Gant said, standing up again with a small turquoise crystal in his hand. He handed me the crystal. "This is an emulator. If you carry meat, you can use this crystal to create more. Hellhounds should never, and I mean never, go hungry."

"The last time I tried to create meat, it didn't go well."

"You're not a mage. Why would you try to create meat?" Gant asked. "Use the emulator. I'm sure the mage can explain it to you."

"What would happen if he did go hungry?" I asked, curious. "I mean, I would never let him go hungry, but it doesn't seem like he can ever get enough."

"Hellhounds," Gant said with a nod. "Bottomless pits of hunger. If it ever happens, you need to—"

The large wooden door slid to the side, revealing a balcony behind it. On the balcony stood a man dressed in a dark suit with his back to us. He beckoned to Gant without turning to face us.

"Magnus?" I asked.

Gant nodded.

"One moment," Gant said, raising a finger. "I need to let him know your status before he comes in here. Standard protocol."

SEVENTEEN

Gant slid the balcony door closed and began speaking to Magnus.

"Our status?" I asked as I observed the conversation between Magnus and Gant. "What does that mean?"

"I would imagine it's a security concern," Monty said, sipping his tea. "He would want to know if we took the stairs, as well as if we passed the other security measures I'm sure are in place."

"I was under the impression dragons were beings of magic."

"That doesn't mean they can't be harmed," Monty said. "His energy signature, even in this place, is considerable. I would not welcome a confrontation."

"I second that," I said. "He's a dragon; he doesn't need to be scared of us, so why all the precautions?"

"It would seem our reputation precedes us," Monty said. "He obviously knows about Slif. I wouldn't doubt he knows about the Kragzimik as well."

"Well, shit," I said. "Not the best way to start a conversation: 'Hello, I go around killing your kind, you said you wanted to chat?'"

"In your defense, both instances were self-defense," Monty said after taking another sip of tea. "Slif had a lethal agenda, and the Kragzimik—well, he wanted to eradicate us all."

"I'm starting to sense a theme, here," I said. "How long has Magnus been the enclave leader?"

"I'm not certain. I do know he's an *old* dragon," Monty said. "That doesn't happen by coincidence. He has remained alive this long because he's careful. Even though this is a neutral zone, Magnus understands the wisdom in taking precautions. James' establishment is proof of that."

"True," I said, "but now Jimmy has Grohn, too. The Randy Rump is super secure as a neutral zone these days."

"Every security measure can be countered," Monty said. "Even powerful runic, or in this case, trollgre, ones. All it takes is patience and power."

"I doubt this Magnus is out there worrying about me, or any of us," I said, glancing at Monty. "He's a dragon. I'm surprised he even wants to speak to me."

"This exercise is called assessing the enemy," Monty said. "Don't misconstrue civility for friendliness. Magnus is not an ally, not even one of convenience. He is here to determine how much of a threat we pose."

"As long as he doesn't lose his mind and go ballistic, I'm good," I said. "I'm not in the mood to fight another one of his kind. Those fights usually end up with body counts and massive destruction."

"This is a neutral zone," Monty said, looking around. "A formidable one. My abilities are greatly diminished in this place. The same will happen to him once he crosses the threshold. He will not attack us here. Even dragons abide the rules of neutral zones."

"I seem to recall a similar speech when you described the Randy Rump," I said. "Then it got blown up several times. You'll excuse me if I keep my weapons close."

"The fact that we were allowed to keep our weapons speaks volumes," Monty said. "Do not forget, we are his guests. Try to refrain from shooting him, or at him."

"It pays to be safe," I said, tapping Grim Whisper with a slight nod. "He may be powerful, but he isn't invulnerable."

Monty gave me a look.

"Fine, I won't shoot unless absolutely necessary," I said. "How much do you want to share with him? I mean, there's a highly trained group of assassins gunning for him. You think he knows?"

"I'm certain he's cognizant of this fact," Monty said. "That, and you also belonged to said group."

"Long ago and lifetimes away," I said, looking at the balcony door as it slid open. "Let's see what he has to say."

Magnus came into the space first. The runes at the threshold shone a brilliant white for a few seconds as he crossed the balcony door. He was followed by Gant, who caused the runes to turn a brilliant mix of green and gold.

Magnus must have shopped in the same place as Hades. His suit was an impeccable Amosu Vanquish bespoke item. The black fabric shimmered with a subtle silver line pattern. Underneath the jacket, he wore a crisp white shirt and a rose tie, which matched the exterior of the building. His shoes were a pair of black Tom Ford customs by Arasheben that gave me pause.

Anyone who would wear a seven-figure pair of shoes

crossed excessive and sailed right into pretentious. Everything about him was meticulous. He could have been the poster boy for mages around the world, with his own tagline. *Dragons: when nothing short of pompous will do.*

He had rugged good looks and reminded me of a young Pierce Brosnan, right around the Bond years, and he definitely had the suave look down. He didn't look a day over thirty, which I knew was a lie. If Monty said he was old, Magnus was counting birthdays in centuries at this point.

He smiled as he approached and that's when the facade slipped. His smile was about as warm as an arctic wind and I could sense the wave of anger and contempt directed at me.

Peaches gave off a low rumble, and I agreed. We did not like Magnus.

Gant moved off to the side and headed to the small bar. Magnus stood in the center of the floor and gazed at us each in turn, before looking at me again. Soft classical music began to play, and Magnus nodded.

"Perfect," Magnus said. "Do you know this piece?"

"Sounds a little somber if you ask me," I said, recognizing the Mozart piece. "I prefer a good Coleman if you want to go for sad and meaningful. This is just people yelling in a language I don't understand."

"Mozart, Requiem in D minor, K626," Monty said. "An interesting choice."

"You killed Slif," Magnus said in a soft baritone. Not a question, just a simple statement of fact. "Did you manage this alone?"

"I'm never alone," I said. "She started it."

"I'm sure she did," Magnus said, walking over to one of the large chairs and sitting. "Shall we discuss how to rectify this situation?" He motioned to another set of chairs. "Please sit. Make yourself comfortable."

Right, that was like wearing a bloody steak and comfortably swimming in shark-infested waters. Everything about Magnus set off alarms in my head. I took a seat and Peaches sat next to me. I could tell he was ready to pounce. Monty, his expression grim, sat in a chair close to me and opposite Magnus.

"Rectify what, exactly?" I asked warily. "I'm not aware we need to rectify anything."

"The stench of the Auer still rests on you," Magnus said with a slight smile. "Am I to assume she was the one who disclosed this location to you?"

I saw no point in lying.

"She gave us a nudge, yes," I said. "I tried to google 'secret dragon club,' but that was a mess. You really need to work on your SEO. The Auer made it so much easier, pointed us right here"—I glanced over where Gant stood —"and said we should speak to Gant."

"I will make sure she is dealt with."

"I'd leave her alone if I were you," I said. "She's not exactly an easy target."

"Are you threatening me?"

"I'm *advising* you. Trying to take her out would be a bad career move."

"I'll take your *advice* into consideration," Magnus said, motioning to Gant, who pressed a panel near the small bar. "Send them."

"Send them?" I asked, looking from Magnus to Gant. "Who did you send?"

"A solution to my Auer...problem, but that's not pertinent to our present discussion," Magnus said, waving my words away. "Do you care to explain yourself?"

"Explain myself? What's there to explain?"

"You killed one of my enclave sisters," Magnus said, getting right to it. "The way I see it, we can approach this one of several ways." He looked over at Gant who nodded holding up a bottle. "No, the Versos 1891. This is a special occasion. Apologies. You'll forgive me; good sherry is one of my weaknesses." Gant handed him a glass. "And this is one of the best. Now, where were we?"

"I killed one of your enclave sisters."

"Yes," Magnus said. "Tradition dictates I respond. This affront cannot stand, but I do have options."

"Is one of those options that we put the incident behind us, seeing as how she tried to kill me and those close to me?"

"Unfortunately, no," Magnus said, holding up his glass and looking at the liquid it contained. "You are not a dragon; therefore, this must be dealt with in the old ways."

"The old ways?" I asked, not liking where this was going. "Are we going to have to meet at dawn with pistols drawn?"

"It's simple, really," Magnus said, ignoring my duel at dawn comment. "Either I kill you; I kill one of your family, blood or chosen; or, you kill me."

"None of those options work for me, thanks. Monty?"

"There is another option," Monty said, "if you are following the traditional ways. The Rite of Fire."

"The Rite of Fire?" I asked. "Why does that sound painful?"

"I thought you were his friend?" Magnus asked. "The Rite of Fire would end him. He is not dragon."

"Correct, I am *not* dragon," I said, staring at Monty before turning to Magnus. "Do you have a Rite of Smoldering, something a few levels below fire? You know, hot enough to be uncomfortable, but not lethal?"

Magnus stared at me.

"Are you always this irritating?"

"Only when I'm awake or facing individuals with delusions of grandeur."

"I have given you the recourses available to me Which do you choose?"

"This Rite of Fire...what is it, exactly?" I asked, remembering Slif's attempts to barbecue me. "Trial by combat, facing off against dragons, or dealing with actual fire?"

"Yes," Magnus said. "All that and more. It *will* kill you. Choose."

"Do I have to face off against you?"

"Against *me*?" Magnus asked, looking over the rim of his glass. "Are you insane? What an absurd notion. Are you suggesting I engage *you* in actual combat? Have you grown tired of living?"

"Then who?"

"You will face Rell, my lead enforcer," Magnus said. "He has much to atone for. This will give him the opportunity to work off some of his debt."

"Really glad I could help Rell out," I said. "When?"

"You have one week to get your affairs in order. Notify your next of kin, and whatever it is you humans do to prepare for death," Magnus said. "One week from today, you will face Rell in my home at the Balfour Estate, and we will settle this matter once and for all."

"And if I refuse?" I asked, because I was suicidal that way. "What if I say no?"

"Then I will start immediately eliminating everyone your life has touched, starting with Mage Montague and your hellhound here."

The rage inside me flared, but I managed to keep it in check. Magnus was not some second-rate enemy. The power he gave off, even inside a neutral zone, told me everything I needed to know. He could back up his words with lethal action.

"You will not touch him or anyone else," I said after taking a deep breath. "You will leave them alone."

"They will be safe," Magnus said, "if you honor your word and accept the Rite of Fire. Yes?"

"I will," I said, feeling a lump of dread in the pit of my stomach. "One week."

"Excellent," Magnus said, dismissing us with a wave of his hand. "This has been quite productive. I expect you here one week from today. Gant, show them out."

Gant gave Magnus a slight bow and led us to the door.

EIGHTEEN

Gant walked us down to the ground floor.

"It was the smart play," Gant said. "Actually, it was the *only* play, but it was the smart one. You bought yourself a week. I'd enjoy it if I were you."

"How dangerous is Rell?" I asked as we stepped outside the restaurant. "Do I have a chance against him?"

Gant shook his head.

"It was great meeting you," he said. "I don't know much about this Rite of Fire—it was before my time, and I'm not a dragon. The last time I heard of one, Rell was standing for the Balfour Enclave against several dragons. None of the challengers survived—and they were dragons. Which you are not."

"Right," I said. "That fills me with confidence. Basically, this is a rite of suicide."

"For you? Yes," Gant said. "But this way, the Balfour Enclave will leave everyone in your life alone, and prevent them from being attacked by *any* dragons. They will be honor bound to do so."

"That's comforting. Too bad I need to be dead to enjoy that level of dragon security," I said. "I need to find a loophole, really."

"Aren't any that I know of," Gant said, "but, like I said, the Rite of Fire is not my thing. Maybe your mage knows?"

"I have a few ideas," Monty said, nodding to Gant. "Thank you for your assistance."

"My pleasure," Gant said. "See you in a week. Try not to do anything stupid, like leave town. Balfour does his homework, and he knows all there is to know about you at this point."

"I get it," I said, walking away. "Don't try to escape or he burns everything to ash."

"Something like that," Gant said, heading back in to the restaurant. "Enjoy the week."

"One more thing," I said. "Who did he send?"

"Magnus plans for every contingency," Gant said, lowering his voice. "He sent a group to deal with the Auer. There's nothing you can do for her now."

"We'll see about that," I said. "Do you know when?"

"I don't, but I know it won't be before the annual enclave meet," Gant said. "Magnus never conducts business this close to the annual event. It will be after, probably a day or two. She's gone; she just doesn't know it yet."

"Knowing her," I said as we stepped away, "I'm sure she does."

We headed to the Dark Goat. I placed my hand on the roof and it unlocked with its usual hammer-on-anvil *clang*, followed by the orange wave of energy across its surface.

I held the door open as the Master of Sprawlesence jumped into the car, executing a superior hellhound stretch, taking up the entire backseat. Monty was strapped in the passenger seat by the time I got behind the wheel.

The engine roared with a scream and settled into a menacing purr. I remained silent for a few seconds before putting the Dark Goat into gear.

"The Auer is quite capable of defending herself," Monty assured me. "That, and she has Roma and the Archive Guard. We need to focus on the immediate threat."

"I'm not blowing myself up with an entropy bomb, and Slif nearly wiped the street with all of us," I said, speeding down the street. "I hope you have an idea."

"Several, actually," Monty said. "Some of it is coming into focus. The rest will have to wait until we meet with Shadow Company."

"I'm glad someone is seeing through all of this, because all I'm seeing is an expiration date a week from now."

"Look closer," Monty said. "What do we know?"

"Magnus wants to kill me?"

"He may not want to, but he has to because of his position as enclave leader," Monty said. "A failure to respond to Slif's death will be perceived as weakness. In dragon society, that would be a death sentence. Obouros would exploit it as an opening."

"He doesn't want to kill me, but he has to?" I said, crossing over to the east side of the city. "Is that supposed to make me feel better?"

"Why now?" Monty asked. "Why not eliminate you shortly after Slif perished?"

"Maybe his schedule was packed with dragon things— you know, terrorize and raze a few villages, hoard some gold, that sort of thing."

"You're conflating fiction with reality," Monty said. "They may still hoard wealth, but now it's done in stock holdings and real estate."

"It probably wasn't convenient before, or maybe Rell was busy killing everything in sight," I countered. "He seems extra angry. Where did you come up with the Rite of Fire?"

"One of my old classes at the Circle focused on dragon hierarchy and how their society evolved over the millennia. The Rite of Fire was used to initiate dragons, to enter certain enclaves, and to settle disputes without wholesale warfare."

"That sounds efficient."

"It is," Monty said pensively, as he looked out of the passenger side window. "What bothers me is that the Rite of Fire is not open to non-dragons, and yet he agreed to let you partake in it. Why?"

"He really wants me dead?" I said, swerving through traffic. "Wants me to suffer?"

"He made no mention of your mark or affiliation to Kali," Monty said. "It's possible the neutralizing effects of the TINY contributed to that, but it seemed odd he would neglect to address it, considering he intends to end your life."

"Is he stronger than Kali?" I asked, concerned—well, more concerned. "She is a goddess with phenomenal cosmic power."

"Dragons were once revered as gods, before gods even existed," Monty said. "I honestly don't know. Magnus is ancient; he could very well be as powerful, if not more powerful, than Kali or Hades."

"Basically what you're saying is he wants to smear me

all over his estate in this rite of his," I said. "At least he will allow his enforcer assassin to do it."

"He could have done that at any time before this meeting," Monty said. "No, there's more. I don't think he expects to see you in a week."

"He thinks I'm going to bail?"

"No," Monty said. "He expects to see you before the week is out. He knows about Shadow Company's mission somehow. The Rite of Fire was all pretense to lull you into a state of complacency."

"Give me a week, but kill me at his earliest convenience sort of thing?"

"Exactly. I wouldn't be surprised if he dispatched Rell right after we left."

"Sounds like the dragon thing to do," I said, avoiding more traffic. We had an hour before our meet with Shadow Company. "Have I told you how much I dislike dragons?"

"You may have mentioned it once or twice," Monty said. "Are you ready for tonight?"

"No, but I don't have much of a choice, do I?"

"There's always a—"

"Not this time," I said, cutting him off along with a few taxis that were jockeying for position behind me. "I have to face this part of my past and put it to rest before it does the same to me."

NINETEEN

"Are you sure you want to come with?" I asked as we approached the place where Cassandra breathed her last. "You realize we're only a block or two away from Haven and Roxanne, right?"

"It can't be helped," Monty said, looking down the block as we parked. "I would imagine that would be them?"

Monty gestured to the large black truck parked down the block. It was similar to an NYTF command and control vehicle, complete with an enormous trailer.

"Nothing says subtle like a huge trailer wide enough to block an entire street," I said, getting out of the Dark Goat. "Let's go say hello."

I opened the door for the Zen Meat Master that had sprawled out into hellhound enlightenment. He stepped out of the Dark Goat with another stretch, causing the car to rock back and forth as he did so.

<*Let's go. Stay alert—these are not friendlies.*>

<Why are we going to see them if they are not friendly? Can I chew on them?>

<No chewing, at least not until I say so.>

<Should I wait until they hit you first, then chew on them?>

<Wait until I say so. Some of them will not want to be around you, and some may want to hurt you. Ignore them and stay close to me, got it?>

<Can we go to the place after this? My stomach feels empty.>

<Once we're done with all of this, I'll make sure you get more meat than even you can devour.>

<That's not possible. I'm a growing hound.>

We were halfway down the block when the rear of the trailer opened. A tall, wiry man stepped out and waited for us to approach. He looked young, easily ten years my junior, about my height, dressed in black combat armor, and was wearing a small arsenal. A dual shoulder rig held two guns, along with dual thigh holsters, equally equipped. I saw the hilts of several blades sheathed along his legs. I imagined there were plenty more weapons hidden out of sight.

"I feel under equipped for this meet," I said under my breath as we closed the distance. "I should have brought a rocket launcher or three."

"He's probably overcompensating for a lack in some other area of his life," Monty replied. "Or possibly he wasn't hugged enough as a child."

The man shifted to the side, blocking the entrance as we reached the trailer.

"You and the Brit can come in," the man said, his voice gruff. "The dog stays out here."

"The hound goes where I go," I said. "We're a package deal. Where's Douglas? Who are you?"

"I'm the one letting you into the trailer, and the mutt stays outside," Tall and Clueless said, letting his hand float over to a thigh holster as he gave me the once over. "Don't even know why we need some washed-up senior citizen. You still know how to hold a gun, old man?"

"Senior citizen?" I said, glancing at Monty. "Did he just call me old?"

"It appears so," Monty said, stepping to the side. "Children these days, no respect for their elders."

I slid forward faster than Clueless could react, drawing Grim Whisper, and placing it gently under his chin. He didn't have time to reach for any of the weapons in his mobile arsenal, and he froze in place.

"What's the point of carrying all these weapons if you can't use them when you need to?" I said close to his ear. "What's your name?"

"Carlos," he said flexing his jaw. "My name is Carlos."

"What do you think, Carlito?" I said, pushing up ever so slightly into his chin with Grim Whisper and forcing his head back an inch. "Do I still know how to hold a gun?"

"You're good," Carlito managed.

"I'm not good, I'm the best," I said. "If I'm here, it's because your team couldn't perform. Is that it, Carlito? You need all these guns because you can't perform?"

Carlos turned a few shades of red as he kept his anger in check. Smart move, especially when the barrel of a gun was poised to redecorate your head into abstract art.

"Negative," Carlos said when he regained some control. "I perform just fine. Maybe one day I'll have the honor of showing you just how good I am."

"I look forward to that day," I said, holstering Grim

Whisper. "Until that day, step aside and don't call my pure-bred hound a mutt, or next time I'll shoot first and let him chew on what's left of you."

Carlos nodded and stepped to the side, allowing Monty, Peaches, and me to enter the trailer. The trailer was a double-wide affair and felt like stepping into an upscale office. We were at one end of a short corridor.

On either side were doorways that led to small rooms. At the end of the corridor, I could see a larger opening that led to a situation room, complete with a small conference table, monitors, and assorted computer equipment.

Carlos stepped in behind us and closed the door, remaining where he was as we moved forward.

"In here, Strong," I heard the rough voice of Douglas call out. "Carlos, go take a walk and get some air."

I glanced back and saw Carlos glare at me.

"Yes, sir," Carlos said, opening the door and stepping out. "Needed to do a perimeter check anyway."

"Who says you don't know how to make friends?" Monty said, as the door slammed shut behind us. "He's seems quite friendly."

"Right," I said, glancing at the door again. "I'll probably have to shoot him before this is all done."

"Maybe you should just give him a firm talking to," Monty said as we moved forward. "Sometimes a strong word is all it takes."

"You'd be amazed at the radical behavior therapy a bullet can produce," I said. "It's life altering."

The situation room was mostly empty. Douglas sat at the conference table with a series of maps rolled out in front of him. Most of the computer terminals were empty of personnel, and standing to the right of the entrance to the situation room was a short woman with a dark complexion.

She was also dressed in black combat armor, and I could tell she had spent some time in the gym. The air of relaxed menace about her let me know she had had extensive training.

Like Carlos, she wore several thigh holsters holding large guns. Unlike Carlos, she carried a shotgun strapped to her back. I could see the runework on the barrel of the Mossberg 590A1 Tactical. Whatever she shot with that thing was in for a bad day.

She stood absolutely still, something much harder than it sounds. If I hadn't sensed her presence, she would have blended into the background. The stillness, along with her posture and gaze, let me know she had been trained in counter-surveillance. I glanced her way and she gave me a slight nod, which I returned. She was ten times the threat Carlos was.

There would be no pissing contest with her; she knew she was dangerous and had no need to prove it to anyone. I made a mental note not to piss her off—not yet, at least.

"Douglas," I said. "You wanted to see me."

"I did," Douglas said. "I see you've met Carlos. Pay him no mind, he's young and full of himself. Reminds me of you a lifetime ago."

"I was young, but never stupid," I said. "I knew better than to underestimate potential threats." I turned to the woman. "And this is?"

"That's Feelds," Douglas said, gesturing to the woman in the corner. "She's on loan to us from an agency I can't divulge. One of the best shooters you want at your back on a breach."

Douglas looked the same as I remembered. A little more gray in the hair, and some noticeable wrinkles around the eyes, but other than normal signs of aging he looked the same. He exercised regularly and it showed. He was still all hard angles and muscle, and looked every bit like the ex-military man he was.

"Feelds," I said with a slight nod, looking around and not seeing George. "Where's Rott?"

"He'll be here shortly," Douglas replied, staring at Monty. "This is the mage?"

"*The* mage? No, he is *a* mage," I said, motioning to Monty. "Douglas, Tristan. Tristan, Douglas."

Monty nodded, but remained silent. Douglas did the same until he saw Peaches.

"What kind of dog is that?" Douglas asked. "His breed doesn't match anything in our databases."

His statement had revealed a few things: they were watching me, which I figured, and their database wasn't extensive enough to explain what breed Peaches was. It meant they had holes in their information—holes I could exploit.

"He's a very rare breed," I said. "Tell me, why am I here, Douglas? I'm guessing it has nothing to do with my hound."

Douglas stood and pointed to a map on the conference table.

"First of all, thank you for coming."

"You didn't leave me much choice," I said, looking at the map. "I still haven't agreed to this mission."

"You're here," Douglas said, confident. "We have a mutual goal in this."

"*I* have a mutual goal with Shadow Company? You must be kidding."

Douglas hardened his expression.

"It wasn't too long ago that you shared the vision," Douglas said, his voice gentle, but dangerous. "That you were one of us."

"I was, right up until you felt that any losses were acceptable to achieve the mission," I said, matching the threat in his voice. "That's the day I realized your vision had blinded you."

"I've learned from my mistakes. You could say I've seen the light. So has Rott."

"Ever since Cassandra, his focus has been dragons."

"His focus is our focus," Douglas said. "We seek out the source instead of going after branches. Now we seek to uproot the entire tree."

"By confronting dragons?" I asked. "That way lies madness."

"Only to the unprepared," Douglas said. "Eliminating dragons means eliminating most of the magical issues in this city. They have their hands in everything. We can remove them from the equation and secure the city—two birds, one fist."

My brain called BS. Men like Douglas were too set in their ways to change. He would disguise and justify his reasoning, rationalizing it was for the greater good, but it always came down to the same thing—power.

"I see you haven't lost your ability for inspirational speeches," I said, giving him a cold stare. "I'm not drinking the Kool-Aid. Tell me, why am I here?"

I saw the anger flit across his face before he got it under control, replacing it with a disingenuous smile.

"I need your help. Shadow Company needs your particular...skill."

"Plenty of other shooters in this city."

"Exactly what I told Rott, but he asked for you specifically."

"Since when do you take suggestions from Rott, or *anyone?*"

"Our purposes align," Douglas said. "He made a cogent argument that you were the best at what you did and I'd prefer we keep this op in-house."

"What is the op?"

He smiled, thinking my curiosity had gotten the better of me. Part of me did want to know how they would attempt to take down a dragon; the other part of me just wanted to put a bullet in his smug face and call it a night. I opted for listening to the op.

"We need to destabilize the balance between the two major dragon enclaves in this city," Douglas said. "We have an opportunity to weaken an enclave, with one mission. It's elegant and simple."

"Nothing is ever simple," I said. "What will weakening an enclave do? You still have the other to deal with."

"A weakened enclave would be the perfect catalyst for a dragon civil war," Douglas said. "We light the match and watch them burn each other to ash."

"A civil war?" I asked. "Wouldn't that cause collateral damage? Serious collateral damage?"

"In order to excise a tumor, an incision must be made," Douglas said turning the map and pointing to a location. "This is our incision. The target is the tumor."

"Who exactly is this target?"

"The dragon enclave leader, Magnus M. Balfour."

TWENTY

"You're insane," I said, looking at the map. He was pointing to the location of the TINY. "He's a dragon enclave leader. How would you even get close to him?"

Douglas looked at me, glanced at Monty, and then looked at me again.

"We have reason to believe Balfour will be vulnerable tomorrow night," Douglas said. "Tomorrow, he will be at this location to pick up a vehicle." He pointed to the map again. "We will arrange the transfer and eliminate the target."

They somehow knew about Balfour picking up the Duezy, which either meant Cecil had a leak, or they had an insider in the Balfour Enclave. Both seemed unlikely, but Douglas appeared confident, which meant his intel was solid. This was bad. I did my best to keep my face impassive.

"How could you possibly know that?" I asked. "I would imagine information like that isn't exactly common knowledge."

"We have an inside man," Douglas said with a tight smile. "Someone you know."

"You managed to turn a dragon to help you?" I asked. "I find that unlikely. Dragons can't stand humans, much less want to help them."

"No, not a dragon. Something better."

"Something better? What are you...?"

I felt the strange energy signature. It caused both Monty and me to turn at the presence entering the situation room.

"Hello, Simon," the unfamiliar man said with George Rott's voice. "It's good to see you again."

"Rott?" I asked. "That you?"

The voice was definitely George Rott's, but the rest wasn't. This man was young and well-built, where I remembered Rott being older and heavyset. Rott had graying black hair, and this person was bald. The real difference was in the face and eyes. Rott had normal human eyes. The eyes I looked into appeared reptilian for a few seconds before shifting to human.

I was staring at a stranger. A much younger and stronger stranger.

"Mostly me, with some upgrades," George said with arms outstretched. "It takes some getting used to." He rubbed his head. "I do miss the hair, though."

"How did you...? I mean, I saw you explode."

"I honestly thought I was dead," Rott said. "When I regained consciousness, no one knew who I was and then I realized why."

He pointed to his face.

"The combination of the synthetic entropy bomb, the Kragzimik, and you must have combined to create this transformation," Monty said. "You were somehow spliced with the energy instead of destroyed by it."

Rott nodded.

"The Kragzimik unleashed some energy there, right at the end, before I detonated the bomb, and I was caught in the blast. It killed the dragon and I came out like this. It was perfect."

"How is this perfect?" I asked. "You don't know what happened to you, to your body. For all you know you could be dy—"

"I know exactly what happened," Rott interrupted, his voice sharp. "I was born again, given a second chance. Don't you see? That dragon died, but I lived. This was meant to be. I am meant for a greater purpose. I have a calling. I rose from the ashes and flames of a dragon, like a phoenix."

I looked deep into Rott's eyes and realized that this had been more than a physical transformation. The man that he had been was gone, replaced with a zealot. I could guess what this "calling" was, but I needed to hear him say it. I needed to know how far off the cliff into madness he had stepped.

"A calling?" I asked, modulating my voice. "What calling, exactly?"

"Don't you see?" Rott asked. "I can blend in with them. I'm not as powerful as one of them, but I could infiltrate their enclave and pass for a dragon. Now, I can attack from within. I can make them pay for what they did to Cassandra, and you're going to help me."

Rott had stepped into Wile E. Coyote territory. He was so far off the cliff, he didn't know he was hanging in midair. I didn't want to think about what would happen when he realized the ground was gone.

The crash was going to be spectacularly fatal. I almost felt sorry for him; this entire crusade had been born in grief. The loss of Cassandra had set him off, and the explosion with the Kragzimik had finished the process, destroying his mind.

"Help you?" I asked warily. "How can I help you? You're the one with the now perfect disguise. Dragons can sniff me out a mile away."

"You're right. I can get close, and I have, but none of us can take the shot," Rott said. "You can. I can get you the ammunition and firing solution you need to make it one and done. One shot, one kill."

"This Balfour is a dragon. Bullets don't really work on them. Trust me, I've tried—they bounce off."

"Normal ordnance would, yes," Douglas said. "But we have something special for Mr. Balfour."

Douglas put a large round on the map. Black wisps of energy floated off its surface. It reminded me of my entropy rounds, but I had never seen one designed like this—much less a .50 caliber round created for a Barrett M82.

"Where did you get that?" Monty asked, concerned. "Who made this for you?"

"That is a need-to-know situation," Douglas said. "And *you* don't need to know."

"What is that?" I said looking at the runed round. "It reads like an—"

"That is a runed entropy round, keyed to Balfour's DNA," Douglas said, with a sense of satisfaction. "It cost a small fortune to produce and we were only able to make a handful, but *you* only need *one*."

"It's a dragon killer," Rott said, his voice soft. "I can finally get some justice for Cassandra."

"Cassandra's killer is dead," I said, keeping my voice even. "Slif is dead. I should know, I was there when she exploded."

"The dragon that killed my little girl is a symptom," Rott said. "I'm going to remove the sickness. It starts with Balfour."

"Where does it end?" I asked. "Are you planning to kill all of the dragons?"

"Yes, except I'm going to let them kill each other," Rott said. "Balfour will be the catalyst. By the time I'm done, they will be tearing each other apart."

"What about the collateral damage? You start a civil war, people will die."

"They deserve to die if they sympathize with dragon scum," Rott snapped. "There will be the loss of some innocents, but that can't be helped. This is a war. War is messy. There will be casualties."

I stared at Rott and then glanced quickly at Monty. He gave me a look that said *Don't even bother, he's a lost cause,* before coughing into his hand.

"How are you going to get close to him?" I asked. "He probably has the best security on the planet."

"He's an entitled self-important prick," Douglas said. "He would never drive his own vehicle. That's why we'll be driving it for him."

"I will be his driver when he picks up his vehicle at his restaurant," Rott said. "I'll make sure you have your shot. You just have to make sure you don't miss—this time."

TWENTY-ONE

Douglas explained the plan to me.

I had to admit that it was clever, yet not too clever, and simple enough to have few moving parts, which gave it a chance of succeeding. A high chance.

Rott had managed to insert himself into Balfour's driver pool. I don't know how he managed it, but tomorrow night Cecil would deliver the Duezy to the TINY. From there, Rott would drive Magnus to an annual enclave meeting, where only the leaders of the enclave would be present.

En route to this meeting, Balfour would have a fatal meeting with one of the special entropy dragon killer rounds. Rott would stage it to make it look like the Obouros Enclave ordered a hit on Balfour and succeeded. It was a classic because it worked, even though a part of me really wanted to ask if we could frame Guilder instead.

I doubted they would get the reference and it would only serve to piss them off. The last thing I needed was a group of trained, trigger-happy assassins trying to kill me more than they already were.

I saw what the play was; if I took the shot and killed Magnus, I was certain the next move was to remove me from the board and claim I was working with the Obouros Enclave. If I didn't take the shot, they'd find a way to remove Magnus, blaming Obouros and me. Shortly after, they would come after me with the help of Obouros. Shadow Company never allowed loose ends. For good measure, they'd try to eliminate Monty, too.

It was lose-lose for me every way I looked at the scenario.

That was the straight play. If I factored in that Rott or Douglas were working with Magnus to loop me into a vendetta mission, it made even more sense. Rott would get his revenge for Cassandra, Magnus would be seen to remove Slif's killer, reinforcing his position as enclave leader. Douglas was the outlier. I couldn't see what he would get out of going along with Rott's plan.

"You will do this for me, for Cassandra," Rott said after the plan was laid out. "You owe me, Strong. You do this, and the scales are even."

"You think starting a dragon war will balance the scales?" I asked, letting my anger get away from me. "What part of this entire op brings your daughter back?"

"I think...starting a dragon war will remove their cancer from my city," Rott said gripping the conference table. "I will do this, and you will help me so that no father has to bury his child because a monster cut her down."

I saw Rott's fingers press into the table, punching holes into the wood. It would seem his transformation was more than cosmetic. There was no rationalizing with him—his course was set and he would follow it to the end, even if it meant the end of his life.

"I don't see why you would need a mage for this op," I said. "I assume you have coms and diversions handled. I'm guessing Carlos is your blaster, and Feelds here is surveillance. If I'm the shooter and Rott is driving, that leaves Douglas to run comms and run tactical. We don't need him."

"He's our insurance," Rott said. "Like you said, we're facing dragons. I'm stronger than I was"—he looked down at the holes in the table—"but I'm not as strong as Balfour. That's where he comes in."

"You are seriously overestimating my abilities," Monty said. "Balfour is stronger than me by orders of magnitude."

"Then it would behoove Strong to put him down quickly, don't you think?" Rott said. "This time, you won't have a choice. You either drop Balfour, or your friend, the mage here, dies when he confronts an angry dragon."

"Why would I do that?" Monty asked. "This entire plan is a disaster."

"I could see how you would think that way," Rott said with a nod. "Let me see if I can help you see the merits of this op. After my transformation, I was able to pick up on particular energy signatures in the city. Specifically those magical in nature."

I didn't like where this was going.

"There's a reason why we're meeting here," Rott said. "Aside from it being the place where I lost my little girl, it's also the place where someone close to you works, isn't it, mage? A certain Director DeMarco?"

"She's in a secure location," Monty said and I could feel the menace in his words. "Surrounded by a security team."

"Not exactly," Rott said. "We couldn't get to Elias, the head of the team, but the rest of the sorcerers we inserted into Haven are ours."

"How many?" Monty asked keeping his voice calm. "How many have you placed in Haven?"

"More than you can easily handle, mage."

"You have no idea how many I can handle."

"Doesn't matter. If you fail to follow the plan, I will instruct them to eliminate everyone in the building, starting with your Director."

"There are hundreds of patients in that building," I said. "What are you saying?"

"They can remain patients or become casualties," Rott said. "That's up to the mage. Imagine how many sorcerers it would take to wipe out the entire facility. I have twice that amount in there. What will it be?"

"You don't want to do this," Monty said, quietly.

"It's already done. One call from me and the place becomes a graveyard."

"You've made a fatal error."

"One I intend to rectify, with your help."

"What do you want?"

"You do what I ask you to do tomorrow night and this will be all over, like a bad dream," Rott said. "You don't, and you will get to bury Roxanne DeMarco—or at least what's left of her. Trust me when I tell you, burying a loved one will make your life an absolute hell."

"What exactly is it that you want?" Monty asked. "Be specific."

"Tomorrow night, Balfour's vehicle will suffer engine trouble," Rott said. "I will make sure he gets out of the car."

"Engine trouble? How are you going to manage that from inside the car?"

"Carlos is our explosives expert. He'll take care of that, as well as making sure Balfour's reinforcements are delayed coming from his estate."

"I'm going to need a clean line of sight for this to work. If Carlos causes too large an explosion I'll be shooting blind. Would hate to hit the wrong target."

"The vehicle damage will be enough to be convincing," Rott said. "The vehicle is armored, but if Balfour refuses to exit, the runes on those rounds will allow you punch through it and him if needed."

"If he doesn't get out I may need to get creative," I said, seeing at least ten ways this could go wrong. "What's my location?"

"Strong, you'll be positioned on a roof here"—Rott pointed to a building on the map—"but I need Balfour distracted. That's where the mage comes in. You will keep him occupied long enough for Strong to take the shot. After Balfour is down, you two are done. We'll take it from there, handling the rest."

"And the sorcerers at Haven?"

"They will be gone five minutes after I have confirmation of the kill."

"One second past and I will show you what a life of hell looks like," Monty said. "When is the vehicle being delivered?"

"Midnight tomorrow, 135 West Broadway, here," Rott said, pointing to a different location on the map. "I'll drive south for two blocks and stop here"—he pointed to the block between Reade and Chambers Streets.—"while you will wait here in Bogardus Plaza. Strong will take up his position four blocks away, on Murray Street. Once Balfour exits the vehicle, you confront him and Strong takes the shot. This whole op should take no more than one minute beginning to end."

"Do not deviate from this plan," Douglas added. "One minute of your life to make the city safer, get justice for Rott, and be free of Shadow Company, forever."

"We meet here tomorrow at ten p.m.," Rott said, rolling up the map. "Douglas will kit you out then. Don't be late, and don't try to contact Haven, your Director friend at the NYTF, or those creatures in the Dark Council. I'd hate to have to start this op with the mass extermination of helpless patients."

We exited the trailer in silence.

TWENTY-TWO

"He's surprisingly well informed," Monty said once we were outside. "How connected *is* Shadow Company?"

"Very," I said. "They're small, but nimble. Douglas knows people in high and low places. Same with Rott, although I don't know if his contacts are willing to work with the new and improved Reptilian Rott."

"They've been planning this for some time," Monty said. "The networks are too extensive. Inserting himself into the Balfour Enclave was ingenious. For a moment, I thought Cecil's security protocols were compromised."

"We could just blow up the trailer," I said, glancing over my shoulder as we walked back to the Dark Goat. "It would be clean and surgical, like a nuke."

Peaches nudged my leg with a low growl of approval. He sounded like I felt. I wanted to tear Rott apart, but knew it would put too many people in danger.

"Rott probably has a failsafe in place to trigger the sorcerers in Haven if he dies of unnatural causes—a failsafe like a surgical nuke," Monty said, the anger and frustration clear in his voice. "Either that or he has regular check-ins to ensure his sleepers remain dormant at Haven until instructed otherwise."

"Monty, I'm sorry," I said. "I didn't think he would threaten Roxanne or Haven."

"That's why he did," Monty said, getting into the Dark Goat. "He counted on the element of surprise to force me to face Balfour. It worked. It's not your fault, but he threatened Roxanne. As long as he lives, he's a threat."

I remained silent for a few seconds, but the message was clear. Rott was living on borrowed time.

"You can't face Magnus," I said, changing the subject, and sliding behind the wheel as my hellhound conquered the backseat. "Even after your schism, he's too strong."

"I have no intention of fighting a dragon, Magnus or otherwise," Monty said as I drove away. "The same way you can't eliminate the leader of a dragon enclave."

"Well, I'm glad we agree on that," I said with a sigh. "How exactly are we not supposed to kill Balfour, but make it look like we did?"

"How good a shot are you, really?"

"No wind, elevated position, a good spotter, and an excellent weapon, 2000 meters," I said. "I won't have a spotter, and I don't know what kind of rifle they have prepped. Factoring for little to no wind, and the elevated position, four city blocks is about 1000 meters, well within my range."

"I have an idea of how we can do this, but it's going to require exceptional accuracy from you," Monty said. "Can you manage that?"

"How exceptional?" I asked, glancing at Monty. This train of thought was beginning to sound like a bad idea.

The problem was that we only had bad ideas and worse ideas at the moment. "What are you thinking?"

"I'm going to need you to shoot through me and into Balfour—without killing me, of course," Monty said. "I can make it look like it was a fatal wound and put Balfour in stasis long enough to convince Rott."

"Shoot? Through you?" I asked in disbelief. "You want me to shoot you?"

"*Through* me," Monty stressed. "Without hitting major organs, would be an added benefit."

"Oh, is that all? Shoot through you and maybe curve the bullet around your major organs so it can look like you were hit and killed along with Balfour. That about the gist of your request?"

"Yes, my suits are runed to neutralize most small-arms fire if I manage to get shot."

"Did you see the round Douglas showed us?" I asked. "*That* is nowhere near small-arms fire. A .22 caliber is small-arms fire: that .50 cal round will punch a hole through your suit, you, and anything behind you. The entrance wound will be the size of my index finger and the exit wound will be you splattered all over the street. No way."

"What would happen if I could decrease the velocity?" Monty asked pensively. "It would diminish the lethality of the round, correct?"

"Considerably, but you're talking about slowing down something coming at you at 853 meters per second. You'd have a little over one second to react from the moment I fire."

"1.1 seconds exactly," Monty said. "Plenty of time. This is what I propose..."

I remained silent as he explained his idea. About two minutes in, I started shaking my head.

"Too many things can go wrong, Monty," I said. "It would be easier to put one in Rott and—"

"You're forgetting Haven," Monty said. "We can't risk Rott unleashing his sorcerers."

"Shit," I said, hitting the steering wheel. "This is too dangerous."

"We have alternatives."

"Really? Like?" I said, heading into the Moscow garage. "Our choices are either bad or horrific."

"If we kill Rott and Douglas, everyone in Haven dies," Monty said. "If you somehow manage to kill Magnus, the resulting war will create untold casualties in the subsequent power struggle created by the void of leadership in the Balfour Enclave."

"I was wrong: our choices are horrific or monstrous."

"I have no doubt that Rott is deranged enough in his newfound cause to order the execution of everyone in Haven."

"Rott wants his justice—at any cost—and Magnus must uphold tradition," I said. "It's all there, but I'm missing something. There's a piece missing, and I can't see it."

"We have a day to figure out what that is," Monty said. "I'm still not seeing Douglas' motivation. He doesn't strike me as one to act out of loyalty to Rott. He's using him to further his agenda, whatever that may be."

"Agreed," I admitted reluctantly. "I'm not buying the 'safer city' line. This is about something else."

I parked the Dark Goat in our spot and we bypassed the lobby, heading directly upstairs through the new personal parking level elevator Olga had recently installed. I think she was tired of Peaches scaring Andrei and anyone else we came across in the lobby. She had announced the new elevator as a building upgrade and renovation, making sure to give us the keycards that allowed its use.

In the short time we had been using it, I never saw anyone else inside. I was beginning to get the distinct feeling Olga was trying to isolate us from the rest of the building.

"I need to make a few calls," Monty said. "We need contingency plans in place when this all goes south. I have no faith in Rott's goodwill. He just threatened Roxanne and an entire hospital to get me to cooperate. He has no intention of letting us walk away from this. You'd better inform your friend in the NYTF."

"Rott said not to—"

"Your phone, please."

"Do not explode my phone, Monty."

He gestured over the phone and pressed some of the buttons on the screen. A soft golden rune pulsed on the back of my phone for a few seconds before fading from sight. He handed me the phone and nodded.

"There you go."

"That's new," I said, examining my phone. "Since when could you do—whatever it is you just did?"

"Since I nearly lost my mind going through a schism," Monty said. "It's a simple matter of scrambling frequencies, and *everything* operates on frequencies."

"You scrambled what?" I asked. "Did you destroy my phone?"

"I re-encrypted your device with new runes," Monty

said, walking away. "If they are monitoring your phone, and we have to assume they are, they'll know you made a call, but won't know who you called. I'd refrain from trying Haven or the Dark Council. The security on their ends is virtually non-existent."

"Who are you calling? Dex? The Ten?"

"We need a scalpel for this, not several bricks of C4," Monty said. "My uncle and the Ten are best used sparingly."

"Sparingly, like when the end of the world as we know it is near?"

"Precisely," Monty said, stepping out of sight. " I need to make some calls. I'll be right back."

I dialed a number as Monty headed to the conference room. I made sure of the encryption before I made the call.

"Strong," Ramirez growled. "Do you know what time it is?"

"Did I wake you?"

"Do you really think I sleep knowing you, your mage, and that hound of yours freely roam the streets of my city?" Ramirez said. "How much damage?"

"What?"

"How much damage have you caused?" Ramirez asked. "Do I need to call EMTes? How extensive is the demolition?"

"Does something have to be destroyed for me to call you?" I asked, mocking offense. "Maybe I just wanted to check up on how my favorite NYTF Director is doing?"

"Cut the shit, Strong. We only speak when the shit has hit the fan or is about to. Since my radio is relatively quiet, I'm going to assume the shit is incoming. How bad?"

"It has the potential to be pretty bad."

"Shit," Angel said. "Casualties? Where?"

"Nothing, yet," I said. "Tomorrow there's going to be some activity downtown, in Tribeca—West Broadway all the way to Murray Street, to be specific. You want to take your time getting there. That will keep any collateral damage to a minimum."

"What are we dealing with? Ogres, werewolves, wereogres?"

"I don't think wereogres are a thing," I said, thinking back to Grohn with a shudder. "At least I hope not. What do you know about dragons?"

"Rare, large, dangerous, breathe fire, impossible to kill, that sort of thing," Ramirez said, alert now, all signs of grogginess gone from his voice. "The NYTF isn't equipped to deal with dragons. It would be sending my men to slaughter."

"I know, which is why you need to give us some room tomorrow night," I said. "Once things are relatively safe, I'll give you the all clear."

"You, the mage, and your creature are going to face off against a dragon?" Ramirez said slowly. "Just you three?"

I looked down at my voracious hellhound who was carrying his bowl in his jaws and padding toward me. He plopped the titanium bowl at my feet, nearly breaking one of my toes in the process.

"I really hope we don't have to," I said with a short sigh. "Can't say more than that. I'll give you a call as soon as I can."

"Understood," Ramirez said. "Try not to get yourself dead."

TWENTY-THREE

Monty returned a few minutes later.

"Where did you go?" I asked. "I thought you were in the conference room?"

"I used Dex's room," Monty said. "One of the calls necessitated a face-to-face meeting."

"Excuse me?"

"I'll explain later," Monty said. "Do you still have that emulator Gant gave you?"

"I do," I said, fishing out the small crystal from my jacket pocket. "Why?"

"May I see it?" Monty asked, outstretching a hand. I passed him the crystal. "Thank you."

"What's going on?" I asked, concerned. "Is that not an emulator?"

"It is," Monty said, examining the crystal. "It's also the way Rell is going to find you."

I looked at the crystal as if it were radioactive.

"Gant's in on this too?" I asked. "I thought he was looking out for my hellhound?"

Monty gave me a look that said, *You can't possibly be this naive*, before looking at the crystal again.

"Gant works for Magnus," Monty said, touching parts of the emulator in sequence. "If he didn't use your creature as a pretense, it would have been something else. The key was to make sure you had this crystal on your person before you left the TINY."

"How did I not see that?" I said, slightly angry at being duped. "I'm usually an excellent judge of character."

"Says the person currently involved with a murderous ancient vampire," Monty said. "Your history in character judgment is somewhat spotty."

I opened my mouth to answer and then closed it. He was right. If I reviewed my recent choices, I'd say spotty was putting it nicely.

"I partnered up with you," I said. "That has to count for good judgment."

"Are you certain you didn't suffer head trauma when you faced Evers?" Monty asked. "Having me as your partner, while probably the most sane decision you've made, is not an indicator of good judgment. Far from it."

"Are you saying it was a bad call?"

"Absolutely not," Monty said. "Having me as your partner has saved your life countless times."

"See? Good call, excellent judge of—"

"Having me as your partner has also jeopardized your life countless times," Monty finished, straightening out a sleeve. "In any case, Gant works for the Balfour Enclave. It's possible the emulator was given with good intentions, but it can be tracked."

"If I were Rell, I'd attack when I was most distracted,"

I said. "That would give me the greatest chance of taking me out easy."

"He may be operating on incomplete information," Monty said, going into a closet and coming out with a jacket. "I had Piero make this for you some time ago."

I looked at the jacket. It was identical to the one I was wearing.

"You asked Piero to make the exact jacket I'm wearing?" I asked. "Why? This one fits perfectly."

"This one has been specially runed," Monty said. "I understand your condition will keep you alive. This jacket has been runed to prevent your perforation."

"You mean it's bulletproof? Nice," I said, taking the jacket and holding it up. "This is like runic Kevlar, thanks."

"Bullet-resistant, not proof. It's more designed to prevent runed rounds from doing damage," Monty said. "I noticed your mala bracelet is gone. Does this mean you lack a shield?"

"I've been upgraded," I said, focusing and creating a small dome of energy around me, which disappeared a few seconds later. My brow was instantly covered in sweat, and my head pounded from the effort. "Kali disintegrated my mala bracelet, but I can make this now. It's hit and miss—well, mostly miss."

"A dawnward?" Monty asked, surprised. "How? Why did it only last a few seconds?"

"I need practice. I can't seem to hold it for long unless I have Ebonsoul materialized, and even then, *pfft*," I said. "I still don't know how it works, but I think it has something to do with the pendant Nana gave you and my being a shieldbearer."

"You don't know how it works. Fascinating," Monty

said, rubbing his chin. "Do you know how you obtained it?"

"Something Kali did when she gave me her upgraded mark," I said, recalling her words. *A shield does not require a shield. You will be my aspis—a shield-warrior.* "That was followed by mind-shattering agony. When she was done, my bonds were straightened out, my brain had been liquefied, my eyes were glowing, and she'd left me with this."

I opened my shirt and showed Monty where the pendant used to rest. It was now a dim violet outline etched into my chest.

"She merged you with it?" Monty asked. "What do you mean, your eyes were glowing? Your eyes aren't glowing."

"They were when she merged me with the pendant," I said. "Anyway, the merging wasn't fun—more like agony. Then she destroyed my mala bracelet, but forgot to leave me an instruction manual for my purple bubble of protection."

"It's called a *dawnward* and it's an incredibly potent defense," Monty said. "Why didn't you use it against Evers?"

"I could barely create it just now," I said, rubbing my temple. "And it's giving me a migraine. I don't think Evers was going to give me the opportunity. She was a little focused on shredding me."

"Have you created it prior to this moment?"

"I only just managed to create it against Dex," I said, shaking my head. "Even then, he managed to slice through it with his psycho mace-axe."

"You never did tell me how you survived facing Nemain, or Dex for that matter."

"It wasn't so much me surviving as Dex refusing to

shred me to nothingness," I said. "He is off-the-charts powerful. Are you sure we can't call him?"

"No, we can't," Monty said. "Since your proficiency with the dawnward is unreliable, you will need to wear the jacket and try not to get shot."

"That's on the top of my to-do list every day," I said, switching jackets along with the contents of my pockets. "I have a bad feeling about this entire op. They're going to try and kill us, aren't they?"

"You said it yourself: Shadow Company doesn't believe in loose ends," Monty said. "The information we possess makes us liabilities. They can't afford to leave us alive."

"Remove all sources of information that can blow back on the Company," I said. "It's SOP. They'll try to sanitize the op, and everyone involved who's not Shadow Company once it's done. Starting with—"

"Us and everyone we care for, yes," Monty said. "We're going to stop them."

"You know what's *not* on my to-do list today?" I asked. "Getting taken out by insane zealots and power-mad assassins looking to exterminate what they perceive as threats to their way of life."

"Now that your to-do list is sorted, I can rest easy," Monty said, heading to the kitchen. "All I need now is a good cuppa."

He grabbed the kettle and began filling it with water. He was acting normally, but I could tell from the number of times he straightened his sleeves that he was upset.

"We're going to keep her safe, Monty, I promise."

"You have no way of keeping that promise," Monty said. "Bloody hell, what about next time? The next time someone like Evers surfaces or some creature decides I need to pay and targets her? Then what?"

"Then we stop them, too," I said, gently, noticing that the water in the kettle was beginning to boil. "Monty? Maybe not melt your favorite kettle?"

He looked down suddenly.

"Bollocks," he said, placing the kettle on the stove and leaving the kitchen. "I'll be in my room. I still have much to prepare."

"I got the tea," I said. "Try not to blast a hole in your room."

<Go with him, boy. Make sure he stays close.>

<He is close. Will you fill my bowl?>

<Later, yes. Make sure he calms down and doesn't break anything.>

<Should I lick him? My saliva will calm him down.>

<I'm sure your multi-purpose saliva is awesome, but don't lick him right now. He needs some quiet time.>

<I'm very good with quiet time. The angry man should take a nap. Naps always make me feel better.>

<I agree. Naps are excellent, but he's not a hellhound. Go and watch him.>

Peaches padded off after Monty. The fact that I didn't hear my name yelled out in anger a few seconds after Peaches invaded Monty's space let me know how serious this was. My hellhound was rarely, if ever, allowed into the Montague inner sanctum.

Monty had declared his space a drool-free zone, and if there was one thing Peaches was exceptional at, it was the creation of his healing saliva. When the kettle had gone from dull orange to normal gray, I grabbed an oven mitt and started the Earl Grey process.

I had learned how to do this some time ago. It was different from the creation of my magnificent Deathwish javambrosia, but I had realized after some time that Monty without tea was a danger to us all. It was a risk I wasn't willing to take. For the sake of the tri-state area, I learned the "proper" way to make boiled leaves in case we ever faced the emergency an out-of-control Montague would be.

I didn't think we were quite there yet, but I knew if Monty could reduce the Shadow Company trailer to dust without risking Roxanne, he would have. They had raised the stakes by threatening her. What they didn't know is that they had signed their own death warrants.

I sat on the Eames to rest my eyes for a few minutes.

TWENTY-FOUR

It was early afternoon when I opened my eyes.

I had managed to catch a few hours of sleep and woke with a start. I dreamed I was drowning, my head being held underwater. I realized the reality wasn't too far off as I pushed Peaches, the saliva monster, away from my face.

<You were napping. That's good. Can you fill my bowl now?>

<Where's Monty?>

<The angry man is sitting on the floor with his eyes closed. Is he napping? I always like to be comfortable when I'm napping. He doesn't look comfortable, he looks angry.>

<That's his default face. He's fine. Let's give him some time. We have a rough day ahead.>

<Will you fight the dragon man?>

<You know about dragons?>

<Yes. Dragons are big fire lizards. They are bad.>

<So do you understand that Frank is not a dragon?>

<He is a special dragon. He is a dragon inside his mind.>

<Inside his mind? What he is is out of his mind.>

<The man in the truck smells bad, like a dragon. Are you going to fight him?>

<He wants to do some bad things. I need to stop him.>

<Can I bite him?>

<Yes, but not until I tell you to. Can you wait?>

Peaches gave me a low rumble and his eyes flickered with red light.

<I can wait.>

Monty came in wearing a new Zegna mageiform. This one was a deeper black than usual with dark gray accents. The menace that radiated from his side of the room was palpable, but I didn't say anything except point to the cup of tea on the counter.

"Thank you," Monty said, causing the cup to glow a soft orange, and bringing the water to a slow boil before taking a sip. "You've improved. I can almost drink this now."

I took a sip from my cold Deathwish and raised my cup in acknowledgement.

"If you drank a real drink, and not boiled grass, you'd know what real power was," I said. "You ready?"

"Yes; one stop before we go."

"Where?"

"We need to rectify our insurance plan."

"Rectify our...? Wait, we're going to see the—"

"No, but I have a solution to our Haven problem."

"What? You're going to ask her to shift the entire place?"

"Don't be daft," Monty said, heading to the door. "That would be impossible. Or at the very least improbable."

"Oh," I said, slightly relieved. "I mean of course, that

would be impossible. Haven is enormous, above and underground."

"Exactly. I'm going to have her shift everyone inside."

The words registered as sound, but my brain failed to process the meaning behind the sounds.

"I'm sorry," I said as we stepped into the garage elevator. "I thought I heard you say you were going to ask her to shift everyone inside Haven. Is this more of that non-funny mage humor?"

"No, the Transporter was one of my calls earlier," Monty said calmly. "The next stop is to secure payment and to preserve history."

"I know you're speaking English, but most of the time it sounds like a foreign language," I said confused. "Can you clarify in non-mage American?"

"Not here," Monty said. "I'll explain everything at James' establishment."

We arrived at the empty Randy Rump a few minutes later. It was still too early for the evening rush. I parked outside and locked the Dark Goat. Monty and Peaches went ahead as I gave the exterior a scan. If Rell was out there, he was making sure I didn't see him. Jimmy was behind the counter, sharpening some blades as I crossed the threshold into the restaurant. He motioned over to the corner with his chin. Peaches padded over behind the counter and nudged Jimmy in the leg, nearly knocking him down. I turned to see where Jimmy had pointed.

Sitting at a table in the far corner was Cecil.

Cecil ran a hand through his short gray hair, pulled on his neatly trimmed goatee, and gave us a tight smile as we approached. A large mug of mead sat on the table in front of him, the sweet smell of honey filling the air as he took a long pull.

"Thank you for coming on such short notice," Monty said, taking a seat. "Were you able to procure my request?"

"I don't understand it, but yes," Cecil said, as his hazel eyes shone with latent power. "How's the Goat? Still intact, I'm assuming."

"Still," I said, apologetically. "Sorry, I think you've created a monster with that one. I don't think we can destroy it."

"On the plus side, I'm not getting requests for non-melting cars or the vehicles that don't explode," Cecil said. "For that, I thank you. It doesn't fix the Beast situation, but I'm still working on that."

"Cecil? Can I ask you a question?"

"Of course," Cecil said. "Do you need extra explosives to see if you can overload the defensive runes? I know we have a small-scale tactical device at the shop you can use."

"You have a nuke? Back at the shop? Really?"

"Not nuclear; runic, much stronger, but no radiation," Cecil corrected. "We could try that, but you'd have to be in the car when we detonated it."

I stared at him for a few seconds.

"What? No, I don't need extra explosives or small tactical devices, thanks," I said, raising a hand. "I thought *you* owned the Duezy."

"Ah, that," Cecil said, looking from Monty to me before taking another pull from his mug. "You're wondering about the delivery tonight."

"It did cross my mind," I said. "I thought there was only one Midnight Ghost made?"

"Two," Cecil said, holding up two fingers. "One I own,

the original. The other…Well, you know who owns that one. Best not to mention names, even in here."

"Emmet and Armand made two? Amazing."

"I never said *they* made two," Cecil answered. "They made one. SuNaTran, *I*, made the second, identical to the first with some minor adjustments."

"Adjustments I need you to implement tonight," Monty said. "Can you do it remotely?"

"It won't be easy, but yes. Do you have a timeframe?"

"Shortly after your delivery for a window of thirty minutes."

"Thirty minutes means we can lose the automobile," Cecil said concerned. "Are you certain? Replacing that one won't be fast or inexpensive."

"Yes," Monty said. "If it's lost, I will commission a second one to be made. How soon can you make the other delivery?"

"Moving that many tons of premium chocolate underground to an undisclosed and abandoned subway station without attracting attention will take some time," Cecil said. "Are you certain it has to be tonight and one drop? There are only so many refrigerated trucks in the fleet."

"Yes to both," Monty said. "Can you do it?"

"I need at least three hours. I can't guarantee less than that."

"Three hours will suffice. Call me the second the delivery is complete."

"Done," Cecil said, taking one last pull from his enormous mug, before turning to me. "If you manage to destroy the car, try to survive long enough to get me some notes and the method of destruction."

"If something or someone manages to destroy the

Dark Goat," I said, "I don't think I'm going to be worrying about taking notes. Have you tried asking some of the heavy-hitters to take a crack at it?"

"No one wants to get close to either that car or the Beast," Cecil said, standing as a red Lamborghini Urus pulled up outside. "That's for me. I wanted to apologize about the blacklist, Strong. Dragons are bad for business, which is why I stay away from them. It's not personal."

"Except for tonight."

"Tonight is the rare exception, and it only happens once every few decades," Cecil said with a small sigh. "It's an honor contract, which is the only reason we fulfill it."

"You may not have to, after tonight," Monty said. "If all goes as planned, you will be free from the obligation."

"That would be the desired outcome, but I'm dealing with you two," Cecil said, shaking his head as he walked away. "The chances of this happening without things exploding are slim to none. Good luck."

"Great to hear how much confidence he has in us," I said as Cecil left the Rump, the door closing softly behind him. "Tons of chocolate?"

"Payment for the shift, which should leave the sorcerers at Haven without victims," Monty said. "James? The back room, please?"

Jimmy pointed to the back.

"Make sure she leaves the way she came," Jimmy said, sounding upset. "I don't want her presence lingering in here. Scares the customers and screws with the defenses."

"Understood," Monty said, heading to the back room. "I will convey your concern."

"Monty?" I asked as he opened the door to the back room. "Who is Jimmy talking about?"

I felt a chill in the air and turned as Monty closed the door to the back room, pressing the runic sequence that would seal us in with an energy signature that kicked my limbic brain into flight overdrive.

"He's talking about me," a female voice said. "Hello, Simon."

I followed the sound of the familiar voice across the room and my blood decided freezing in place was an excellent idea. Dressed in all black and sitting on one of the chairs around the large table, I could just make out a figure obscured by a dark nimbus of energy.

"Do I know you?" I asked, opening my jacket to give me access to Grim Whisper. "Who are you?"

"You don't know me in this form, no," the woman said. "But you know of me, and his uncle knows me"—she pointed to Monty—"intimately."

It was the Morrigan.

TWENTY-FIVE

Worse—it was the Badb Catha.

"Monty, why are we in a locked room with the scary aspect of the Chooser of the Slain?" I asked, barely keeping my voice under control.

It wasn't fear I was feeling exactly. Fear had packed its bags and run screaming out of the Randy Rump. What I was feeling was a deep, paralyzing, underlying, soul-gripping dread, that squeezed me into mind-numbing shock. I took a few deep breaths and tried to get a grip without losing all control of my bodily functions.

"She was the second-to-last call I made," Monty said, his jaw set. "We're here to arrange terms."

"Terms?" I asked, worried. "What terms? What are you talking about?"

"Simon, we're out of our element," Monty said. "Neither of us is strong enough or wields enough power to confront an enclave of dragons."

"An enclave of dragons? Since when are we confronting

an enclave of dragons?" I asked, trying to keep my voice calm. "We're confronting Magnus and possibly Rell. When did an enclave enter the picture?"

"The moment we agreed to be part of this operation," Monty said. "Word will go out that we challenged Magnus. If we manage to kill him what do you think the response will be?"

I paused and gave Monty's words thought.

"The enclave will be out for blood."

"And if we don't?"

"Magnus *and* the enclave will be out for blood," I said, seeing the no-win scenario. "Goddammit, how could I not see this? They outplayed us."

"You wanted to do the honorable thing," Monty said. "You wanted to reconcile Rott's pain regarding his daughter's death, but we are dealing with honorless individuals. Men who would threaten an entire hospital of defenseless patients, who would plunge this city into a dragon war, without regard for the consequences Then there is a dragon who only sees tradition and your death."

"But her?" I asked, pointing at Badb. "Isn't this a little extreme? Why would she help us?"

A large crow about twice the size of a normal crow sat perched on one of the other chairs. It screeched, making me jump as it flapped its wings. Then it really creeped me out by wailing.

"Where there is war, carnage, rage, and violence," Badb said softly, her voice clear in the emptiness of the room, "I am there. If forces are arrayed against you, then I will welcome them into my garden and reap their lives. Do you agree to the terms, mage?"

"Terms? What are these terms, Monty? Why are we discussing terms with her?"

The dread in the pit of my stomach clenched into a fist of apprehension. Was Monty going uber dark this time? Dealing with the Morrigan was shady enough, but this aspect of hers had only one purpose...death.

"I agree," Monty said, his voice steel. "All on the battlefield who are not under my aegis are yours to do with as you please."

"How speaks your shieldbearer, the Marked of Kali?"

"Why does she care about my opinion?"

"Part of the terms requires we be in alignment. If you need to adjust the terms, now is the time to do so."

I turned slowly to face Badb. A few deep breaths later, I managed to get my emotions under control.

"We will deal with the leaders of Shadow Company, Peter Douglas and George Rott," I said, staring at Badb. "You can have any sorcerers at Haven who want to harm innocents. It would be great if you could squish Magnus without killing him, but let him know that coming after us and ours would be bad for his health."

"You want me to 'squish' a dragon?" Badb asked. "I do not *squish* my foes. I crush bones and spill blood. I lay waste to entire battlefields and destroy enemies."

"That's a little much," I said, slightly taken aback at her calmness. "We only need to stop the Balfour dragons from coming after those"—I glanced at Monty, who nodded—"under our aegis. If they try, *then* you can do all the crushing and spilling with the laying of waste."

"The sorcerers who wish harm upon yours in this place, Haven, are mine to feast upon?"

"Feast away," I said with a nod. "Only those working for Shadow Company."

"I am to persuade the dragons of this Balfour Enclave without killing the leader to leave you and those under your aegis alone?"

"Yes. Just persuade, not kill."

"Are you in accord, mage?" Badb asked. "Do you accept these terms put forth by the Marked of Kali?"

"I do," Monty said. "On my word as a mage and a Montague."

There was an energy shift in the room and the nimbus of black around Badb flashed with red and gold for a few seconds before she slowly disappeared.

"It is done," Badb's voice said. "The terms are accepted. I will leave you my totem. When you require my unkindness, the Marked of Kali must destroy it."

The massive crow flapped its giant wings and took off, flying full speed at the far wall. It vanished a second later. A single black feather floated down to the table. Monty picked up the feather, and handed it to me.

The black feather shone with violet light as I examined it. I put it inside my jacket with an uneasy sensation.

"Do you remember what to do with that?" Monty asked.

"Yes," I said, remembering our short, destructive visit to London. "Do I need to be in Haven, or will this set off remote death by goddess?"

"Better not to be in the vicinity when you do summon her," Monty said. "Do not call her until I let you know Haven is clear. From what I understand, her missions of death are heavy on the collateral damage. She has a tendency to kill everything on what she perceives to be the battlefield."

"This is the surgical scalpel option? You've got to be kidding."

"It's the only option that can act on both Haven and the Balfour Enclave," Monty said, grimly. "*We* must deal with everything else."

In that moment I realized it was too easy.

"Monty, what exactly did we just do?"

"We evened the playing field."

"Evened the playing field?" I asked. "Don't you mean, evened the odds or leveled the playing field? Are you feeling okay?"

"I'm fine. You know what I mean," Monty said, waving my words away. "We now have the advantage on the playing field."

"This feels like we just obliterated the playing field, the stands, all of the parking around the field, and whatever city the playing field sits in."

"Anyone who stands against us tonight will realize they have made a fatal error," Monty said, creeping into semi-Darthness. "They threaten death; we will unleash it upon them tenfold."

"When you start speaking like that, my inner Jedi starts the Darth alarm."

"How many lives have you touched with your own?" Monty asked, quietly. "Can you name any which you're willing to lose?"

"No."

"Magnus or the Shadow Company will go after them all."

"What's the fine print to these terms?" I said, the dread still seizing my midsection. "That seemed too easy."

"There was nothing easy about what we just did."

"Why would she agree? What does she get out of this? I mean, besides the whole wiping out of everything she sees."

"I agreed to her terms," Monty said. "Which requires repayment in the future."

"You indebted yourself to Badb Catha?" I said, raising my voice. "Are. You. Insane?"

"No. *We* are out of options," Monty said, his jaw set and his tone cold. "If we don't get help—her help—we've lost. Do you understand? *We lose.* Even with her help, we may still lose. At least this way, we stand a chance."

"Dex, The Ten, any of the insane mages willing to work with you?" I asked, as my anger rose. "Are you telling me none of them were an option, not one? We had to resort to this?"

"No, *none* of them," Monty said, flatly. "Those insane enough to face off against a dragon enclave aren't powerful enough. Those powerful enough to do so would never consider it, even for me. I will not put more people I care for in harm's way."

"At the very least we could have asked them."

"What did you think I was doing?" Monty asked, exasperated. "Badb Catha was my second-to-last call. I reached out to everyone I thought could help. It did not go well."

"Who was last on the list?"

"What you would call the thermonuclear option. Even I wouldn't go that far—not that he would agree, but I didn't dare, just in case he did."

"Who?" I asked, my brain still jolted by the fact that

Badb Catha had agreed. "Who would be the nuclear option?"

"Ezra."

The name stopped me cold. For a brief second, I understood how desperate Monty had truly been.

"Would he have said yes?"

"I'm glad we don't have to find out," Monty said with a sigh. "Unleashing her will be dangerous enough. She is an aspect of the triune Morrigan...the deadliest and most fear-inducing of the three."

"Yet you called *her*?" I asked, incredulously. "Why not one of the other less scary aspects? The one dating Dex would have been a better choice."

"They are *all* dating my uncle," Monty said. "There are no major distinctions here. Why do you think most consider my uncle mad to be with her?"

"That would actually explain why," I admitted. "Are you certain the schism didn't fry some circuits in that mage brain of yours?"

"I'm certain I will not be held hostage by the Shadow Company or Magnus," Monty said, his voice and expression dark. "I will not lose those close to me. If that means dealing with Badb, then so be it."

"Again, making statements like that—I start hearing the Imperial March. Are you okay? You're not feeling a desire to wear a deep Zegna cowl or give in to the hate?"

"Stop spouting gibberish. I'm not going dark, nor will I," Monty assured me. "I also recognize when a situation is beyond my capabilities. We can't be everywhere at once. The Transporter and Badb will buy us some time; not much, but hopefully enough that we can do what we need to do to walk away from this."

"While stopping Shadow Company."

"While eliminating Shadow Company and stopping Magnus."

I nodded, trying to take it all in.

"Shit, I still can't believe you accepted her terms," I said, still angry. "I mean I understand, but damn, Monty, that was a bad idea."

"I'm glad you understand," Monty said, pressing the runic sequence to open the back room door. "Because *you* accepted the same terms."

"You want to repeat that?" I said, steadying my voice. "What do you mean *I* accepted the same terms...No."

The realization hit me like a gut-check.

"Yes," Monty said, opening the door. "We do what we must to keep those near us safe. She is following the terms *you* laid out for her. My agreement was to follow whatever you determined. Technically, it was you making the terms."

"Technically? Technically?" I yelled. "We now owe Badb a favor?"

"Yes," Monty said, quietly, "and if we want to be alive to negotiate extricating ourselves out of it, we need to survive tonight."

I opened my mouth to disagree, but realized Monty was right. We would have to deal with Badb's terms later. Right now, we had to deal with getting through tonight...alive.

This is why you always read the fine print. Monty hadn't exactly tricked me; it was more like inviting me into the carnage Badb Catha was going to unleash. Part of me still felt this was dangerous overkill. The other part—the part that understood Magnus and Shadow Company would only respect power—knew this was, if not the right course, then an acceptable course of action.

"I'm not working or doing any favors for her," I said. "There better be some kind of exit clause."

"If our actions spark a dragon war, it won't matter," Monty said. "At that point we will have greater concerns."

"Like staying alive," I said as we stepped out of the back room.

TWENTY-SIX

"We need to speak to Dex," I said. "After this is all through, and if we somehow make it out alive, I need to speak to Dex."

"Agreed," Monty said as we stepped into the main dining area. "James, a word?"

Jimmy came over to where we stood as the door to the back room closed silently behind us.

"What's going on?" Jimmy asked. "Is she gone? Tell me she's gone."

"She's gone," Monty said. "I strongly advise against conducting business for a few days. There will be backlash from tonight and I'd rather you not bear the brunt of it."

"Got it," Jimmy said. "I was due a mini-vacation anyway."

"Where's Grohn?" I asked, looking around. It's not like he was easy to miss.

"Out back, unloading another truck. I better go tell him we're going to be off for a few days. Do you need anything before you go?"

"No thanks," I growled, still somewhat pissed. "Stay safe, though, okay?"

"I'll be fine. Grohn and I will go spend some time in the mountains with my sleuth," Jimmy said. "It'll be good for him, and I'll get to catch up with family."

"Family sounds good," I said. "They're all you have"—I glanced at Monty—"even if you want to strangle them sometimes."

"You two going to be okay?" Jimmy asked with a note of concern in his voice. "I couldn't get the details, but it sounded heated in there for a minute."

"Nothing we can't resolve," Monty said. "I'd appreciate your discretion regarding our guest this evening."

"The less I know about her the better," Jimmy said, raising a hand. "She is Grade-A petrifying, and there isn't much that scares my kind."

"Thanks for feeding my black hole," I said, stepping out of the way and letting my hellhound move toward the door. "We'll see you when you get back."

Jimmy nodded and took off his apron before heading to the back. He paused and turned, his face serious.

"You're dealing with the Morrigan; make sure *you're* the ones that get back. Be careful out there."

"We will," I said as we left the Randy Rump.

At least I hoped we'd be back.

We made our way to the Dark Goat and got in. My hellhound tested the limits of his backseat domain with a magnificent sprawl, taking up all of the space in one long stretch. I thought I heard the doors creak as he pushed against them with his massive legs.

We drove in silence for a few minutes. I was still set to

slow burn. I didn't enjoy being roped into owing Badb Catha, but I understood why Monty did it.

"Would you have agreed if I had taken the time to explain the option to you?" Monty asked after some time, reading my thoughts. "I apologize if this feels like a deception."

"Not *like* a deception," I snapped. "No, I wouldn't have agreed. I would've told you to take your insane plan and take a long walk off a short cliff. This is crazy, Monty, you have to see that."

"No crazier than anything else we have done."

"No crazier? Wrong, much crazier!"

"What would you have proposed?" Monty asked, glancing at me. "We go in and destroy them all in a hail of orbs and bullets? That plan would have lasted exactly two seconds before either Magnus cut through us or Haven became a killing ground."

I kept silent for a few seconds, because he was right.

"Can you get them out? The people at Haven? Can you get them out in time?"

"I don't know," Monty said, turning to look out the window. "I've never heard of a Transporter moving so many people at once. It's not just the patients; she has to move staff, too. Fortunately, it's the evening shift and the staff will be minimal."

"What about the detention level?"

"It should be safe from the attack," Monty said. "I doubt any of Shadow Company's sorcerers will gain access to those levels. Badb Catha won't give them time. They will focus on the soft targets."

"How do we call her off?" I asked, concerned. "Does the Death Goddess have an off switch?"

"None that I'm aware of," Monty said. "It's best to let her run her course and stay out of her way."

"Right, nothing can go wrong with *that* strategy," I growled. "Sorry, this whole op is such a flustercuck."

"Excuse me? I think the correct term is cluster—"

"No, a flustercuck is before it happens," I corrected. "The clusterfuck starts the moment I pull that trigger to shoot you."

"About that," Monty said. "Please try to avoid my head. I'm slowing down the round, not stopping it."

I glanced at him again.

"You want me to aim at some non-lethal part of your body with a round designed to drop a dragon. Do you hear yourself?"

"Correct. I'm placing my life in your aim."

"Do you realize how batshit that sounds?"

"Which part? Asking you to take a non-lethal shot or trusting you enough to place my life in your hands?"

"Both, Monty," I said with a sigh. "This is beyond dangerous. What if...what if I miss?"

"I won't exactly be in a position to chastise you about it, now, will I?" Monty said. "You won't miss. I know you won't."

It was my turn to pinch the bridge of my nose.

"I think the schism scrambled what little sense you had left," I said. "If we make it through this op, you go back to Haven for a full eval."

"Agreed," Monty said with a slight nod. "If we don't, it won't matter much, will it?"

"I'm not feeling the nihilist Monty," I said. "Don't mages ever try to encourage each other before a major battle?"

"Mages deal in reality, not false hope or wishful thinking. I fail to see anything to be encouraged about," Monty said, staring at me. "We face overwhelming odds. We risk losing everyone we care for, along with our own lives in the process. Even you, with your curse, will not be able to stand against a dragon of Magnus' power and age. What we need is to go into this evening armed with all the facts and operate on complete information, not hope or luck."

"Mage pep talks suck," I said. "My morale feels so lifted right now, thanks."

"You're welcome."

We arrived at the trailer with ten minutes to spare.

TWENTY-SEVEN

Carlos was standing at the door as we approached.

"You're early," he said, glaring at me. "Douglas said ten o'clock."

"Actually it was Rott, and early is better than late," I said, returning his glare. "You plan on blocking our way, or do I have to shoot you this time?"

"You caught me off guard last time, old man," Carlos mocked. "I didn't expect someone of your advanced age capable of moving like that. It won't happen again."

I slid forward, moving much faster than out last 'conversation', but this time, I materialized Ebonsoul. The look on Carlos' face let me know he just wasn't ready and never would be. I placed the blade of Ebonsoul gently against his neck. Peaches gave off a low growl.

"Do you know why it won't happen again?" I asked, applying pressure to the blade as I spoke into his ear.

Carlos froze, realizing that any sudden movement could instantly make him a head shorter.

"No, sir," Carlos managed to whisper. "I don't."

"Because next time, if there is a next time, I won't be warning you," I said. "I'll be ending you."

I reabsorbed Ebonsoul and stepped back.

"What the hell are you?" Carlos asked, rubbing his neck. "You're like them, some kind of freak."

"Step aside before I stop feeling cordial."

Carlos moved quickly to the side and opened the door. His actions showed respect, but his eyes radiated hatred. I'd have to watch him during the op. The last thing I wanted was to be shot by a stray round or blown up by a misplaced explosive. This time he remained outside.

"I'd say that your social skills need some polish," Monty said as we moved inside. "But that would require you to possess social skills."

"I have plenty of social skills," I said as I headed down the corridor. "He called me a freak. I'm not a freak."

"Not at all, you're just abnormal."

I glanced at Monty, but he had a straight face and I left the comment alone. I didn't want to go into what I could or could not do in front of Douglas. I knew Rott wouldn't be here. He would be with Magnus arranging to be his driver for the night, but if I knew Shadow Company, the entire trailer was equipped with listening devices.

"You're early, good," Douglas said when we entered the situation room. He pointed to the conference table. "Here are your kits."

I saw the long case and imagined it was the rifle I was supposed to use.

"Open it," Douglas said. "Wouldn't want you to feel uncomfortable."

I opened the case and saw my old rifle. Memories flooded me as I ran a finger along the barrel.

"My rifle. You kept it?"

"Once Shadow Company, always Shadow Company," Douglas said. "You never really leave."

I ran a cursory check of the equipment. Someone had been keeping it in working order and giving it regular maintenance. Part of me was surprised, but it made sense. Douglas was arrogant enough to believe that one day, I would come back, because I couldn't function without Shadow Company indefinitely.

"It's been maintained."

"Expensive piece of hardware," Douglas said with a curt nod. "Nothing wrong with the rifle. It's the operator"—he gave me a pointed look—"that concerns me. Ammunition is next to it."

Beside the rifle was a small, clear case with five rounds of ammunition. The case was covered in black wisps of energy. Next to that was a smaller version of the main map with locations circled in red. Sitting next to the map were a pair of high-frequency burst comms—one each for Monty and me.

"The comms are on a scrambled frequency," Douglas said, tapping the comm in his ear. "We go in radio silent until Rott shows up, and then I will coordinate, understood?"

"You weren't kidding about only making a handful," I said, taking the small ammo case and the rifle. "Five rounds?"

"You only need one," Douglas said with a growl. "I didn't prep anything for you, mage. Figured you have your own weaponry."

"I do," Monty said, looking over the table at the combat armor. "Is that for us?"

"Experimental armor," Douglas said tapping his chest. "Lightweight and designed to stop almost anything short of a rocket. There's a set there for each of you."

"My clothing is more than adequate," Monty said, feeling the material of the combat armor. "Is this runed?"

"Enhanced," Douglas corrected. "We fight fire with fire. Strong?"

"No, thanks," I said, tapping my jacket. "I'm good."

"Your choice. One more thing," Douglas said. "Feelds will be your spotter. I don't want a repeat of last time. Any objections?"

"Has she done this before?" I asked, knowing objections would be futile. I was pretty sure her job was to put a round in my head a second after I took down Magnus. "Is she a shooter?"

"She's one of the best. She'll make sure the shot is clean."

"I'm sure she will," I said. "Doesn't seem like I have a choice."

"You don't."

Monty stared at Douglas. I could tell he was trying to figure him out.

"Why are you part of this operation?" Monty asked. "Why are you helping Rott? Do you bear the dragons that much hatred?"

"I don't care about dragons," Douglas said, surprising me. "I care that the power structure of my city has been skewed for too long. No one group should wield that much power unchecked."

"You feel causing their implosion will restore balance?"

"Or wipe them out completely," Douglas said. "Either works in my book."

"The vacuum left by their elimination would be filled by another," Monty said. "Someone else will step in to take control."

"Not if we stop them," Douglas replied. "This plane belongs to humans. Only humans. Anything else needs to go or needs to be removed."

"Things are never that simple," Monty said. "There are beings on this plane beyond your understanding."

"If they aren't human, they're not welcome. We start the cleansing tonight. You can use one of the rooms off the corridor to get situated. We leave in two. Any more questions?"

We were about to leave the situation room when I turned and faced Douglas again.

"You said if they aren't human then they need to go, right?"

"That's what I said," Douglas replied, gruffly. "What of it?"

"That apply to Rott, or does he get a pass?" I asked. "I'm just curious if your *cleansing* applies to him, too."

I saw a brief flash of anger, which he quickly masked.

"Rott is serving our cause," Douglas said, giving me a hard look. "He shares in our vision, unlike some. What happened to him was an accident, and he uses his power for good. Those others out there? They will be dealt with, along with anyone sympathetic to their presence on our plane. They will all be expunged, starting with the dragon. You may go."

It wasn't a request. Douglas turned from me, ending the discussion, and pressed a button on a console next to him. I heard the engine start up.

We stepped out of the situation room as a steel door

slid closed, cutting off the area from the rest of the trailer. I saw Carlos at the other end of the corridor. He gave me a smile and a mocking salute as he glared my way.

I felt the trailer move as we stepped into one of the rooms. I made sure to remain silent. Monty had come to the same conclusion I had: the rooms were under surveillance. There was a good chance Douglas or Feelds was listening and watching us.

There was a small table and several chairs. I placed the long case on the floor next to me and smoothed out the map on the table, pretending to examine it.

"Let's run over the op again," I said, looking at my smaller copy of the map. "You will be situated where, again?"

Monty pointed to the map.

"Here," he said, subtly placing three fingers on the map signaling every third word. "I think Rott will have to arrange to be here"—Monty placed five fingers on the map this time—"before the engine is killed."

"Agreed," I said. "Will you be able to distract Magnus long enough?"

Monty nodded.

"I will turn him away from you and position him near the automobile," Monty said. "That will give you your opportunity. Don't miss."

"I won't," I said.

"Perhaps you should instruct your creature on his behavior," Monty said. "We don't want him to create a larger problem. You know he has a tendency to magnify the situation, increasing things to immense proportions."

I nodded.

<Hey, boy. I'm going to need you to go into XL battle mode soon.>

<This place is too small. It would break.>

<Not in here. Outside, when things go south.>

<You want me to go south? Why?>

<Not you going south. When we face off against these guys.>

<You want to take someone's face off?>

<When the danger starts, you go large and stay close to me. I'll let you know.>

<I'm your bondmate I go where you go.>

<I'll be far away from the danger. Monty will be in the middle of it. We need to keep him safe.>

It was a slight exaggeration. I knew Feelds would try to put me down. She looked trained and dangerous, but I didn't want Peaches focused only on me. Something told me Magnus wasn't going to cooperate.

<I will keep him safe and then I will be next to you.>

<Fine. You make sure he's safe and then you come right back.>

Some time later, the trailer stopped and Feelds appeared at the doorway.

"This is our stop," she said, looking at me. "Let's go."

TWENTY-EIGHT

We reached my location, the roof of the Weill Cornell center, four blocks away from the designated distraction. I lay on the roof and set up my rifle, a Barrett Light Fifty beast that would easily fire past the four blocks without so much as breaking a sweat.

It all came back in a rush. The muscle memory was instant, and I assembled the pieces in a silent meditation, putting the rifle together in quick, smooth movements. I opened the tripod and stretched out on the roof.

I had a clear line of sight about a mile down West Broadway all the way past Canal Street and beyond. Feelds set up close to me and pulled out a specialized telescope.

She sighted down West Broadway and gave me a short nod with a thumbs up. Peaches grumbled on the floor next to my prone position.

"Good to go," Feelds said. I heard her voice over the comms: "Firing solution in five."

I looked down the scope and realized it was equipped with night vision. I scanned down the street. The entrance to the TINY was unobstructed. I moved the scope down a few blocks and saw Monty standing in the center of Bogardus Plaza, a small park taking up the corner of the block between Chambers and Reade Streets.

"Eyes up," Douglas said over the comms. "Delivery incoming."

I moved the rifle slightly and spotted the Duezy heading down West Broadway. A few seconds later, I saw Gant come outside the restaurant and wait. The Midnight Ghost came to a stop in front of the TINY. It was as incredible as I imagined it would be. It was truly a piece of automotive art, and I could see why Magnus would opt for using it. The car made an impression. I saw Cecil get out and extend a clipboard to Gant, who signed it, taking the keys.

Cecil got into a waiting Urus and pulled away. Gant waited outside as Magnus and Rott stepped out of the restaurant. Gant handed Rott the keys, had some words with Magnus, then headed back inside.

"We have eyes on target," Feelds said. "Package is being loaded. Thirty seconds to intercept."

Rott held the door open for Magnus, who looked up in my direction for a brief second before getting in the Duezy. Rott got in, started the Duezy, and began heading south down West Broadway. The streets were mostly deserted this late at night, which meant little-to-no traffic. I took a deep breath and let it out slowly as I followed the progress of the Duezy.

One block and nothing. On the second block, I started seeing white smoke escape from under the hood.

"Engage target once out of the vehicle," Douglas said

over the comms. "Blaster will cover our tracks. Strong, you make sure you take the damn shot."

Rott pulled over and got out, opening the hood. He was shaking his head and walked over to the other side of the Duezy, gesturing to Magnus to exit the vehicle.

"Sir, you need to get out," I heard Rott over the comms. "It's overheating and this is dangerous. I'll call for a replacement. We should head back to the restaurant."

"Can you fix it?"

"No, sir," Rott said. "I'm not a mechanic. Especially not for a vehicle as unique as this."

"Then what good *are* you?" Magnus asked angrily, as he stepped out of the Duezy and slammed the door. "This is unacceptable. Cecil and I will have words."

"I understand, sir," Rott said, closing the hood. "Please stand over there, sir." Rott pointed to the sidewalk. "The street isn't safe."

"I am not a child—what's your name again?"

"My name is Rott, sir."

I scanned the area and saw Monty approaching. I scanned up the street and saw Gant along with several large men exiting the TINY. This was not good.

"We have incoming," I said. "Four unfriendlies just exited the restaurant. I recommend we abort."

"Negative," Douglas said. "Blaster, stop them."

"Copy that," Carlos said over the comms. "This is going to screw the timetable, though."

"It can't be helped—do it," Douglas said. "Do not let them reach Balfour. Mage, engage the dragon now. Strong, when you get the shot, take it. I don't care who's in the way. You take the shot, or everyone in Haven dies."

I heard Carlos laugh.

"Lighting it up in three, two, one," Carlos said counting it down. "Starting the party."

I saw a barrage of rockets scream their way toward Gant and the men. As soon as the rockets impacted, the front of the restaurant exploded in an enormous bloom of flame.

"Now! Mage," Douglas yelled, and Monty crossed the street. "Get him into position."

"Magnus," Monty said when he drew close. "It's over."

"You?" Magnus said, momentarily surprised. "What are *you* doing here?"

"Ending you," Monty said, rushing Magnus as he gestured. "Your madness ends tonight."

Magnus recovered fast, but not before Monty crashed into him. They collided and slammed into the Duezy in a flash of golden light. Monty held Magnus in a rear choke-hold as he gestured with his free hand. From the way Magnus moved I could tell the hold wasn't going to last.

"I was only going to kill Strong," Magnus said. "But I can accommodate your demise as well, Montague."

Magnus began moving Monty's arm away from his neck.

"Take the shot, Strong!" Douglas called out. "Do it now!"

"Monty is in the way. I repeat, target is not clear."

"You take it or I do," Rott said, reaching into his jacket. "I'll burn them both."

"No," I said. "This shot is mine."

I took a deep breath, aimed, and squeezed the trigger.

TWENTY-NINE

The round raced at Monty, hitting him in the shoulder and punching through Magnus' chest, 1.1 seconds after I fired. A spray of blood created a cloud of death around the two men as they launched forward several feet from the impact.

"Carlos, plant the Obouros assassin," Douglas said. "Rott, check vitals. Make sure Balfour is gone."

I saw Rott crouch over the bloody body of Magnus as Carlos carried a body bag near the Duezy. He opened it and pulled out the body of a man I didn't recognize. A few seconds later, Douglas came into view.

"Balfour is down," Rott said, standing up as Douglas drew a weapon. "That's one down, and—"

"I'm sorry, old friend," Douglas said, pointing the gun at Rott. "I want you to know your death won't be in vain."

"What are you doing?" Rott said. "We're taking them out, the dragons."

"No, *I'm* taking them out," Douglas said. "Carlos."

Carlos crouched over Magnus and pulled out a syringe.

He drew blood from Magnus' arm and then walked over to Douglas.

"Are you sure?" Carlos asked, hesitating. "We don't know..."

"Do it," Douglas barked. "Now."

Carlos plunged the syringe into Douglas, injecting the blood into his arm.

"No!" Rott exclaimed in shock. "What have you done?"

"I've acquired power, George. The power to eliminate my enemies—the enemies of Shadow Company."

"Dragon blood is poison to humans," Rott said, stepping back. "You've lost your damn mind."

"No, George, for the first time I can see clearly," Douglas said. "A grief-stricken father who could never get over the loss of his daughter, who tracked and murdered the dragon he felt was responsible...before taking his own life. It's quite tragic, really."

"Bullshit," Rott said, lunging forward as Douglas fired. Rott collapsed to the ground as blood flowed freely from several wounds. "How?"

"Runed rounds," Douglas said, glancing at his gun, "I had a few made for you, too. Can never be too careful."

"You basta—" Rott started.

Douglas fired a double-tap to the head, ending Rott's life. I scanned over and saw that Monty was hurt, but looked intact. Sirens were wailing in the night and I knew they would be swarming over the area soon. Explosions in the city had a tendency to attract attention. A flash of violet light from Monty caught my attention as Douglas pulled out a phone.

"Terminate them all," Douglas said into the phone. "No survivors."

A beam of white light filled the sky. It was bright enough to temporarily convert the night into day for a few seconds. I triangulated its location and my stomach fell.

Haven.

"That was some excellent marksmanship, Strong," Douglas said, looking in my direction. "It's a pity we're restructuring the Company, or else I'd invite you to join us."

"Fuck you, Douglas."

"I had a feeling you'd say that," Douglas said. "Feelds, escort Strong along to his next life."

I felt the barrel of her gun against my side.

"It's not personal," Feelds said. "We don't need two shooters, and Shadow Company doesn't—"

"Leave loose ends, I know. You don't want to do this. He'll betray you the same way he did Rott."

"I'm not Rott," Feelds said. "I'm one hundred percent human, and you, your mage, and that thing you call a dog aren't. Goodbye, Strong."

She pulled the trigger three times. The kinetic energy shoved me across the roof. The jacket Monty gave me held up. My ribs took the brunt of the impact, breaking at least two. My body flushed hot as it repaired the damage. I rolled to a stop several feet away in agony.

I could sense her get to her feet as she approached to deliver the killing blow.

<Stop her, but don't hurt her, not yet.>

<Can I bite her? She tried to hurt you.>

<No, we need her alive right now. Maybe later you can bite her.>

Peaches blinked out, taking her by surprise. He reappeared a second later, tackling her down to the floor.

She landed hard on her back with his jaws around her neck. She was good and kept it together, but the fear in her eyes betrayed her. I didn't blame her—I'd be scared shitless, too.

"Feelds? Report," I heard Douglas demand over the comms. "Is it done?"

I walked over to where Feelds lay, kicked her gun away, and drew Grim Whisper. The absence of blood or wounds on me only served to ratchet up her fear. I nodded to her and motioned for her to answer Douglas.

"He's down, sir," Feelds replied with a slight rasp. "Him and that dog of his."

"Good job," Douglas said. "Regroup at the trailer in ten."

"Roger that," Feelds said. "See you in ten."

I removed Feelds' comm and tossed it off the roof along with mine.

"I'm going to make this simple for you," I said, my body hot from the healing. "I don't like being shot, which means right now I'm in a bad mood. My hound doesn't like people trying to hurt me, and he's pissed. So pissed that he's ready to bite through your throat."

"How are you still alive?" she asked, fear gripping her words. "I shot you point blank. Three times. Your heart should be shredded right now."

"I think the important question is: Do you want to see the sunrise?"

She took a few moments to consider the question, and then nodded.

"Yes," she said. "What do you want?"

"Shadow Company is finished as of tonight," I said. "I'm going to end them. Douglas said you belonged to another agency; I suggest you forget Douglas and Shadow Company and either retire or go back to your previous agency."

"Sounds like...sounds like a solid plan," she said. "You're going to let me go?"

"I am, but understand me. If you come after me again..." I materialized Ebonsoul, and that caused her to lose all pretense, the fear clear on her face. "I will kill you without thinking twice. We clear?"

"Crystal," Feelds said with a slight tremble in her voice. "Can you call off your demondog?"

"Let her go, boy," I said. "She's going to behave."

Peaches stepped off her chest and Feelds got quickly to her feet. She stood still for a moment looking at us, and I wondered if she was considering throwing her life away by attacking. She shook her head and ran off the roof.

I looked through the scope again and saw that Douglas and Carlos were gone. Monty still lay on the ground near the Duezy. I scanned up West Broadway and saw the devastation. Most of the street two blocks away was gone. The facade of the TINY was obliterated. Beyond that I could see first responders on their way.

<Should I get big now?>

<I don't know if the roof can handle your weight at XL. Stay this size for now. Unless you see a dragon.>

Peaches looked over the edge of the roof.

<The angry man is hurt.>

<We need to get to Monty, boy. Can you—>

I didn't get to finish before my hellhound blinked us out. We reappeared next to Monty. He was still face down, and I dreaded turning him over.

"Monty?" I said, reaching to turn him on his back. My hand passed through his body. "What the hell?"

"Over here, Simon," Monty called out from inside the Duezy. His face was pale and he spoke with a grimace. "That was...was an excellent shot. Thank you for not removing my head. I'm afraid I underestimated the force of the round. It appears I'm bleeding out."

"Shit, Monty!" I yelled, applying pressure to his wound. "I don't know a healing finger wiggle!"

"Ha...Haven," he managed with effort. "Take...take Balfour, too. Can't leave him here."

"He wants to kill me," I argued. "It's clear you've lost too much blood."

"We need him...need to take with us...take with us to Haven."

"There's no one at Haven," I said my voice grim. "Douglas gave the order...they're all dead."

"No. I activated the Transporter as soon as you took the shot. Roxanne is still there, she's in my room. Shadow Company sorcerers still there."

"How could you possibly know that? Haven is across town."

"Bond. Created a bond to monitor," Monty said and coughed up blood. "We need to get to her before it's too late. Before they kill her."

"We won't all fit in the Duezy," I said, looking around for a solution. "We don't have time for two trips."

"Use...use your creature,"Monty said. "He can do it."

The next moment, Monty's head fell back as he lost consciousness. I stepped away from the Duezy and crouched down next to Peaches.

*<You heard him. Can you do it? Can you take us all to Haven?
To Roxanne, the scary lady who likes Monty?>*

*<I can take him and the dragon. I don't know if I can come
back to take you. I'm so tired.>*

*<Do it. Take them to the scary lady, now. I'll get there on my
own.>*

Peaches hunched down and let out a low rumble,
followed by a eardrum-shattering bark. The next second
they were gone. I jumped into the Duezy, started the
engine and floored the gas.

THIRTY

I made it to Haven in record time.

I parked the Duezy in front of Haven and got out. Douglas' words came back to me: *Imagine how many sorcerers it would take to wipe out the entire facility. I have twice that amount in there.*

I wasn't going to take any chances.

I pulled out the crow's feather and held it in my hand as I whispered, "*Ignisvitae.*" The feather disintegrated in a violet flame. A second later, a presence of cold fear gripped me.

"Marked of Kali," Badb said from behind me. "I am here."

It took all I had not to run away from her screaming. I took a few deep breaths, stomped down on the irrational fear attempting to take over my mind, and turned.

"Thank you for coming," I said, measuring my words. "Monty, Roxanne, and Magnus are on the top floor. The rest of the place is empty except for the Shadow Company sorcerers, I think."

Badb closed her eyes for a second and smiled.

In that moment, I knew true fear. This was the kind of fear that rooted you to the spot while death came and snuffed you out. She turned away from me and headed for the entrance.

"Marked of Kali," Badb said as she approached the entrance, shattering all of the glass in the lobby. "Do not cross my path."

The black nimbus of energy spread out from her as she walked in. A few seconds later I heard the first screams. I stepped in and took the elevator to the top floor. Monty's room was in restricted access, two levels above me. I ran for the stairwell and blasted the door with Grim Whisper.

Nothing happened.

I holstered my gun and formed Ebonsoul, black and red energy radiated out from my blade. I jammed the blade into the door jamb, then took a step back and slammed the door hard with my shoulder. The door exploded open. I ran up the two flights and shoved hard against the door. This one opened easily and I slid into the corridor. It was empty and I moved fast, taking the corner at speed until I slid to a stop.

Right behind a group of three sorcerers.

I looked down the corridor and saw Elias Paul Bunyan blocking the space in front of Monty's door. He was barely standing; and bruises covered his face and arms. He had one vicious cut over an eye that bled freely, and the other eye had been swollen shut. One of his legs looked like it had been barbecued—the skin was an exposed, angry red.

"Step aside, Elias," one of the sorcerers said. "This has nothing to do with you."

"Layton, you plan on killing someone I swore to

protect," Elias answered, his voice grim. "I'd say it has everything to do with me."

Elias formed two large orbs of black energy.

"You should've joined Shadow Company when you had the chance," Layton said, forming a nasty black and red orb. "It's too late now."

"Shadow Company is no longer hiring," I said, absorbing Ebonsoul and drawing Grim Whisper before opening fire. "I'm closing them down."

I dove around the corner, avoiding the barrage of orbs they sent my way.

"Who the hell was that?" one of the sorcerers asked.

"Doesn't matter. He dies, too," Layton said. "Kill him. I'll take care of Elias."

A scream filled the corridor a second later, followed by two sets of footsteps. I hoped the scream wasn't Elias, but the odds were against him. I ducked into the nearest stairwell and closed my eyes, focusing my energy into Ebonsoul, hoping this would work; if not, I was about to get pummeled silly by sorcerous orbs of death.

When I opened my eyes, my body was covered in a tight violet shield. I hoped it held as I stepped out of the stairwell and around the corner, opening fire with Grim Whisper. I caught one of the sorcerers by surprise, dropping him. The second one had better reflexes and threw up a shield while unleashing another barrage of orbs at me.

I ran forward, slashing through the barrage with Ebonsoul as I closed the distance. He tried to backpedal, but it was too late—I had too much momentum, and slammed into him, blade first.

I buried Ebonsoul into his chest and felt the siphon of energy a second later. It ripped the air from my lungs and nearly brought me to my knees. I staggered back and leaned against the wall.

"What the hell?" I murmured to myself as I absorbed Ebonsoul. "That wasn't like last time. Definitely higher on the creepy meter."

I turned the corner, leading with Grim Whisper.

Layton lay on the floor...well, what was left of him. Elias had shredded most of Layton into a bloody smear. He didn't look much better as he sat against a wall near Monty's door.

"You look like shit," I said, crouching down to help him up. He groaned in pain as he stood shakily. "What the hell happened?"

"Turns out they were confused," Elias said, followed by a grunt as I propped him up against the wall. "I merely brought them clarity of thought."

I glanced over at what was left of Layton.

"Remind me to never get confused around you."

Elias tried to laugh and ended up coughing up blood.

"That isn't good," he said, looking at the blood. "You may as well leave me here. It's not like I can face any more of them in this condition."

"You don't have to," I said. "I brought backup."

"You brought backup?" Elias asked, gripping my arm with a iron grip. "You're not even a mage. How could you bring backup?"

"I know people. Scary people in very scary places," I said. "Now stop talking."

He nodded and rested his head back against the wall, closing his eyes.

I pounded on the door.

"It's me," I yelled, glancing behind me. "Open up!"

The last thing I wanted was to be in the corridor when Badb's black nimbus of energy filled it. The door opened a second later, and we stumbled in. I made sure to keep Elias from falling as I took in the scene. He swayed unsteadily as I held him up.

Roxanne was covered in blood and for a second I thought she had been wounded. I saw Monty in the large industrial bed, and two more, smaller beds next to Monty's. One held Magnus, who looked worse than Monty, the other bed was empty.

I stood there in shock for a few seconds.

"Put him over there," Roxanne snapped, bringing me out of my shock. "Simon, move, now."

I placed Elias in the empty bed and stepped back. Roxanne gestured and Elias was immediately covered in a cocoon of red energy.

"Why are you still here?" I asked. "You were supposed to have been shifted."

"I was in my office when it happened," Roxanne answered. "By the time I realized what had occurred, we were under attack. Elias and a handful of others managed to hold them off while we made our way in here."

"They're not going to be an issue for much longer," I said, glancing at the door. "I don't recommend going out there, though."

"There may be others who need help," Roxanne protested. "I have to do a sweep of the floors to check."

"You may want to wait," I said, my voice serious. "Badb is out there and she's not exactly what I would call friendly right now."

"Badb? Badb Catha?" Roxanne asked. "You summoned Badb Catha? Are you mad? This facility is full of people."

I pointed at Monty.

"Not at the moment," Monty said, getting slowly out of bed. "They've been temporarily shifted away."

"Where do you think you're going?" Roxanne demanded. "You're in no condition to move, much less leave Haven."

"We need to go, and she's going to help," Monty said, making no sense. "Simon and I need to finish this."

"Who's going to help?" Roxanne asked exasperated. "What are you going on about?"

"Haven is empty," Monty said. "But you need to remain in this room, at least until we return."

"I know that's what you said, but it's impossible," Roxanne said. "Not even Dex could teleport the entire facility."

There was a soft knock at the door.

"I'd open that, if I were you," I said, quietly. "I doubt its one of the sorcerers."

Roxanne gestured with a hand and the door clicked ajar. It was gently pushed open the rest of the way, and Badb stepped in. She stepped over to Monty and rested a hand on his chest.

Black tendrils shot out from her hand and entered Monty's wound. He gasped with pain and grimaced as the wound healed. A few seconds later, he was completely healed. She moved over to the bed where Magnus lay and did the same thing.

Magnus shot up in the bed a moment later.

"You," Magnus said, looking at Monty and gathering energy. "You will pay for this."

"He just saved your life," I said, turning to Monty. "Maybe we should have left him on the street?"

"He attacked me," Magnus accused. "He will die."

"He saved you," I said. "You were targeted by Shadow Company. They were going to retire you, permanently. If it wasn't for Monty—"

"And Simon, you'd be deceased," Monty finished. "Your driver, Rott, betrayed you."

"Impossible," Magnus scoffed. "He was my kind, a dragon."

"No, actually, he wasn't," I corrected. "He was Shadow Company. Slif killed his daughter and he wanted to make you pay for that."

"I cannot let this attack go unanswered," Magnus said, finally. "You two have just forfeited your lives."

"All that power and still so dense," I said, moving back. "Is that your final answer? We need to die?"

"You attacked the leader of an enclave, you nearly killed me, and you expect me to what? Forgive and forget?"

Badb Catha stepped closer to Magnus.

"You will seek retribution against the Marked of Kali and Mage Montague?" she asked. "Are you certain?"

"The marked of who?" Magnus asked, confused. "It doesn't matter. Do you know who I am? I am Magnus M. Balfour, leader of the Balfour Enclave and these...these scum dared to lay a hand on me. I will eliminate you, everyone you know, and everyone they know. My wrath will be absolute."

"Will you not turn away from this path?" Badb asked with a small smile. "Will you extend these two clemency?"

"Never," Magnus seethed. "Their destruction will become my purpose. I will see them reduced to dust."

"That is some grudge," I said under my breath. "Don't say you weren't given a chance."

Magnus gestured, ready to unleash some death spell in our direction. Badb Catha placed a hand on his cheek and all magic fled the room in an instant. One of Magnus' eyes clouded over into a milky white, and then he sagged back into his bed.

"Know that you still live because of the mercy extended to you by Mage Montague and the Marked of Kali," Badb said, moving away. "You will not have access to your magical ability, and I have taken the sight from one eye to allow you a constant reminder of your blindness to see reason."

"Who...who are you?" Magnus asked, fear lacing his words. "*What* are you?"

"I am war, violence, carnage, and rage. I am the one who will return to rip your life from your body should you seek to threaten them or any they hold dear. I am the last face you will see before you die. I am Death. I am Badb Catha. Remember my words."

Badb waved a hand and Magnus disappeared.

"Did you?" I asked. "You didn't?"

"Our terms were clear," Badb said. "Persuade, but not kill. I would think he is sufficiently persuaded, yes?"

"Yes, but where did you send him?"

"I have sent him home to nurse his wounded pride. His ability will return in a few centuries. Long enough to teach him some humility."

"Or really, really piss him off."

"Perhaps. We will see what, if anything, he learns over that time."

"Thank you."

"Do not thank me," she said with a smile that chilled

my blood. "We have...terms, Marked of Kali. I will call on you both, soon."

Badb Catha disappeared a moment later, leaving the room hovering around arctic temperatures. I exhaled and saw my breath.

"I still need to stop Shadow Company," I said. "They got away after everything with Magnus. Douglas managed to get injected with dragon blood."

"Dragon blood?" Roxanne asked. "He's going to kill himself?"

"He thinks it's going to give him power to fix what he sees is wrong with the world. Basically, he's a megalomaniacal xenophobe. For once, just once, I'd like to face an enemy that believes all humanity should be forced to drink coffee. I can deal with that kind of insane. Not, 'Let's wipe out everything that isn't human,' off-the-deep-end psychosis."

"The dragon's blood won't kill him," Monty said. "Not immediately."

"He's right," Roxanne said. "It will give him power and access to energy manipulation, and *then* it will kill him."

"How long before he becomes a memory?"

"Hard to say," Roxanne said. "It depends on his physiology, whether he has a propensity for magic. It could be days, years, decades, or centuries. Dragon's blood can extend his life if he refrains from using the power it gives him. There's no real way of telling. Surprisingly there aren't many candidates willing to take the chance of having dragon's blood injected into their body."

"Centuries? I can't wait that long," I said. "Douglas isn't going to refrain from using power. He's going to wipe out anyone or anything that isn't human."

"Do you know where he is?" Roxanne asked. "Your hellhound needs rest. You can't have him search for this Douglas. He barely made it here with Tristan and that dragon. It seems like he made too many concurrent jumps."

"Will he be okay?" I asked, suddenly concerned about my hellhound. "The last jump was extreme."

"Nothing a large bowl of sausage can't cure," Roxanne said, glancing at my hellhound. Peaches' ears perked up at the mention of sausage, but he didn't move. "He'll be fine."

"I know where we can find out," Monty said after a few moments. "If she's still alive."

"Who?"

"The Auer."

THIRTY-ONE

Monty formed a teleportation circle while I rubbed Peaches' belly.

<I need to go find the bad man.>

<Wherever you go, I go. I'm your bondmate.>

<I know, but not this time, boy. You need to rest.>

<If I had some meat, I wouldn't need to rest. Meat would make me stronger. Can you ask the scary lady to make me some meat?>

I gave him a short laugh.

<Stay here. The scary lady will make sausage for you while you get your strength back.>

<I have never been tired before. I think I am growing.>

<I don't know what that means, but I promise we'll look into it when I get back. Maybe Hades knows.>

"I'll make sure he's well fed and taken care of," Roxanne said. "He's safe here. Apparently, the facility is still empty"—she glanced at Monty—"so I only have him and Elias to watch until everyone is returned."

"The Transporter should return them in a day or so,"

Monty said, placing a hand on Roxanne's shoulder. "Time functions differently for her. She placed them in stasis before the shift. No time will have passed for them."

"That will make things easier," Roxanne said, placing her hand over Monty's. "I won't have to explain how they managed to disappear."

The large green teleportation circle pulsed with power as Monty stepped in.

"Ready?" Monty asked. "The sooner we move—"

"Let's go," I said, stepping into the circle. "We need to end this tonight."

The circle flashed green and Haven disappeared.

We appeared inside the Auer's compound, except it looked like a warzone. The neat rows of bookcases had been blasted apart. I saw the bodies of the Archive Guard. Most of them died hard. Several of them had gone fast; their horrific wounds were visible even in the dim light.

"What happened here, Monty?" I asked, looking around. "Who could do this?"

"This looks like the work of a—"

A cough from one of the destroyed bookcases caught our attention.

"Tristan," a voice rasped, "is that you?"

We moved one of the precariously balanced bookcases to uncover the body of Roma. Even without being a doctor, I knew she had little time left. A huge gaping wound exposed part of her left ribcage. Her entire left side was a charred mess.

"Roma," Monty said and began gesturing. Golden runes flowed from his hand and landed on Roma's body. "Remain still."

Roma reached up and grabbed his hand, stopping him.

"I'm afraid my dueling days are over," she said with a tight smile that became a grimace of pain. "It's too late for me. Too much damage."

"Who did this?" Monty asked, his voice cold and menacing. "Tell me."

"Balf—Balfour Enforcer, Rell," Roma managed. "You need to get to the Auer before it's too late. Lower archives, safe room. Go, now."

Roma's hand dropped to her side as her lifeless eyes looked up at us. Monty placed a hand over her face and closed them. He stood and I could sense the anger radiating from him.

"Monty?" I asked. "We'll stop him. I just don't want—"

"No," Monty said his voice dark as black energy crackled around his body. "Not stop, *finish*. He is not an enclave leader. His death will not upset the balance." Monty glanced down at Roma's body. "He *dies* for this."

I didn't have an argument for him. Every dragon I had encountered had wanted to maim or kill me. One less dragon in the world was a good thing in my opinion, especially one who went around murdering mages.

I nodded after a few seconds, looking around the carnage for a way downstairs.

"Where is the entrance to the lower archives?" I asked, giving Monty extra space. "Can we get there from here?"

Monty pointed to a staircase partially blocked by a ruined bookcase.

"That will take us downstairs," Monty said, moving fast. "Stand back."

He slashed an arm forward and the bookcase slid to one side, clearing the staircase.

"Are you sure you can't use the Force?" I said as we moved downstairs. "Because that looked—"

"Not now, Simon," Monty said when we reached the lower archives. "The safe room is on the other end of the floor."

The lower archives were mostly open space compared to the upper level. Bookcases lined the walls, but the center was dominated by desks and research stations. It looked like someone had taken a wrecking ball to the place. Desks and chairs lay in pieces all around the floor. Some of the bookcases were shattered, with books tossed everywhere, while others had been rendered to ash and completely destroyed.

"It's a shame you'll never reach the other end of this floor," a voice said from behind a mound of destroyed bookcases. "The bitch ran and hid, but I managed to give her a parting gift. She won't last long."

Rell.

He was dressed the same way I remembered. Black combat armor, overpowering energy signature, and a seriously bad attitude.

Monty unleashed a beam of black and red energy. Rell dodged to the side and unleashed a swarm of black orbs. Monty made a circle with his hand and created a violet shield, which swallowed them.

They appeared behind Rell a moment later, causing him to dodge again.

"Why?" I asked, materializing Ebonsoul. "Why did you attack her? Why did you kill the Archive Guard?"

"Why?" Rell jeered. "Because I could. Who's going to stop me? You? You're both pathetic, rushing down here to your deaths. This is why humans are mindless cattle.

Everything is emotions with you. She divulged the location of our enclave, and for that alone, she deserves to die."

"That's the reason? Because she revealed the location of your secret dragon club?" I asked as the rage increased. "You are a real piece of—"

"No, wait. There was another reason," Rell said, holding up a finger. "I remember now—because it was fun."

"No more talking," Monty said calmly. "You die now, dragon."

"Come kill me, mage," Rell taunted, drawing a blade. "I'm not going anywhere."

I closed the distance with a growl.

THIRTY-TWO

Rell's blade was a runed weapon, covered in flames.

Every time he parried or swung it my way, I could feel the heat coming off of it. He was fast, managing to keep us both back, while unleashing black orbs at us, which Monty destroyed.

It looked even until I heard Monty whisper something under his breath. The Sorrows were instantly covered in black and violet energy. If they were creepy before with the crying, now they increased the cringe factor by ten. The space was suddenly filled by sobbing and wailing as Monty pressed the attack.

For the first time I saw real concern on Rell's face as he parried Monty's thrusts and slashes. Rell unleashed an orb designed to slam into Monty's chest. Monty made no move to dodge and brought the Sorrows down in a cross block.

The blades absorbed the orb, then and I saw real worry on Rell's face. He backed up as the Sorrows turned black, and the next second a black orb leapt forward from them and raced at Rell.

"You think I can't deal with my own orb?" Rell asked with a smirk. "You may be stronger than most mages, but you're nothing compared to me. Nothing."

Rell held his hand out as the orb closed on him. It slammed into his palm and hovered in place.

"I will never compare myself to you," Monty said, gesturing. "I am beyond dragon filth."

"This won't stop me," Rell said, but his voice was strained as the orb started pushing him back. "What did you *do*?"

"Distracted you," Monty said, pulling me back away from Rell. "Move, Simon, now!"

"What the hell, he's still over there!"

"Not for long," Monty said, hurriedly, creating a barrier of golden energy. "The dawnward. Can you create it?"

"I told you, I don't really—"

"Bloody hell, in five seconds this place is going to be blasted by a beam of absolute death!" Monty yelled. "Use it!"

I closed my eyes and focused my energy through Ebonsoul. A few seconds later we were under a violet dome of energy as a beam of pure white light punched through a surprised Rell. The beam widened as the lower level was bathed in the light, forcing me to look away. The light washed over the dawnward, obliterating Monty's shield and everything around us.

Ten seconds later the beam dissipated, fading to nothing. Even with my eyes closed I felt the aftereffects. Spots danced in my vision as we headed to the other end of the floor. I saw the Auer take two steps and collapse to the ground.

"No," Monty said and rushed over to her. He began to

gesture, but the Auer stopped him. My heart sank; it was Roma all over again. "Not like this."

"Tristan," the Auer said, "we all have a purpose. I have fulfilled mine. It's time for me to go."

The right side of her body was covered in liquid darkness. It was slowly traveling across her body.

"You can't," Monty said. "Not like this."

He gestured and formed an immense orb of golden light, one nearly as bright as the beam the Auer had unleashed on Rell. With a word, he released it, and it cascaded gently onto her body, obliterating the darkness from sight. Several seconds passed until I could see clearly again.

When I could, the liquid darkness was still there, shifting and creeping across her body. Monty began to gesture again, but the Auer stopped him this time.

"Enough," she said, her voice firm. "This cast is beyond you, Tristan Montague."

"I'm certain I can...I'm sure if I...There must be something," Monty struggled to find the words. "I can help. There must be something I can do."

"Yes, there is," the Auer said. "You can let me go with some dignity. You can't undo this; it's too late. Help me over to that chair." She motioned for Monty to move her. "There. That's better."

Monty had lifted her to a large chair that had been blown back in the earlier conflict. She suddenly appeared so small.

"I'm so sorry," Monty said. "If only we had—"

"I will not have you shedding tears for me," the Auer groused as she rested her head back in the chair. "You're a war mage, start acting like it. And you"—she pointed at me—"are the Marked of Kali, an *aspis* and Kali's undying chosen. Death cannot touch you, not yet at least, but you will become intimate with it before your end. It will not do if you dissolve into tears every time someone dies. Compose yourself."

I took a deep breath and wiped my eyes. It wasn't that I was crying. The lower archive was extra dusty from the Auer's mega beam of death, and it caused my eyes to water.

That's my story and I'm sticking to it.

"Can we do anything to—"

"You have little time," she said. "Douglas is going to destroy Haven. He knows about the detention levels and the fact that the facility treats non-humans."

"He wants to make a statement," I said. "He's not that powerful. Haven is immense."

"He is now," the Auer said. "The dragon blood coursing through his veins will give him the power. He knows his time is short."

"He plans to take Haven with him?"

"Haven and most of the city, it seems," the Auer said as more of the liquid darkness covered her body. "Get upstairs and teleport from there. I'd do it"—she gestured to the darkness—"but this seems to be stopping me from accessing my power. Go stop him. Now leave, before I transition and you're trapped down here with me. Go on, it's time to go."

Monty stepped back and I followed him. He took a few steps before moving faster. By the time we were at the stairs we were at a dead run. We took the stairs two at time and Monty skidded to a stop at the top floor.

He began gesturing as I noticed a bright light emanating from downstairs.

"Monty, what's that?" I asked, focusing my gaze on the light getting brighter. "That looks like—"

He grabbed me by the arm and pulled me into the teleportation circle. A flash of green energy later and we were standing at the end of the road that led to the Unisphere.

A massive beam of white light shot up into the sky from the center of the tripod that held up the Unisphere. That was followed by a shockwave that knocked us back several feet. Monty gestured and we were slowed by a cushion of air. I turned back to look at the Unisphere and saw it tilt slightly as it rolled off the tripod.

The three rings around the globe signifying famous orbits shattered, flying off into different parts of the park. The thin plates representing continents warped and twisted as the bolts holding them in place flew through the night, shooting in every direction. The stress from the rolling globe shrugged off each of the continents as it kept moving.

Heading straight for us.

"Can you stop that?" I asked as the globe kept coming. "It looks heavy. Real heavy."

"It weighs approximately three hundred and eighteen thousand kilograms," Monty said matter-of-factly. "I don't believe I possess enough power to stop a mass that large."

"Why would you even know that?" I asked, staring at him. "It doesn't look like it's going to stop."

"It will," Monty said, glancing behind us and pointing. "It will stop there."

"Where?" I said looking in the direction he was

pointing and seeing nothing—nothing except the Arthur Ashe tennis stadium. "No. The stadium?"

Monty nodded and began gesturing.

"Time to go," he said under his breath. "We don't want to be here when a world collides."

He created another circle under us. I felt the surge of energy and Flushing Meadows Park disappeared in a green flash. We reappeared moments later in front of Haven. I barely had a moment to get my bearings when Monty hit me with a blast of air, launching me across the street.

I bounced for a few feet and rolled for several more before coming to a sudden stop against a wall.

"Ow," I groaned, rubbing my side and feeling the heat flush my body as my curse repaired the damage. "What the hell, Monty?"

I slowly got to my feet and caught sight of Monty creating a golden lattice of energy in front of him.

"Get down!" Monty yelled, running from the lattice and diving over a car. "It's him!"

"It's who?" I asked and turned just in time to see Douglas drop onto the Duezy, exploding it into little Duezy components all over the street.

THIRTY-THREE

The only thing that saved me from being instantly impaled was Monty's lattice shield.

I ducked behind a parked car as several pieces of Duezy shrapnel embedded themselves in the car I had ducked behind, as well as the wall behind me. I looked across to see Monty gesturing again.

"Shit," I said, peeking over my makeshift *carricade*. "Cecil is going to be *so* pissed."

"Not relevant," Monty said, unleashing a swarm of six orbs. "We have to deal with Douglas. His energy signature is—"

"It's growing...Oh no."

"Yes," Monty said, creating more orbs. "At this rate he will hit critical mass within ten minutes."

"When you say critical mass...?"

"Haven and most of the East Side will be gone, to start with," Monty said. "And that's only an educated guess. I fear the damage will be even more extensive."

"Strong, come out," Douglas called. "I want you to see what real power looks like."

"Pass, thanks," I called out, feeling a surge of power coming from Douglas. I dove to the side as a blast of flame cut through the car I was hiding behind, slamming into the wall, and punching a hole into the building. "Can you not destroy the building? Then we get called. Everyone gets pissy and starts blaming us. Insurance premiums go through the roof and—"

Another blast punched into the building, narrowly missing me.

"You think this is a joke?" Douglas asked as I felt him spool more energy into his body. "This facility treats non-human scum as if they were human, as if they deserve to live among us."

Douglas turned and extended an arm.

A beam of flame poured from his hand into the side of Haven. The beam of fire was white, tinged with edges of blue. Even from across the street I could feel the intense heat as the beam melted a chunk of the exterior of the building into slag.

"That is bad," I said, looking at the melting exterior. "He's getting stronger."

"I'm going to need you to distract him," Monty said. "For just a moment."

"Look, I know Kali's curse is powerful," I said, peeking over the car again; Douglas seemed distracted. "I don't think it's Death Star beam resistant."

"Use the dawnward, it should protect you until you get to cover."

"The dawnward?" I asked. "Oh, you mean the shield I barely know how to use? That dawnward?"

"It should protect you against a direct blow," Monty said. "I only need a second or two."

"We went from a moment to a second or two," I hissed. "What are you going to be doing while I imitate a target? Is he taking a break? Why aren't we being blasted right now?"

I sensed Douglas spooling up energy again.

"It seems he can't sustain a continuous burst, at least for now," Monty said. "The intervals between blasts is shorter, though."

"So we're running out of time," I said, getting ready to dodge another blast.

"He's a ticking time bomb we can't defuse," Monty said as he started gesturing. "The next best thing is removing the bomb itself."

"One day, it would be great if you could just explain things plainly."

"I thought I just did. Get your dawnward up. When I give you the signal, cross the street over to Haven."

"Across the street, over to where the maniac with flame beams wants to melt me into nothingness?"

"Exactly," Monty said. "It will be the last thing he expects."

"Last thing I expected, too," I grumbled under my breath. "This sounds like a one-way trip."

"It will be," Monty said, focused on his gestures, "for him. Get your shield ready."

I materialized Ebonsoul and closed my eyes. I took several deep breaths and channeled the energy into my blade. When I opened my eyes, an iridescent violet shield covered my skin.

Monty's brow was covered in sweat and I saw him

juggling a pair of larger teleportation circles—only, these were perpendicular to the ground, not flat on it.

"Now!" Monty yelled, getting to his feet. "Go!"

I jumped over the hood of the car and slid across in my best TJ Hooker move. Douglas turned at my sudden movement and extended a hand in my direction.

"*Ignisvitae!*" I yelled as I charged him, extending my own arm.

A beam of bright violet energy shot forward, slamming into Douglas. He fell to one knee and began laughing. I kept charging. He extended his arm palm first, aimed at me. The now blue beam of energy punched into me, but I still kept charging. Douglas opened his eyes wide in surprise and poured more energy into the beam.

It turned a deep blue and I could feel the heat cooking my skin even through the dawnward. My charge had been reduced to a slow walk and I could hear Douglas laugh.

"Your shield can't hold out forever, Strong," Douglas yelled. "I'm going to end you where you stand, and then I'm going to blast this place to atoms."

Douglas extended his other arm, firing another beam of deep blue heat. The two beams merged into one as it hit my dawnward. I was no longer moving forward. Douglas was covered in orange energy as he poured more power into reducing me to ashes.

I didn't dare look away. Keeping the dawnward up was taking all of my concentration. If I looked away, even for a second, I would lose its protection and Douglas would disintegrate me.

"Anytime you feel like lending a hand would be great," I said through clenched teeth as I started slipping back and losing ground. "I'm beginning to get a third-degree suntan here."

"No one is going to mourn you, Strong," Douglas said with another laugh. "You will be forgotten. Your life was meaningless, but your death will help me usher in a new age. Goodbye."

Douglas took a deep breath and poured even more power into his attack. I started seeing parts of the dawnward thin. Douglas was bathed in orange energy and I saw blood start to pour from his nose and eyes.

"Shit! Monty?" I yelled. "He's going to blow!"

"I know," Monty said. "Hold on."

I saw the first teleportation circle hit Douglas and disappear him just as my dawnward failed. When he reappeared, he was easily a hundred feet above us and falling. Monty moved his hands in a circular motion and whispered something I couldn't understand. The second circle turned on its axis and became parallel to the ground. It went from green to violet tinged with black.

Monty stepped forward and stomped on the ground, creating a shockwave that blasted me away as he extended his arms upward into the second circle.

The second circle raced upward and intercepted the falling Douglas, vanishing him from sight.

"Where did he go?" I said, stumbling over to where Monty stood looking up.

"There," Monty said, pointing. "That's him."

I saw a distant orange glow that looked like a mini-sun. It pulsed several times, increasing in size.

"That's him?" I asked, surprised. "How far up is he?"

"I would say about fifty kilometers," Monty said, gesturing again. "Avert your gaze."

I turned away as the mini-sun exploded. Monty formed a dark violet shield above us, diffusing the light from the blast. I felt a flash of heat as Douglas detonated in the atmosphere and lit up the night sky.

All of the windows in the buildings adjacent to Haven shattered, along with the glass in all of the vehicles surrounding the building for several blocks.

Car alarms screamed into the night, a symphony of chaos as the blast from Douglas' explosion slowly expanded across the sky.

"He's dead?" I asked. "I mean, really dead?"

Monty narrowed his eyes and looked up into the night sky. After a few seconds, he nodded.

"He's gone," Monty said, before heading toward Haven's lobby. "It's over."

"Can we not do that again, ever?"

"I didn't want to do it this time," Monty said and touched my arm. "It would seem the jacket was projectile resistant, but not heat resistant."

I looked down and realized I was in my charred shirt. My arms were baked a dark red, but my curse was working overtime to heal the damage from Douglas' blue beam of death.

"It did its job," I said as we walked slowly into Haven. "Feelds tried to put three in me. It stopped them all."

"Did you...?"

"I let her go," I said. "Maybe she won't make the stupid choice next time, if there is a next time."

"There is *always* a next time, Simon," Monty said, pressing the button to the elevator. It took us a moment to realize all the electronics in the building were disabled. "The explosion must have unleashed an EMP."

I pulled out my phone as it rang.

"I guess the pulse wasn't strong enough, or Hack has some next level equipment," I said, looking at the number and wincing. "Ramirez."

"That one is all yours," Monty said. "I'm going to go upstairs and sleep for a few days. Enjoy the conversation."

Monty headed for the stairwell and went upstairs.

"Angel," I said in my most cordial voice. "How are things?"

"How are things?" Angel said, then took a deep breath. "HOW ARE THINGS?"

I held the phone away from my head as Angel spent the next five minutes cursing me out. Most of the curses were in Spanish, and all of them were extra creative. I winced at some of the suggestions. A few of them were just anatomically impossible, though that didn't stop him from repeating them several times. When I felt he had calmed down, I brought the phone to my head again.

"You might get a call from the government about an explosion above the city," I said and held my breath waiting for another outburst. All I got was silence. "Angel?"

"Why would I be getting a call from the government about an explosion above my city, Simon?" Ramirez asked, his voice sounding tired. "Don't you dare bullshit me about this. I need all the details. If not, I will be directing them to a certain explosive detective agency I know."

"I'll explain it all over dinner," I said. "Masa, on me."

"You better believe it's on you," Ramirez said, somewhat mollified. He loved Masa and leapt at any chance he got to eat there. "Bring your wallet, because I'm bringing my appetite."

"Deal," I said, suddenly weary. "It's been a long night, Angel. I'll call you in a few days."

"You do that," Ramirez said. "West Broadway is a mess, with some fatalities."

"How bad?"

"One John Doe and plenty of property damage. The manager of the TINYs got caught in some kind of blast a few blocks away, but he's going to pull through. His staff wasn't so lucky, though. Three of them were incinerated on the spot; I don't know how he survived."

"It wasn't his time, I guess."

"Guess not."

"Any information on what caused the blast?"

"My team is leaning toward to gas main Why? You have any information?'

"No," I lied. "Just wondering. I'm going to call it a night. Be safe out there."

"If you're going to be indoors, it's safer already."

Ramirez hung up and I looked up into the night sky. Douglas' blast cloud was still spreading out like a borealis. My curse had restored my body, healing me. It couldn't do anything about my mental exhaustion; I would have to deal with that on my own. I shook myself alert and headed over to 2nd Avenue.

I just had one more stop to make.

THIRTY-FOUR

Douglas' trailer sat alone near the pier on the East River.

I knew it was a trap. I was counting on it. It had taken me the better part of three hours to find it. I reached out to some old contacts and needed to call in several favors, but eventually, I managed to locate the double-wide trailer.

I knew it was too large to hide in a conventional parking garage. The damn thing was just too wide to fit down any of the ramps. No self-respecting garage in the city would let that beast in. The only alternative was to get it out of the city by boat.

My contacts had informed me of the ghost ferry: an illegal ferry service used to move contraband. Anything you wanted could be smuggled out of the city—for a price. Douglas' trailer was on the schedule for tonight.

The ferry was scheduled to arrive in an hour. There was no way I was going to let that trailer leave the city. This was going to be a world of pain, and register high in the suckage factor, but it was the only way to make it look real.

It was still early. The East River esplanade was empty in the early hours of the morning, except for the Shadow Company trailer, which easily took up four spots. I walked down 34th Street to the parking lot, keeping an eye on Pier 11, which was where the ghost ferry would dock to pick up its cargo.

This was going to go one of two ways: Either I would reach the trailer and together, we would go up in a blaze of glory, or I would reach the trailer and get dropped the second I reached the door. Both options required pain, but I was tired of being flambéed tonight. I was really hoping for the second option.

I smiled and shook my head when I realized that out of the two options, getting gunned down was the one I preferred. My life had seriously become twisted.

I reached the trailer door and felt the first suppressed round hit me. Contrary to the illusion of film, suppressed rounds aren't whisper quiet. That only happens in the imaginations of directors. A real suppressed round isn't much quieter than a normal round fired from an unsuppressed weapon.

A rapid series of *clack clack* punched into my midsection, spinning me away from the door. I drew Grim Whisper, staggered for a few feet and collapsed, falling backward and remaining still—waiting. My body flushed hot as it dealt with the rounds and damage. They hurt like hell, and I wished I still had the runed jacket. I heard the footsteps a few minutes later.

"That's what happens when you get old and slow," Carlos said into the night. "You get dead."

He raised his weapon for the killing blow. Shadow Company SOP was three body shots center mass and a double-tap to the head. I was counting on Carlos following protocol. I got lucky—if he had managed the double-tap, I'd still be recovering.

Or I'd be dead.

I raised Grim Whisper and fired twice, blowing out each of his knees. He screamed into the night. Combat armor is especially good at keeping major organs protected; the joints, less so. The material around the knees is thinner by design to allow for mobility and running. Great for evasion, horrible for stopping rounds. He fell to his ruined knees with a grunt of agony.

"Hello, Carlos," I said, stripping him of his gun. "You waiting for Douglas?"

"He's going to fuck you up, freak," Carlos snarled. "When he gets here, you'll see."

He started laughing and for a brief moment, I pitied him. He had drunk the Kool-Aid and bought into Douglas' line of human superiority. Together, they were going to cleanse the world of all non-humans and create a utopia where Douglas would rule, and all who didn't fall in line would be eliminated, or cast out.

"You are truly too clueless to live."

"Douglas is going to end you, old man," Carlos said in between the laughter. "You are *so* dead."

"You first," I said, putting a round through his temple and ending his life.

I picked up his lifeless body and placed it in the trailer. I moved back what I thought was a safe distance and focused.

"*Ignisvitae*," I whispered, sending a beam of violet energy at the trailer.

The beam widened as it crossed the esplanade until it

was two feet wide. It punched into the side of the trailer, detonating the ordnance inside. A massive fireball bloomed into the sky. I stepped back and sent two more beams of energy at the trailer, making sure nothing was left except molten slag.

A few minutes later, I heard the helicopter and walked away, staying under the FDR overpass until I was several blocks away. Sirens filled the night and my phone rang.

I looked at the screen and saw Ramirez's number. I let it go to voicemail. I would explain it to Angel in a few days. Right now, all I wanted was a strong cup of coffee and my bed.

I made my way over to 1st Avenue and hailed a taxi. I took my life into my hands and stepped into the first one that stopped.

"Out late tonight," the driver said with an infectious smile. "Where to?"

From his accent, I could tell he was from Southeast Asia. The Randy Rump would be an unwise choice right now, so I opted for my fallback coffee shop.

"Last Gasp," I said. "Do you know it?"

The driver nodded. I read his identification tag on the dash and saw his name was Raj Chandran. His picture was next to his name. The same infectious smile beamed at me. At least he enjoyed his job.

"Best coffee in the city," Raj said with a chuckle. "Crutch keeps it open 24/7 now. All the cabbies drink there after the night shift. Before, too; all the time, actually."

"Perfect," I said, resting my head back and closing my eyes as the sun peeked over the horizon. "Coffee is what I need right now. That, and about a week of sleep. Raj, I'll double the meter if you get me there in one piece."

"No guarantees," Raj said with a head wobble, laughing as he floored the gas. "Hold on."

I held on.

THE END

AUTHOR NOTES

Thank you for reading this story and jumping back into the Monty & Strong World.

Disclaimer: The Author Notes are written at the very end of the process. This section is not seen by the ART or my amazing Jeditor—Audrey. Any typos or errors following this disclaimer are mine and mine alone.

Here we are...13 books in and counting! WOW!

Thank you for joining me in this incredible adventure. If you had asked me when I first started writing Monty & Strong how many books long the series would be, I would have answered, this is going to be a trilogy.

No more.

Obviously MS&P had other ideas. Those of you who are in the MoB Family know of my trials and tribulations keeping my stories to a predetermined length. In the case of M&S, I never thought it would go this long back when I started Tombyards & Butterflies. That quickly changed.

REQUIEM was a nice departure from the usual M&S

story. We uncovered some of Simon's past (Monty's too) and dealt with the subject of our present being formed by the choices of our past. This will come up in future books. Badb Catha will *not* forget the terms.

The next few books will deal with themes that have been interwoven in the previous 13 books. There will be much upheaval, danger, death, and explosions—or what M&S call Friday. The next book, DIVINE INTERVENTION, will touch on some deities crashing into Monty & Simon's lives. Some we know, others, not so much. All of them will have their own agendas, with some of them wishing harm on the Terrible Trio.

Simon will get to experience firsthand what it means to be the 'Marked of Kali'. It promises to be dangerous and fun, well, maybe not so much fun for him. Monty still has to deal with the effects of his schism and increase in power, plus there is the small matter of owing Badb Catha a favor. I think Dex may have a few (loud) words to say about that conversation.

I didn't forget SEPIA BLUE. Her last book DEMON will be out sometime this year as well as the next Night Warden story NOCTURNE MELODY, which promises to be a fun, if dark book, which is the usual for Grey & Co. It's possible Simon makes a cameo in that one. It's way past time he and Frank had a 'conversation' about Frank's influence on a certain hellhound.

As I have always said, out of the several series I have the privilege of writing(quite a few at this point), this one is by far one of the easiest for me. The stories flow freely and it's usually a matter of my trying to keep up with the story as it unfolds in my head.

As I write these author notes, it gets harder and harder

to share what's coming without revealing spoilers. I can only say that the next batch of books in the M&S series will be a blast and I hope that you join me on that adventure. I will also be focusing on closing some of the short story series, most of which are trilogies. This will allow me to focus on the larger books(M&S, Night Warden Sepia Blue, Darkin, Designers, John Kane, to name a few off the top of my head. I'm sure I missed one or two) that are in the schedule.

As always, this book answered some questions, and in so doing raised a ton more. It can't be helped. I promise to get to all the questions eventually. It may take 30-40 books, but I'll get there at some point.

As long as you keep reading, I'll keep writing.

Once again, I wanted to share what an incredible honor and pleasure it is to be able to write these stories for you, my amazing readers. On the days when it's more work than play (there are a few), knowing that I'm writing this story for you helps me get through the rough patches when I want to just a fling a asteroid at the planet and call it a day.

Thank you again for taking the time to read this story. I wrote it for you and I hope you enjoyed spending some time with Simon as he confronted the parts of his past he preferred to keep buried. This time, it was Monty who did his best to be a good friend and brother to the reluctant immortal. Simon will continue to grow, maybe even getting a hang of the dawnward. If not, I'm sure there is no shortage of mages willing to give him a few lessons on the painful execution of certain casts.

Whether or not Simon gets it, will be discovered in future books, What I do know, is that he will always do his best while striving to be a worthy bondmate to his ever-ravenous hellhound, Peaches—who we all love.

If you enjoyed this story—please leave a review. It's really important and helps the book (and me).

Thank you again for jumping into this adventure with me!

SPECIAL MENTIONS

Larry & Tammy—The WOUF: Because even when you aren't there...you're there.

Stacey Stein: For sitzfleisch, the ability to sit still for the long periods of time required to be truly productive. Simon still needs to learn this, I'm just getting the hang of it.

Jeanette Auer: Our first "official" Redshirt. Congratulations on your "death"!

John Fauver: Urban Renewal Fiction will be a genre... I promise, LOL!

Dolly Sanchez: Reptilian Rott is an awesome description. Thank you.

Orlando A. Sanchez
www.orlandoasanchez.com

Orlando has been writing ever since his teens when he was immersed in creating scenarios for playing Dungeons and Dragons with his friends every weekend.

The worlds of his books are urban settings with a twist of the paranormal lurking just behind the scenes and with generous doses of magic, martial arts, and mayhem.

He currently resides in Queens, NY with his wife and children.

John Kane
The Deepest Cut*•Blur

Sepia Blue
The Last Dance*•Rise of the Night•Sisters•Nightmare

Chronicles of the Modern Mystics
The Dark Flame•A Dream of Ashes

Montague & Strong Detective Agency Novels
Tombyards & Butterflies•Full Moon Howl•Blood is
Thicker•Silver Clouds Dirty Sky•Homecoming•Dragons &
Demigods•Bullets & Blades•Hell Hath No Fury•Reaping
Wind•The Golem•Dark Glass•Walking the
Razor•Requiem

Montague & Strong Detective Agency Stories
No God is Safe•The Date•The War Mage•A Proper
Hellhound•The Perfect Cup•Saving Mr. K

Brew & Chew Adventures
Hellhound Blues

Night Warden Novels
Wander•ShadowStrut

Division 13
The Operative•The Magekiller

Blackjack Chronicles
The Dread Warlock

The Assassin's Apprentice
The Birth of Death

Gideon Shepherd Thrillers
Sheepdog

DAMNED
Aftermath

RULE OF THE COUNCIL
Blood Ascension•Blood Betrayal•Blood Rule

NYXIA WHITE
They Bite•They Rend•They Kill

*Books denoted with an asterisk are **FREE** via my website—www.orlandoasanchez.com

ACKNOWLEDEGEMENTS

With each book, I realize that every time I learn something about this craft, it highlights so many things I still have to learn. Each book, each creative expression, has a large group of people behind it.

This book is no different.

Even though you see one name on the cover, it is with the knowledge that I am standing on the shoulders of the literary giants that informed my youth, and am supported by my generous readers who give of their time to jump into the adventures of my overactive imagination.

I would like to take a moment to express my most sincere thanks:

To Dolly: My wife and greatest support. You make all this possible each and every day. You keep me grounded when I get lost in the forest of ideas. Thank you for asking the right questions when needed, and listening intently when I go off on tangents. Thank you for who you are and the space you create—I love you.

To my Tribe: You are the reason I have stories to tell. You cannot possibly fathom how much and how deeply I love you all.

To Lee: Because you were the first audience I ever had. I love you, sis.

To the Logsdon Family: The words *thank you* are insufficient to describe the gratitude in my heart for each of you. JL, your support always demands I bring my best, my A-game, and produce the best story I can. Both you and Lorelei (my Uber Jeditor) and now, Audrey, are the reason I am where I am today. My thank you for the notes, challenges, corrections, advice, and laughter. Your patience is truly infinite. *Arigatogozaimasu.*

To The Montague & Strong Case Files Group— AKA The MoB (Mages of Badassery): When I wrote T&B there were fifty-five members in The MoB. As of this release, there are over one thousand four hundred members in the MoB. I am honored to be able to call you my MoB Family. Thank you for being part of this group and M&S.

You make this possible. **THANK YOU.**

To the ever-vigilant PACK: You help make the MoB... the MoB. Keeping it a safe place for us to share and just...

be. Thank you for your selfless vigilance. You truly are the Sentries of Sanity.

Chris Christman II: A real-life technomancer who makes the **MoBTV LIVEvents +Kaffeeklatsch** on YouTube amazing. Thank you for your tireless work and wisdom. Everything is connected...you totally rock!

To the WTA—The Incorrigibles: JL, Ben Z. Eric QK., S.S., and Noah.

They sound like a bunch of badass misfits, because they are. My exposure to the deranged and deviant brain trust you all represent helped me be the author I am today. I have officially gone to the *dark side* thanks to all of you. I humbly give you my thanks, and...it's all your fault.

To my fellow Indie Authors: Thank you for making this solitary craft a little less solitary. You have created a space where authors can feel listened to, and encouraged to continue on this path. Your generosity, humor, and work ethic inspire me daily. A rising tide lifts all the ships indeed.

To The English Advisory: Aaron, Penny, Carrie, Davina, and all of the UK MoB. For all things English...thank you.

To DEATH WISH COFFEE: This book (and every book I write) has been fueled by generous amounts of the only coffee on the planet (and in space) strong enough to power my very twisted imagination. Is there any other coffee that can compare? I think not. DEATHWISH —thank you!

To Deranged Doctor Design: Kim, Darja, Tanja, Jovana, and Milo (Designer Extraordinaire).

If you've seen the covers of my books and been amazed, you can thank the very talented and gifted creative team at DDD. They take the rough ideas I give them, and produce incredible covers that continue to surprise and amaze me. Each time, I find myself striving to write a story worthy of the covers they produce. DDD, you embody professionalism and creativity. Thank you for the great service and spectacular covers. **YOU GUYS RULE!**

To you, the reader: I was always taught to save the best for last. I write these stories for **you**. Thank you for jumping down the rabbit holes of *what if?* with me. You are the reason I write the stories I do.

You keep reading...I'll keep writing.

Thank you for your support and encouragement.

CONTACT ME

I really do appreciate your feedback. You can let me know
what you thought of the story by emailing me at:
orlando@orlandoasanchez.com

To get **FREE** stories please visit my page at:
www.orlandoasanchez.com

For more information on the M&S World...come join the
MoB Family on Facebook!
You can find us at:
Montague & Strong Case Files

Visit our online M&S World Swag Store located at:
Emandes

If you enjoyed the book, **please leave a review**. Reviews
help the book, and also help other readers find good
stories to read.
THANK YOU!

ART SHREDDERS

I want to take a moment to extend a special thanks to the ART SHREDDERS.

No book is the work of one person. I am fortunate enough to have an amazing team of advance readers and shredders.

Thank you for giving of your time and keen eyes to provide notes, insights, answers to the questions, and corrections (dealing wonderfully with my extreme dreaded comma allergy). You help make every book and story go from good to great. Each and every one of you helped make this book fantastic, and I couldn't do this without each and every one of you.

THANK YOU

ART SHREDDERS

Amber, Anne Morando, Audrey Cienki
Bethany Showell, Beverly Collie

Cam Skaggs, Carrie Anne O'Leary, Cat, Chris Christman II, Colleen Taylor

Darren Musson, Davina 'the Tao of the Comma' Noble, Dawn McQueen Mortimer, Denise King, Diana Gray, Diane Craig, Dolly Sanchez, Donna Young Hatridge

Hal Bass, Helen Gibson

Jasmine Breeden, Jasmine Davis, Jeanette Auer, Jen Cooper, John Fauver, Joy Kiili, Joy Ollier, Julie Peckett

Karen Hollyhead

Larry Diaz Tushman, Laura Tallman I, Leslie Watts, Luann Zipp

Malcolm Robertson, Marcia Campbell, Maryelaine Eckerle-Foster, Melissa Miller, Melody DeLoach

Nick Church

Paige Guido, Pat (the silly sister), Penny Noble

RC Battels, Rob Farnham

Sara Mason Branson, Sean Trout, Stacey Stein, Susie Johnson

Tami Cowles, Tammy Tushman, Tanya Anderson, Ted Camer, Terri Adkisson, Tina Jonhson

Vikki Brannagan

Wendy Schindler

Thanks for Reading

If you enjoyed this book, would you **please leave a review** at the site you purchased it from? It doesn't have to be a book report...just a line or two would be fantastic and it would really help us out!

Made in the USA
Middletown, DE
11 May 2022

65631053R00194